The *Other* *Road*

a novel

S.L. ARRINGTON

SL ARRINGTON PUBLISHING GROUP,
ARRINGTON, TENNESSEE

The Other Road. Copyright © 2024 by S.L. Arrington

Published by SL Arrington Publishing Group

Arrington, Tennessee

www.SLArrington.com

Cover design and interior formatting by Damonza

Printed in the United States

ISBN: 979-8-9913584-0-8 (Hardback)
ISBN: 979-8-9913584-1-5 (Paperback)
ISBN: 979-8-9913584-2-2 (Ebook)
ISBN" 979-8-9913584-4-9 (Audiobook)

For Connie Arrington,
my amazing mother for loving me with the strength and patience I needed. I couldn't have been blessed with a better mama.

For Ginger Arrington,
my extraordinary wife and chief content editor who has supported me and encouraged me on this writing journey every step of the way.

For Ashley, Amanda and Alyssa,
my beautiful daughters; your honest feedback, editing and support were essential in my perseverance to complete this work.

And in memory of Mildred Hale Gay,
my grandma, who constantly encouraged me through her personality and actions to *be free, take risks and live life*

CHAPTER 1

Present Day

HE ALWAYS SAID he wouldn't live past ninety-five. As a little girl, ninety-five had seemed like an eternity. Now I wish he would have said one hundred.

The man I lovingly knew as Pawpaw, only one week before his ninety-fifth birthday, died peacefully in his sleep. Mother told me that Grandma knew he had passed away because she woke to silence in the middle of the night.

Grandma had a way with words. She always knew what to say to quell my inner fears; even so, the thought of walking through the front door of their old bungalow, knowing Pawpaw would not be there, was almost more than I could bear. I hadn't seen anyone in my family for ten years, and it took Pawpaw's death to bring me home. With a deep breath, I closed my eyes and knocked.

Staring down at the welcome mat, I heard the lock rattle as it was unfastened from inside. The door opened slowly. I was instantly transported to my childhood; standing at that door, anticipating the showering of affection that rained down on me every summer of my youth. But at the same time, I knew I wasn't. I was thirty years old, and anxious to see a family I hadn't visited in a decade. I was afraid of how Grandma might react to the wayward grandchild who didn't make time to say goodbye. I knew she loved me then, would she still? Then, I heard a sound I had been longing to hear for over ten years. It was the tender voice of my grandma, Marina.

"Welcome home, Izzy Bee."

All of my guilt and sadness boiled over. The lengthy apology I had rehearsed became moot. I lunged forward and embraced her, burying my head into her shoulder. Her scent was so familiar and comforting. Like the smell of fresh cut flowers interlaced with delicate chocolate. It wrapped around me like a freshly washed blanket that had just been air dried on a cool fall day. I immediately relived the night my high school boyfriend crushed my heart. Grandma sat with me on the couch and allowed me to cry on her shoulder for hours. Her embrace was always the perfect medicine for a broken heart.

The tears began to flow as all of my emotions poured out. I kept my head buried in her long white hair.

"I needed this," I whispered through my tears.

"Me too, Izzy, me too"

I glanced at the small table near the front door. A photo of the two of them sat in a simple frame. They were much younger then. I've always loved that photo because neither of them was looking at the camera; they were too busy smiling at each other.

Pawpaw was a handsome man, a few inches over six feet tall, slender but not too skinny and he had a head full of thick light brown hair. It had a slight wave to it but he kept it neat. I remember staring into his eyes while he told me stories when I was a little girl; they were a soft blue color and seemed to soak up everyone's problems and concerns.

Grandma noticed my eyes were beginning to well up, so she quickly took my hand and began to console me.

"I'm sure glad you made it; I know Pawpaw is as happy to see you as I am. Did you know the spirit hangs about for three days before making its way to heaven?" Her eyes fluttered around the room imagining him in different places.

I could sense the optimism and sincerity in her voice. Her eccentricity, although at times awkward, was one of the traits that I loved about her. She led me from the entry and straight into her small but comfortable kitchen.

"You look like you could use a bite to eat, let's make you a plate," Grandma insisted.

"Yes, she does look like she could use a bite to eat. Hello Isabella. I guess better late than never seems to work for you." I knew that voice. In fact, it was the voice that set me on my path of self-discovery and total family avoidance ten years earlier.

"Hello Mother," I said to her, in as much of a 'not glad to see you' tone as I could muster. "Thank you for the phone call."

"Honestly… I didn't think you would come," she snapped back at me, standing up from behind the small dinette in the corner of the kitchen.

"Be nice, Susan Jane, your father is watching, and this is not about you!"

"Good Lord, Mom. Dad died two days ago. He's not here, no matter what you say."

"You hush your mouth young lady, he's here for one more day and I'll be damned if you are going to spoil my goodbye!"

Watching my mother and grandma fight like this was rewarding in and of itself. I was rooting for Grandma. Not that I disagreed with Mother, but anybody willing to go toe to toe with 'mommy dearest' had my support any day.

Mother and I haven't always seen eye to eye, in fact, it's probably safe to say we've never seen eye to eye… on anything. Her controlling nature and desire to manage every aspect of my life, while screwing hers all up, was often a topic of fiery debate. Our last battle happened ten years ago when I decided not everyone was cut out for college, and I dropped out after completing my sophomore year at the University of Southern California. It wasn't that it was too hard, in fact it was fairly easy. It just wasn't something I wanted to do. I don't believe I had ever seen her that angry, and to top it off, it was like Grandma and Pawpaw took her side on the whole matter. I packed up all my things and I went to live my life, on my terms, and for ten years my stubbornness got the best of me. Standing in my Pawpaw's house knowing I had missed every opportunity to see him again, was more heart wrenching than any fight I had ever had with my mother.

"Eat as much as you want, Isabella, there is plenty. People have been dropping food off all day, and my guess is it will continue until we've had daddy's memorial service." With that, Mother gave me a cautious hug, a kiss on my cheek and made her way to the garage.

Grandma grabbed two plates from the cupboard and began filling them up for both of us. We sat there for a while, eating together and catching up.

"You know she loves you very much, don't you?"

I nodded in response to her question. I've always known Mother loved me. She worked tirelessly for years to give me everything I needed and then some. From the day I was born, it was just the two of us. I never knew my father. Mother said she thought they were 'in love' when she got pregnant during her last year of college, but then he just vanished without any further discussion. I guess that was another reason my bond with my pawpaw was so wonderful, for he was the closest thing to a father-figure I had ever known.

"How have you been Izzy Bee?" Unlike most, I noticed Grandma would always ask questions that truly demonstrated she cared.

"I've been well."

"You look good, are you happy?"

I gazed into her compassionate eyes before responding truthfully. "Most of the time."

She nodded and grinned, then took a bite of the fold-over sandwich she had made.

Mother waltzed back into the kitchen and looked at us rather suspiciously, and proclaimed, "Well, luckily, I was able to rearrange some things in the refrigerator out in the garage. I think I will put all of this food out there and then I'm headed to bed. It's been a long day and I think I need some time to reflect. Isabella, will you be staying here tonight?"

"Of course she will" injected Grandma, "I wouldn't have it any other way. We have some catching up to do tomorrow. If the last two days have reminded me of anything, it's that we've not much time on this earth. Izzy Bee, you can have the guest room upstairs if you'd like."

"Yes ma'am, thank you."

Grandma slowly made her way to the mantle and retrieved a small, framed photo of Pawpaw. I could see the veins through the thin skin on her hands as she clutched the photo to her chest and slowly walked down the hall to her room. As the door came to a close and I heard her call out, "Goodnight girls, I have a feeling tomorrow is going to be quite a day."

I volunteered to help Mother take the remaining dishes out to the refrigerator in the garage.

"Thank you, sweetheart," Mother stated while giving me another hug. "I really am glad you were able to make it."

"Me too." I stared at my mother's aging face. A part of me wanted to apologize for staying away for so long, but I decided to save it for another day. "I guess I will see you in the morning. Goodnight, Mother."

"Goodnight Isabella."

Making my way up the staircase and onto the landing outside the guest room, I paused to take in the old house. It was eerily quiet and for a moment, I thought I sensed my pawpaw standing there with me, reaching out to give me a hug and a kiss on the forehead.

I slipped into the feather bed I had slept in many times during my youth and pulled the quilt up to my chin. My head sank into those cool, soft pillows, and my body experienced a peace I had not felt in a long, long time.

I drifted off to sleep not knowing how prophetic Grandma's words would be and how the next day would alter my life forever.

CHAPTER 2

Present Day

I WOKE THE NEXT morning to the sound of muffled voices. Mother and Grandma were talking, but no matter how hard I tried, I couldn't make out the words. Regardless of how tired you might be, it's difficult to fall back asleep once you hear voices and your nose detects the smell of coffee and bacon wafting through the house. I pulled up out of bed and clumsily made my way into the bathroom for a hot shower. The bathroom seemed smaller than I remembered, but I swear the towels, rugs and décor were the same sea foam green I recalled from my childhood years in the house. After getting dressed, it was time to venture downstairs.

"I thought you were going to sleep all day. Is this how you live your life? No wonder you still haven't found stability."

"Well good morning to you too, Mother," I retorted with dry sarcasm.

Standing in the kitchen with an apron on and pressing out a few homemade biscuits with her fragile hands, was my beautiful grandma. Her hair was still fairly long with tight curls, but instead of the almost black hue that had graced her for years it was now the color of fresh fallen snow. She saw me coming down the stairs and smiled.

"Good morning, Izzy Bee," she said in her kind voice. "I'm making some biscuits for us. Can you look in the pantry for a little jar with a red-checkered lid? I believe it's still in there. It's homemade blackberry jelly from some friends of ours in Mississippi. I hope it's still good. William sure did like blackberry jelly."

I walked into the pantry and located the jar she had described. "Grandma, this looks pretty old, are you sure it's still good?"

"Of course, dear, it's not that old. I think William and I brought it back with us the last time we visited the Barclay's down in Vicksburg."

"Haven't they both been dead for fifteen years?" Mother questioned.

"Hmmm? I don't think so," Grandma stammered.

The three of us sat around the small kitchen table with our bacon, biscuits and coffee.

"Tell me Isabella, what have you been up to?" Mother asked in a prying manner. "Do you have a job?"

After washing a mouthful of biscuit down with some coffee I decided to reply, "I've been working as a waitress for a while now."

Grandma smiled at me, sipping on her coffee.

"Thirty years old and waitressing? Sounds…"

As Mother uncomfortably searched for the right word, Grandma interrupted, "Delightful."

"Ha," Mother chirped, "miserable, was more like the word I was looking for."

Grandma frowned at Mother and was preparing to defend me, when I decided I should speak for myself. "It's actually rewarding. I get to meet new people every day. We have regulars who have become my friends. It gives me more freedom to live my life and the money, it isn't great, but it's not bad either."

"To each their own, I suppose," Mother snipped before picking up another piece of bacon. "Where do you live?"

"I had an apartment for a while, but I lost it."

"You couldn't pay the rent?" Mother questioned.

"No," I defended, "it was a small room over a detached garage and the people who were renting it to me had their son return from college and they needed it for him. Now, I stay with friends who are willing to let me crash with them, and I help them out with chores and offer up a small amount of rent."

"Good Lord Isabella, that's no way to live your life. You need a plan and a budget. It sounds to me like you are 'winging it'. What kind of life is that?"

Grandma chimed in, "Sounds to me like you are doing just fine dear."

I smiled in delight at my wonderful grandma's support. "Thank you," I mouthed silently to her.

Mother scolded her and glared in disapproval, "You're not helping at all."

Raising her eyebrows at Mother in defiance, Grandma winked at me and grinned in delight.

"I don't understand how you can live your life without any plan or direction. It is wasteful and non-productive to me," Mother explained.

"You are just like your daddy," Grandma mumbled while smiling and shaking her head in disbelief.

"To each their own, I suppose," I responded. Grandma and I grinned back and forth to each other.

Mother huffed as she conceded her argument for now.

Grandma and I ate half of that small jar of jelly all by ourselves.

Mother wouldn't touch it, she just kept mentioning how there was no telling what type of stomach ailment would befall us for even trying it. We sat there together for almost an hour, mostly Mother and Grandma sharing predictions about who would attend Pawpaw's memorial service in a couple of days. Once the topics had begun to run dry, I knew I had better select the subject or risk becoming the subject, again.

"So, what's the plan for the day Grandma?"

"No plans, I'd just like to spend some time with the two of you."

We cleaned up the kitchen and made our way into the parlor.

Grandma and Pawpaw loved to travel and made many friends over the years. This was obvious given all the photos and items displayed throughout their home. Not feeling the need to sit immediately, I became mesmerized, looking at each picture within the room.

A picture of Mother when she was a little girl, a photo of me as a baby, a picture of Mother, Pawpaw and Grandma on the beach together, the memories were endless. I focused in on one small picture buried behind the others on the center shelf of an antique curio cabinet. It was an older photo of a beautiful lady with blonde hair.

"Hey Grandma, who is this?" I asked, while picking up the photo.

She pretended not to hear me so I shot a curious stare at Mother.

Mother shrugged before answering, "I think that's an old friend of the family, right Mom?"

"Her name was Susan Jane," Grandma whispered with a smile on her face.

"Susan Jane?" I asked. "Mother, were you named after her?"

She shrugged before inquiring, "Mom, wasn't she dad's first wife?"

Grandma didn't reply, she just sat there and sipped her coffee with a look of satisfaction on her face. I could tell her thoughts were somewhere else.

Pawpaw was married before? My curiosity was off the charts, and I wanted to know more, but I realized our conversation had moved into an awkward place. Placing the photo back, I moved on to another old picture that was also tucked away in the curio cabinet. It was a picture of Grandma and Pawpaw. It had to have been taken many years ago and appeared to be in some type of lodge or cabin with a fireplace behind them. "Grandma, where was this taken?"

She glanced across the room at the photo I was holding, smiled and replied, "Aspen, Colorado."

"Was this on one of your trips to visit us when we lived in Denver?" Mother asked.

"No," Grandma answered quietly. "That's from when William and I first met." She reminisced in her mind; her face had a glow I had rarely seen before.

"I'm confused," Mother admitted, "I thought the two of you met in California."

"There are a lot of things you don't know," teased Grandma.

I interrupted, "How did you and Pawpaw meet?"

There was a quiet pause. Mother and I both waited curiously as Grandma took a sip of her coffee before placing it down on the small table beside her.

"Izzy, can you go to the hall closet for me? There should be a lockbox on the top shelf. Go ahead and get it down and bring it in here please." Her smile had changed to an expression of nervousness and anticipation.

My mind fluttered with curiosity. I opened the hall closet door and located the small box. It was about the size of a boot box, but made of metal. Despite its name, there was no lock, just a small latch that was closed. I lowered the box down from the top shelf. I could feel its contents shift inside. I brought the box back into the parlor and offered it to Grandma.

She stretched her palm out toward me and stated softly, "Will you open it for me?"

I sat down on the sofa next to Mother and placed the lockbox between the two of us. I gripped the latch and opened it up. We took turns removing the handful of items within the box.

A shell, a hospital bracelet, a rock, a small stone turtle, a pocketknife, a silver locket on a chain and a stack of pages held together with a large clip. "What is all of this?" Mother asked.

"You asked me how we met, well… there it is," she responded. "In all honesty, I asked William a few years ago if he remembered how we met. He left the room and came back with this box and those items. William always dreamed of being a writer, so back in the nineties he wrote our story; of how we met. He also made the stipulation that it was not to be read while he was alive. He said 'he didn't want us to argue if his recollection of events were different from mine'."

"So, you've never read this or even know what these objects are?" Mother inquired.

"Oh, I recognize each and every one of those objects, but I've been waiting a long time to hear our story. Izzy, will you do the honors?"

I took the stack of pages out of the box and carefully turned to the first page and began to read.

CHAPTER 3

December 1, 1970

I CAN REMEMBER THAT day as if it were yesterday. It was mid-morning and unseasonably warm for early December in Hudson, Ohio. Highway 91 ran straight as an arrow north and south from the city of Cleveland down to the smaller metropolitan area of Akron. Hudson sat right in between. There wasn't much to it, in fact, the highway was called Main Street from one city limit to the other. I had driven through that beautiful little township several times, but other than the clock tower and Saywell's Drug Store, I couldn't remember much about it.

There were a few clouds hanging low in the blue sky, while a faint smell of smoke still lingered; the little town had battled through a tragic fire a couple of weeks before. It was a Tuesday, so there wasn't much going on other than locals going about their day.

A diner sat along Main Street, nestled amongst a few other shops and businesses, each with their own unique personalities. I had passed it several times over the last five years. It had an aged façade about it. The white paint on the building wasn't very white anymore and was flaking off in several spots. The striped awning that hung out over the sidewalk had seen its better days, and there was a sign made of wood hanging on the wall above the awning that read, *MILDRED'S DINER*. Someone had taken the time to paint 'Best Fried Pies in Ohio' on the glass window overlooking the street. Standing outside, I paused to reflect on my life. With a deep breath, I decided today was as perfect a day as any to try the best fried pie in Ohio.

As I opened the door, an old bell mounted precariously above it jingled.

"Find yourself a seat, anywhere you'd like," yelled a lady from behind the counter, as the door closed firmly behind me.

I made my way to a small table with four mismatched chairs and took a seat. The age and need for replenishment was apparent, but regardless of the wear and tear on the little diner, it was one of the cleanest establishments I had ever patronized. Not a crumb or speck on the tile floor. It had a glow about it that could only come from frequent mopping or polishing. Even the salt and pepper shakers looked new. Someone loved and cared for this place.

I noticed there was only one other customer. He was sitting at the counter with a cup of coffee, while the older lady who welcomed me was wiping it down and putting away dishes.

"Be right with you!" yelled out a younger voice.

I was staring out the front window to my right in a daze when I heard footsteps approaching me from my left.

As I turned and saw her for the first time, rays of sunlight were traversing through the front window and dancing across her face. A small curl of her hair had snuck down past the bright pink scarf that was wrapped around her forehead and was dangling playfully in front of her eyes. Her wavy hair was dark like the midnight sky and had it not been pulled back into a ponytail, would have easily rippled down beyond her shoulders. She was wearing a short-sleeve light blue dress that stopped just below her knees and was adorned with a white lace collar. And the white belt she wore brought attention to her dainty waistline. An order pad was tucked into the pocket of her soft yellow apron.

I must have been staring at her, because as she approached my table she exclaimed sarcastically, "You must be from another planet, I've never seen you in here before." She gently flicked the independent curl out of her eyes.

The comment caught me a little off guard. "What?"

She repeated much slower and in a louder tone, "I SAID, YOU MUST BE FROM ANOTHER PLANET, I'VE NEVER SEEN YOU IN HERE BEFORE."

"I'm from Cleveland. Why, why would you think I'm from another planet?" I asked nervously.

"Cause you were staring at me like you've never seen a waitress before, and I've never seen you around Hudson."

"Oh, I'm sorry… it's just… the sun… your hair…you know?" I stammered.

She peered at me like I was an ugly puppy. "You're so weird. But this is your lucky day."

"Why is this my lucky day?"

"Well, if you had waited until tomorrow to stop in, you would've never had the pleasure of having me as your waitress. So - as you can see - it's your lucky day."

Her attitude, her smile, her energy for life, everything about her was mesmerizing. I must have been staring again because she snapped her fingers at me as if trying to wake me from a trance. "You wanna order something, or did you just come in for some inspiring conversation? I have places to be you know."

"Oh, yes please. The fried pie, is it the best in Ohio?"

"I'll let you be the judge, okay?" she answered in a non-convincing manner.

"Okay. I'll have a pie and a cup of coffee for here, and uh… can I get a cup of ice water to go?"

"Is that all?" She seemed disappointed at my small order.

"That's all, thanks."

As she headed back to the kitchen, I heard the gentleman at the counter ask, "Hey Mar, you're not really gonna leave us are you?"

"As soon as this guy over here finishes his coffee and pie, I will be done."

"Well, I'll believe it when I see it," cried the older lady behind the counter. "Tommy, she's been saying she was gonna leave for almost a year now."

"Oh, I am," snarked the young waitress. She headed my way with my coffee and a small carafe with some cream in it.

"Thank you," I said.

"You look like a creamer kind of guy, am I right?"

"Uh, yes… wait, what do you mean I look like a creamer kind of guy?"

She gave me a little squinty-eyed smile and turned back around, I noticed her eyes were a sea of emerald green, well at least one of them was, while the other was drifting into more of a hazel green with hints of brown.

Ignoring me but continuing her conversation with the two at the counter she pronounced, "I have saved up; I told you both I would be leaving, and now it's up to me to take that leap of faith. You won't miss me anyway Tommy, you know I spit in your food." As she passed by the older gentleman, who I presumed to be Tommy, she patted him on his bald head.

"Mar, don't say that out loud," the lady behind the counter scolded. "The other customers might hear you and think it's true."

"Oh, come on Aunt Mildred, there's not but one other customer in this place right now and he doesn't care if I spit in his
food, do you mister?"

I looked up and noticed her staring at me as she finished that
statement. She handed me the fried apple pie on which she had so
curiously drawn a smiley face with whipped cream.

She giggled and winked at me while turning back toward the
kitchen. The cares of the world, or at least my world, flushed from
body in an instant. A blast of energy passed through me and for a
moment I felt more alive than I had for the past five years.

It was obvious the woman behind the counter, referred to as
Aunt Mildred, must be the owner of this fine establishment since
the restaurant itself was named 'Mildred's Diner'. She was an older
lady, short in stature, motherly in her demeanor, and I could tell
she cared deeply for this young waitress whom they called 'Mar'.

The conversation turned a little more serious when Mildred
confronted the young waitress.

"Mar, you know I don't like the idea of you travelling by yourself. You've never done anything like this before. The world is a
dangerous place."

"Hudson Ohio can be a dangerous place! The explosion a
couple of weeks ago could've killed us all." The young waitress
paused. "I'm not a child Mildred; I'm thirty years old for Christ's
sake. I can take care of myself. Have a little faith in me, okay?"

"I do, and don't you ever mistake my concern as a lack of faith.
I'm just gonna miss you if you go," declared Mildred, her eyes
beginning to tear up a bit. I watched the two of them embrace. It
reminded me more of a mother and her child, than an aunt and
her niece.

Finishing off the last bite of pie, I wiped my mouth with my
napkin and tried to pretend I was not paying attention to any of

their conversation, although I don't know how anyone could in such close quarters.

"Here," interrupted Tommy, "I know ten dollars isn't much, but maybe it can help you find your way. You take care of yourself Mar."

"Thanks Tommy." She gave Tommy a hug before she turned and headed my way.

"I hope you are a big tipper!" She set her left knee on the chair across from mine. "I'm trying to pad my travel fund."

"So, Mar?"

"Marina," she interrupted "my name is Marina Payne."

"Oh… sorry," I apologized. "So, Marina, you're not only leaving your job, you're leaving Hudson?"

Marina sat down in the seat across from me and gave me a look of a woman who desperately wanted her point of view to be heard. "Listen, I've always done what everyone else has said that I should do. I've always been convinced by others to not try, to not fail. I'm not one to follow the herd. I don't want to plan; I want to just go. Haven't you ever felt that way?"

I paused and chuckled as I let her passionate words sink in. "I've always been the planner. I have a hard time letting go. Your view on life, your urge to fly, it both fascinates me and scares the hell out of me."

"What did you say your name was again?" Marina asked, remembering I was a stranger.

"Oh, sorry, I'm William, William Massey."

"Well, William, it seems like a boring way to spend your life if you ask me. It's actually what I don't want to fall into for the rest of my life. I've never left Hudson, at least not the area. I went to school here and I've worked in this diner for my whole life, but come tomorrow morning I will be setting myself free." She smiled while she glanced upwards, imagining how great the experience would be. "I've never been to the ocean, that's my dream, the coast of California; San Diego to be exact."

"So, you've mapped out your trip? Where you will stay along the way? How much gas it will take? What will you do when you get there?" This was a paradigm I couldn't wrap my head around.

Marina laughed, "Holy cow, you have way too many questions. I just want to see the world, on my terms, you know?"

Staring at this young woman, I felt conflicted. On one hand, it seemed very careless. On the other hand, the idea was quite exhilarating. "I'm sorry," I apologized, "this is intriguing to me."

"You know, I've saved up some money, I'm not sure it's enough to get me all the way to California, but I'll deal with that if I have to." She rose from the chair and headed back toward the counter before looking back toward me with a smile.

I began to stare out the window, contemplating life and admiring the courage and freewill this young lady had, when the most beautiful bluejay I had ever seen landed upon the light post outside. It fluttered its wings and pranced about, trying to get my attention. I watched with delight as it tilted its head and stared straight at me through the window; Like it was trying to speak to me.

My trance was interrupted one last time. "I'm glad I got to meet you William Massey, thanks for coming in."

She handed me my ticket and a small cup of ice water. Leaving the money for my bill on the table, I looked back as I passed through the door and noticed Marina removing her apron and handing it to Mildred.

Sitting in my car, clutching the silver locket around my neck in my left hand, my heart raced and I could hear an imaginary timer counting down. A little voice in my head was telling me this was not the end. *Open your mind, be spontaneous and quit planning everything.*

The tiny bell jingled loudly as I hurried back into the diner at the same moment Marina was coming toward the front door to leave.

She looked a little surprised to see me standing there.

"Why Mr. Massey? Hello, again. I had a feeling the ten-dollar bill was a mistake. I'm guessing you forgot your change?"

"Oh no, it's yours." I set the cup of ice water down on the table and began to explain. "Listen, I have a question for you. A proposition of sorts I suppose; if you'll hear me out." I couldn't believe what I was saying. It was like a stranger had taken over my body and was steering me in a direction I had no plan for.

"Okay?" She sounded nervous.

"Umm... oh... how do I say this?" I paused and wrung my hands together, "I…uh… I want to go to California with you." The whole universe paused while I waited for a response.

She stood there a little shocked and suspicious. I could see over Marina's shoulder that Mildred and Tommy were also focused in on our conversation.

"Listen… I will pay my own way. Heck, I'll pay your way. I can cover all of our expenses and ensure you make it to California." I paused, waiting for the rejection.

"Mr. Massey, I don't know who you are. For all I know, you could be some sort of weirdo or killer."

"I know, I know, but I'm not. I promise."

"That's exactly how a weirdo or killer would respond, Mr. Massey."

"I know. In fact, this is not who I am; spontaneity isn't my thing. But someone once told me, not so long ago, that I needed to venture out and redefine who I am. I know it's strange. It is for me too, but I promise you, no funny business. Just two adults sharing a car ride, a journey if you will, for a few days. You know it's safer to not travel alone."

"I don't know about this Mr. Massey. This is a little unusual."

"I'm sorry, but I had to try. Don't ask me why, but I had to give it a shot. How about this? We can meet here at the diner in the morning at 7 o'clock. If you're not here, then I will know what your decision is. If I'm not here, you will know I've changed my mind. If we're both here... we go with it, you know, spontaneity, okay?"

Marina stood there in shock. I noticed a concerned yet sincere look on Mildred's face and the look of a protective dad on the face of Tommy. I didn't stick around for arguments; I bolted out the door, jumped into my car and headed on my way.

CHAPTER 4

December 2, 1970

I TOOK A TAXI from Cleveland to Hudson the next morning. The ride felt excruciatingly long, in slow-motion at times. Thinking twenty minutes had passed, I would glance down at my watch to realize it had only been five. *It's funny, the more eager you are to arrive, the longer it seems to take.* Staring out the window at the flat ground and dense forest, I started second guessing my decision to open my mouth at the diner the day before.

When we finally pulled up in front of Mildred's Diner, I felt like a schoolboy at his first dance— a bundle of nervous anxiety. My body and eyes were tired because I hadn't slept much all night. Every scenario had played out in my mind since leaving the day before. Would she be there or not? This was all so new for me. I grabbed my duffel bag, paid the driver and gave him a little extra to wait a few minutes longer, just in case. Exiting the cab, I wondered, *is this one of those forks in the road I am always hearing about but never taking?*

I approached the diner, hesitated, took a deep breath, exhaled, and then opened the door.

The bell jingled above me and I stepped through and looked around. The diner was about half full, and I realized Marina wasn't there. A lump formed in the back of my throat and I suddenly felt like someone had landed a sucker punch straight to my gut. A melancholy cloud swept over me as I approached the counter. Mildred was pouring some coffee when she noticed me.

"You're back. What can I get for you?" Mildred asked.

"Have you seen Marina today?"

"Sorry hon, She's not here. She might be somewhere in Indiana by now."

I paused before continuing. "Okay… Can I get a cup of ice water to go please?"

"Sure thing. You sure you don't want another one of my pies?"

"No, ma'am. I'm afraid the ice water is all I need today." I set my bag down by the counter and made my way to the restroom.

As I stared into the mirror, I thought, *what a damn fool you are!*

Unaware that Marina had entered the diner, I turned the corner from the restroom and stated to Mildred, "Thank you for the ice water…" My eyes locked onto Marina's eyes and in unison we both whispered, "You're here."

We approached each other slowly. Her dark hair wasn't up in a ponytail anymore, but instead was parted slightly to the right and flowed in graceful waves down past her shoulders. Her pale olive skin was highlighted almost perfectly with a simple kiss of makeup that contrasted her high cheekbones and round face. Her waitress uniform was replaced by a striped aquamarine tunic top with long puffy sleeves cinched at the waist and transitioned down to the frayed flair-bottomed jeans that fit her perfectly.

We both smiled as I stammered to find the words to say. "I didn't think you would show up."

Marina's smile shifted to a look of concern. She glanced at the cup of ice water I was now holding. "What is it with you and ice water?"

"Oh… nothing… I'm just thirsty…" I took a long gulp of the water and placed it on the counter.

We both stood there uncomfortably waiting for the other to say something. You could cut the discomfort with a knife.

"So, I guess we're going to do this?" Marina stated in a matter-of-fact way, hoping to trigger some reaction.

Mildred was smiling from behind the counter. I noticed her attempting to camouflage her eavesdropping by wiping the same spot on the counter, continuously. I wasn't sure if it was because she found the whole situation to be entertaining or if she was happy Marina wasn't going to be travelling alone, either way my mind couldn't help but think, *this is really happening.*

Marina gave Mildred a hug and a kiss on the cheek and whispered, "I'll call you soon." She then barked out as she turned and headed for the door, "Grab your things William Massey, I'm ready to hit the road."

"You want your ice water?" asked Mildred.

"No thanks, I don't need it anymore," I yelled back.

Marina approached a turquoise 1965 Ford Mustang and opened the driver's side door.

As I started to open the passenger door, I noticed her staring at me impatiently.

"I have a few ground rules. First, I am the only person allowed to drive my car. Second, I don't know if you smoke or chew, but if you do, it won't be in my car. Third, I need to know you can actually hold up your end of the deal. Did you bring any money with you?"

It was obvious that one of Marina's tactics for dealing with uneasiness or uncertainty was to try and exude leadership and control. I found it adorable and endearing, but I tried not to let that show in my response for fear she would take offense. "I'm okay with not driving, but I have never been able to sleep while someone else is. I don't smoke and I don't use tobacco of any kind." Reaching into my pocket I pulled out a stack of bills. "I brought some cash with me. Here's five hundred dollars for you to hang on to so you know I meant what I said."

Marina gawked at the stack of bills.

She walked around and opened the trunk of the car for me. "You can throw your bag in the trunk if you'd like, or the back seat."

I looked in the back seat and noticed a large worn-out duffle bag with a brown paisley design, that I suspected once belonged to Mildred given its aged appearance and older style. Next to it sat a pillow, a crocheted throw, a cotton blanket, and a couple of small canvas totes with various personal belongings hanging out of them. Venturing around to the trunk, I noticed a larger green suitcase and a mustard-colored leather tote. I thought, *wow… this appears to be everything she owns.* Setting my bag next to the spare tire, I closed the trunk and took my place in the passenger seat.

My first impression of her car was that it was extremely clean and well kept. The seats and steering wheel showed no signs of wear and the smell the carpet and vinyl emitted was almost like new. Nothing fancy, just a standard hardtop three speed automatic transmission with all the basics; AM radio, air conditioning, heater and defroster. I could tell she was proud of this car and it had to be one of her most prized possessions.

"Well, let's hit the road, William Massey." Marina cranked the car and we pulled away from Mildred's Diner.

CHAPTER 5

December 2, 1970

I NEVER DREAMED IN a million years that one day I might go on a road trip across the country with a total stranger; a female stranger at that. This was the type of thing some people would love, but for me… this is the stuff nightmares are made of. I contemplated, *you could still back out*, but like an uneasy virgin sailor who is staring back at shore; that ship had sailed.

At first, the car felt like a steel trap with wheels; turquoise vinyl was surrounding me on all sides and an unknown firecracker with dark curly hair driving at full throttle down the interstate. I watched Marina straighten her sunglasses in the rearview mirror; try different buttons on the AM radio looking for a more satisfactory station, or my favorite, turn her head to admire each house and building in every town we passed through. I'm certain I was making a bigger deal of it all in my head at the time, and I would become more accustomed to her driving and the confines of her car, but for the time being, my nerves were shot.

I tried staring out the window, admiring the beautiful forests of Ohio whizzing by at what seemed like a record pace. The leaves had long fallen from the trees and what remained was a somber tapestry of twisted branches and limbs almost begging for a beautiful snowfall or the onset of spring buds to lighten nature's mood.

Soon we entered Columbus and shortly after we exited the capital of Ohio, but not in the direction I would have expected. Instead of heading toward Indianapolis, we were on our way to Cincinnati. Vacuous of what to say and not wanting to second guess my host, I decided to say nothing at all.

It was an uncomfortable silence.

Not completely void of sound however, since we did have the radio that was picking up a few stations, but altogether it was eerily quiet. Neither one of us knew what to say. Two complete strangers with no prior knowledge about one another, only a few hours into a multi-day, possibly multi-week journey across the countryside. What could go wrong?

"So, you like water?" Marina asked in an admirable attempt to break the silence.

"Yep"

More silence.

"So you're a waitress?" I asked.

"Pretty much my whole life."

More silence.

"How about you, what do you do for a living, Mr. Massey?"

"Industrial sales," I answered, like everyone knows what that means.

We continued our trek through rural Ohio, listening to a radio station that kept fading in and out. We were both getting hungry and lunchtime was approaching.

Marina again broke through the silence. "Why don't we stop for a break and some lunch."

"Okay," I responded. I noticed Marina roll her eyes and let out an exaggerated breath. I could tell something was wrong, but I didn't know if it was something I said or something I did. I started thinking about what to say, I was now overanalyzing and over-thinking my every move.

At this point she offered up a softball question, "What are you hungry for?" She glanced over at me almost appearing to be poised for my next mistake.

Contemplating the question, I cautiously answered back with what I thought was a considerate response, "Whatever you want is fine with me." I smiled, but her body language let me know my answer was not what she wanted to hear.

We pulled into a small truck stop diner, one of those places known for their pancakes at 11 o'clock at night. No sooner than we had sat down in a booth next to the front window, an energetic waitress approached us.

"What can I get you two lovebirds?"

Marina looked up from her menu rather flustered by the waitress's assumption. "Oh, we're not together… we're just trav-eling together."

I smiled as the waitress looked at me then looked back at Marina and shrugged her shoulders, before continuing, "What can I get you two travelers today?"

Marina smiled and nodded at the retraction. "I'll have lemon-ade, and for my meal, can you surprise me?" She turned my way, daring me to do the same.

I peered up at the waitress from my menu and specified, "I'll have water and the ham and cheese sandwich please."

Marina scoffed, unsurprised by my order. After the waitress hurried back to the kitchen, I noticed Marina was now staring stoically out the window at the eighteen wheelers coming and going from the parking lot. I didn't like the feeling that I might be responsible for the sudden waning of her cheery disposition.

"Are you mad at me?" I pleaded in frustration, "because I don't know what I've said or done, but I can't get back in the car and stare out the window thinking you are going to be mad at me."

"What you've said?" Marina shot back. "What you've said? You've hardly said two words for the last four hours. I have tried to start conversations with you only to get one word answers in return." She waited for my response.

"Okay," I replied, oblivious to what I was doing.

She tilted her head ever so slightly to the side and peered up at me with raised eyebrows. "You did it again."

Luckily for me, the waitress arrived with our drinks and our food which distracted Marina. I realized she had been given a plate with fried chicken livers, mashed potatoes, green beans, a roll and what appeared to be a small jar filled with honey. I was unable to hold back my smile and soft chuckles as I witnessed the most perplexing yet enchanting expression on Marina's face I had experienced up to that point in our short time together.

"Why are you laughing?"

I chose not to respond but instead raised my eyebrows and shrugged my shoulders with childlike confusion.

"William, what is this meat?" she whispered. Her expression reminded me of the frightened pure innocence of a little girl.

"They appear to be fried chicken livers, with a side of honey for dipping."

"People eat chicken livers? With honey?"

Marina stared endlessly at the pile of chicken livers on her plate. It was almost like she was trying to wish them away. Then without further hesitation, she picked one up with all the determination in the world, dipped it into the honey and took a bite.

The timing of our server was impeccable; at the moment when Marina's brain told her mouth to expel the chewed-up liver, the waitress appeared.

"Aren't those the best chicken livers you've ever had? They're my favorite."

Marina proceeded to smile and chew the chicken liver for what felt like an eternity, all along nodding her head in agreement with the waitress. While she struggled to swallow the bite, our eager server smiled and turned to head back to the kitchen. I knew better than to laugh at this point. I simply pushed my ham and cheese sandwich toward Marina and gave her a cordial nod and a wink. She humbly passed her plate to me while washing the taste out of her mouth with a large swig of lemonade.

"Thank you, Will Massey," she whispered.

"No problem, Marina."

"Call me Mar." She looked at me and smiled with a certain degree of concession.

A warmth ran through me like a cup of hot cocoa. It's a feeling I will never forget. It was like a barrier had been removed for both of us, the formality of two strangers softened by a simple gesture.

She finished off the ham and cheese sandwich, folded and placed her napkin neatly on the table next to her plate and picked up her glass of lemonade. "I have an idea to make our trip more bearable."

"I'm listening," I countered with a suspicious smile.

"What if we take turns? Each day one of us is allowed to ask the other a deep question. You know… something requiring elaboration or at least more than a one-word answer. I figure the more we get to know about each other, the less we feel like strangers and it might make our drive a little less boring. What do you think?"

"Nothing too uncomfortable, right?"

"If something is too uncomfortable, maybe we give each other a pass to come back to the question before our trip is finished… Deal?" She extended her hand to shake on it.

I contemplated the offer, then reached out and shook her hand. "Deal"

This was the first time we had physically touched. I believe it was the first physical contact I had with another human being for five years. I have no words to describe it, other than… unforgettable. We finished up our lunch break and headed to the car.

Reflecting back on Marina's desire for more conversation, I asked as we pulled back onto the road, "Now that we've established you don't like chicken livers, what's your favorite food?"

She smiled in approval at my attempt to start a conversation. "I'm very much a meat and potatoes girl. I'd say my favorite food would be a tender pot roast with some mashed potatoes and carrots. How about you Will?"

I thought about it, and replied, "I don't get to have them much, but I actually like oysters. I'll eat them raw or deep fried, but my favorite would be Oysters Rockefeller. Have you ever had them?"

She stared at me blankly.

"They take a nice mix of chopped spinach, parmesan cheese and seasonings and cook it to perfection right on top of the oyster in half of its shell." I explained.

Marina raised her eyebrows, unsure of my choice.

I snickered, picturing her eating and reacting to oysters the same way she did with the chicken livers.

Approaching the outskirts of Cincinnati we encountered a road construction project and at least two bad car accidents. That perfect storm brought our journey to a standstill. Facing miles of snarled traffic, the first day of our journey slowed from the speed of a cheetah to the stroll of a turtle in a matter of seconds.

I exhaled in frustration before glancing over at Marina. "What now?"

She hesitated and then initiated her plan. "Do I get to ask the first question?"

I raised my eyebrows playfully and conceded to her request.

"Based on what you've told me so far, you are an industrial salesman in Cleveland… is that where you were born and raised Will Massey?"

"No. I was actually born and raised in Memphis, Tennessee."

"Like Elvis?" She quipped playfully.

"Sort of," I replied, "although I think he may have been born in Mississippi."

"Does your family still live there?"

Easing into the question, I paused, shaking my head from side to side and staring straight ahead. "No, they've all passed away."

"I'm sorry, Will. I didn't mean to…"

I interrupted her apology. "It's okay, it was a while ago."

Marina respectfully paused her questioning, but that didn't last very long. "So I guess you were an only child?"

"I had two older brothers, Walt and Drew, but they both died on the beaches of France back in forty-four."

Marina processed that comment, before asking, "In the war?"

"Yeah, they were part of the D-Day invasion."

"Were you in the war?"

"How old do you think I am?" I joked, trying to inject a small amount of levity to the conversation. "I was too young to enlist. Walt and Drew were a few years older than me."

Although a little glum, Marina did appear pleased that her plan was working. "I'm sure you've missed them."

"I do miss them and I think of them sometimes. It was so long ago, you know? But at the same time, it feels like it was yesterday."

Luckily for us, the traffic was keeping us at a manageable speed, allowing Marina to safely split her time between driving and listening to my story.

"We were quite the team, the three of us boys."

Marina smiled and her eyes glistened with excitement.

I continued. "I remember this one time when Walt, Drew and I all decided we were going to go fishing in an old slough down where the Mississippi River would flood sometimes. We headed out with some egg sandwiches Walt had thrown together and a couple of canteens of water. Carrying our cane poles over our shoulders, we probably walked four miles to get to the slough, barefoot and in nothing but our old overalls. When we got there, we realized it had been so hot and arid, that the ground around the old marsh had dried up like clay bricks. Our plan all along was to dig us up some worms and use them for bait. Well, we forgot the shovel, so the three of us were down on our hands and knees for about an hour clawing at the hard ground, with no luck at all. Drew decided that'd had enough, so he sat down under an old cypress tree close by. He ripped back the wax paper that Walt had wrapped around the sandwiches and took a bite. You should've seen the look on his face. It was almost as bad as the look you had when you bit into those chicken livers."

Marina blushed.

"Anyway, Drew was the type to not offend anyone. So, he swallowed down about half of his sandwich before setting it aside. Walt and I joined him under the tree and pulled out the other two sandwiches. Walt took a bite of his and commenced to spitting and gagging. He yelled and cussed at Drew saying 'why in the hell didn't you tell me I over salted them eggs?' Drew started laughing so hard he nearly pissed himself. I didn't know what to think, but about that time, the overdose of salt hit Drew's intestines and he began to head around the tree and started getting sick."

I shook my head and smiled, remembering the moment so vividly in my mind.

"We let him drink our portions of the water and after resting for about an hour, he started to feel a little better. So, Walt gets the idea to use the eggs in the sandwiches for bait. We struggled for darn near another hour to try and catch something with those eggs before we realized those fish cared for over-salted eggs about as much as we did."

I went quiet, remembering the faces of my brothers.

"Are you okay?" she asked.

I grimaced. "Yeah. You know… death is a pretty cruel thing."

Marina searched for something to say, before asking, "Well, did you ever catch anything?"

Her question made me smile. "As a matter of fact, I wadded some of the bread into a ball and put it on my hook; I caught the biggest channel cat any of us had ever seen. We packed it up and headed home. I think Walt and Drew were a little irritated that I was the only one who caught anything."

There was respectful delay before I continued.

"You know, the war ended before I could enlist. Momma sent her only remaining son off to college and I never went back to Memphis."

"You never went back to see your parents?"

"Never had the chance; they took a trip over to France in forty nine to see where Walt and Drew were buried. They died in a boat accident on the way back home. At least they got to see where my brothers were buried before they went to join them in heaven."

We continued further down the road and after about an hour

of no talking, Marina finally spoke up, "I'm sorry about your family, Will. What did you do after that?"

I looked over at her, smiled and replied, "That's another question for another day."

She pouted and gave me a look of displeasure that was actually kind of cute, to which I replied "You made the rules Mar, not me."

The unexpected traffic delays had cost us about four hours on our day. Night was settling in on our drive, and we were both getting tired. It had also started to rain, so we decided to find the next decent motel with a vacancy and get ourselves a room for the night.

As we pulled into the parking lot of this little travel motel, I looked over at Marina nervously. "I can try to get us two rooms if you'd like."

She looked at me with a cautious grin. "No, I think you're a good man Will Massey. I believe I'd feel safer with you in the room with me than not."

"I'll get two beds then," I emphatically and gallantly proclaimed.

After going into the office and haggling with the manager for fifteen minutes, I returned with the key and we proceeded to room number three.

"We're lucky; the manager said this was his last available room." I fumbled around with the key until Marina took it from me and opened the door.

I couldn't believe my eyes; there, in the middle of that little hotel room, sat one queen-sized bed. I immediately began to apologize.

"Marina, I swear I told him two beds. He said that's what this was. If I'd known…"

She stopped me mid-sentence and goaded, "Aren't you a sneaky little man there Mr. Massey?"

"No, I swear!" My heart began to race at the implication against my honor.

"I'm just pulling your chain Will. If it's their last room, then there wasn't much you could do."

"But I swear I told him two beds. I'm not the kind of guy who takes advantage of the vulnerabilities of a young woman…"

My mouth gaped open and I instantly recognized my mistake in choosing those words. One thing I had learned early on about Marina was her quick-acting defense mechanism, triggered whenever someone suggested she was weak. Her face drained of any sunshine and she let me have it. "William Massey, I am thirty years old. I am not a little girl. I can take care of myself and I am not, I repeat *not*, vulnerable! This room is fine, and we will make due. We're both tired and we need some rest."

I stood inside the doorway like a statue, hoping I was invisible after that small misstep.

She made her way into the bathroom to wash up and get ready for bed, so I pulled the extra blanket onto the floor along with one of the pillows. Lying there thinking about this predicament I had gotten into, my mind wandered again toward Marina and how there was this feeling like I had known her all of my life. It was comforting.

"What are you doing?" Marina exclaimed, exiting the bathroom.

"I'll sleep on the floor. I'm a gentleman first and foremost. You can have the bed."

Her body language revealed she wanted to debate this decision, but then she softened and nodded at me bashfully. She slipped into the bed and turned off the light. The last thing I heard that night was her soft, sweet voice whispering, "Thank you, Will."

CHAPTER 6

December 3, 1970

I WOKE TO A sound I have never gotten used to, but I have learned I could never live without.

Marina had risen early to shower. Now, I wouldn't say that it was the most in-tune or melodious voice I had ever heard. In fact, she was often pitchy and flat. Yet, to describe her voice as anything but angelic would be an understatement for me. I truly believe God can manipulate our senses to interpret things the way He intends them. For me, her voice was mesmerizing and comforting. There I lay on the hard floor, eyes closed, pretending to be asleep. On one hand, I was embracing the emotions stirring within me towards a woman I scarcely knew. On the other, I was a little confused and guilty about how deeply these feelings were already affecting me.

She came out of the bathroom ready for the day. "Wake up sleepy head. It's time to hit the road."

I rolled over and stretched, making a show out of a cavernous yawn and pretending to wipe sleep from my eyes. Marina stood there looking at me impatiently. The light orange jumpsuit she wore clung to her figure, mirroring her vibrant energy and fiery spirit. Her long, dark curls were neatly pulled back from her face, restrained by a white scarf tied elegantly at the back. I became lost, admiring how striking she looked. Debating whether to compliment her appearance or keep my thoughts private, I opted for a safer, more lighthearted response. Flashing a goofy smile, I assured her, "I'll only be a few minutes."

After a short time, I emerged to find Marina had already packed up our belongings and placed them into the car. Her eagerness and excitement was noticeable. We walked over to the little diner connected to the motel and took a seat.

"What's the plan for today?" I asked.

That small nudge was all she needed to get her going. Marina pulled a Hammond Road Atlas and a pencil out of her bag and began to trace a route from Hudson, Ohio to Louisville, Kentucky.

"I think we are a little north of Louisville," she explained, using the pencil to point to the direct spot on the map. "We can either go south from here through Nashville, or we can go west toward St. Louis."

Looking at the map from the other side of the table, I used my finger to trace the most direct route I could from Hudson, Ohio to San Diego, California.

"Before you say it, I realize I probably should have headed toward Indianapolis when we were coming through Columbus, but what's done is done," Marina acknowledged. "And I know I said my goal was to see the coast of California, but I wouldn't mind experiencing a little bit more along the way." She peeked up from the atlas long enough to make eye contact in the most pleading way possible.

My tendency to find a pragmatic and practical solution had

taken over again, and I back-tracked quickly, "Oh, of course, I wasn't implying…"

"I know you weren't implying anything," she assured me with a flirtatious grin.

Marina studied the map again, allowing herself to be distracted long enough to thank the waitress for our coffee when it arrived. "Nashville might be a fun place to visit."

"Nashville it is," I confirmed, holding my coffee mug up and tapping it against hers.

Marina pushed the keys across the table to me. "Are you okay to drive for a while?"

I picked up the keys and started to make a wise-crack, but realized she was trusting me with her most valuable possession. "Thank you for trusting me. I would be happy to drive."

As we continued our journey, I noticed the closer we got to Nashville, the harder it was to avoid country music on the radio. We tried numerous times to find other stations before settling on the one with the clearest signal. It's not that I didn't like country music, it was just that most of the songs they were playing either talked about loves lost, fighting, people making dumb decisions, or all of the above, and none of those themes would make a long road trip any more enjoyable. I was trying to pay attention to the road, but my restlessness was getting the better of me. Hill after grassy hill passed by outside while the sun continued to stay tucked behind an overcast sky. Marina must have sensed a question was about to come her way because out of nowhere she began to sing along with the radio.

Everything faded from my mind and I was drawn into her performance as she sang along with Patsy Cline to every word of "Crazy". After the song ended, a moment of silence filled the air.

I believe if she could've kept singing non-stop for thirty hours, I would've driven us all the way to San Diego and not realized it.

"So Mar, how did you end up in Hudson, Ohio? Were you born there?"

She glanced over my way with a look and tilt of the head that seemed to let me know I had asked an acceptable question.

"Although I've spent most of my life there, I'm not originally from there," she stated in a matter-of-fact way. "I moved to Hudson to live with my Aunt Mildred when I was about six years old."

"So the lady in the diner is your aunt?"

"Will, it's my turn to speak," Marina replied, firm but still smiling. "Yes, Mildred is my aunt; she was my dad's youngest sister. I never met my mom. She died when I was a baby. My dad raised me and my brothers and sisters from that point on. I don't remember him much at all. He was a coal miner in Pennsylvania. I remember when I did see him; he was always coughing and sick. He died from black lung and I was sent to live with Mildred in Hudson."

I wasn't quite sure how to respond. Before I could probe a little more, she began again.

"Mildred was like a mother and a big sister to me. She took care of me even though she didn't have much. Of course, I started helping out at the diner as soon as I was big enough to clean tables and wash dishes." Marina smiled and added, "I'm sure going to miss that diner, and Aunt Mildred. Anyway, I was always told my mother looked like a gypsy. Dark hair down to the middle of her back; 'short in stature, but tall in attitude,' Aunt Mildred always said. I guess she got sick in the spring and by winter she had died."

"Sounds like you take after your mother in looks and personality," I responded without thinking first.

Marina cocked her head to one side and raised her eyebrows. "What's that supposed to mean?"

I chuckled at first, before realizing that my charm and humor wasn't enough to explain my comment. "I meant the description of her hair and height sounds a lot like you. That's all?"

Marina smirked suspiciously and mumbled, "Uh-huh."

"And maybe a little bit of the attitude thing," I uttered while smiling from ear to ear.

Marina swiped at my arm, playfully reprimanding me.

"Or do you take after your dad?" I deflected.

"No, I guess you are right. My dad was tall and slender with dark hair and a stubborn streak. Mildred said he got his strong work habit from their daddy, but he also got his inability to love correctly. Not quite sure what she meant; I just wish I could have known both of them more."

Trying to extend the conversation, and without seeming to pry too much, I reflected, "Sounds like Mildred loves you and cares about you."

"Oh yes, Mildred definitely knows how to love and to care. She taught me how to be a woman, how to work hard, how to survive and how to love."

"Speaking of love," I stated, "why aren't you married? You're smart; you're beautiful in more ways than just your looks. Haven't found Mr. Right yet?" I mused.

It appeared that I caught Marina a little off guard with my compliment. "Now Will Massey, if I didn't know any better, I would say you're trying to sneak another question in."

"No. That's not what I was trying to do. I just... you know... the conversation... I'm enjoying getting to know you."

"You know the rules," she scolded in a playful manner.

"Okay, continue telling me about Mildred."

"What about her?"

I could tell Marina was enjoying this back and forth banter. To be honest, I was too, so I continued, "You said she taught you how to love, is Mildred married or has she ever been married?"

Marina nodded 'yes' with a reserved smile before explaining, "Mildred married her sweetheart, Jesse, before he was shipped off to the war in 1942. She always said he died on some beautiful island in the Pacific in a not so beautiful war. By the time I arrived on her doorstep four years later, she had opened up the diner and was frying up her pies for everyone."

"She never met anyone else and remarried?"

"She was never given the chance," Marina retorted. "Do you know, most men in the 1940's had no interest in a young woman who already had a child?"

"I don't know about that."

"Trust me Will, I watched as she would go out on a date. Once the guy would see me, they would never be heard from again." Marina paused, reflecting on that situation. "She gave up a lot for me. She took me in as her own."

Marina's facial expression suddenly shifted. It was obvious she had never truly considered that sacrifice before. "She's really been more of a mother to me than an aunt." She smiled proudly and glanced over at me.

I realized I had been so engrossed in her story that I had driven right through Nashville.

"Umm… I think we drove through Nashville," I admitted.

"Oh well, maybe another time." Marina said.

It dawned on me we were headed straight for Memphis, Tennessee. I hadn't been there since I left for college. The cloud of anxiety and trepidation must have been apparent because Marina asked, "Are you okay Will?"

"I'm fine… really… I am."

Sensing I needed a little quiet time, she fluffed her pillow against the window and proceeded to close her eyes for a while.

My mind drifted upstream, against the currents of time, to my childhood. I wondered if the old house where we flourished as a family was still around. Would it look the same?

I began to smell ham fresh out of the oven on a Sunday afternoon. My mouth watered and I could taste the purple hulled peas and cornbread dancing across my tongue. I could hear my mama's voice singing "The Old Rugged Cross" while she set the dishes on the table. I could vividly see Daddy holding Mama from behind as he whispered something into her ear that made her smile and blush with delight before turning around and kissing him.

I wondered, yet again, if I could have protected Walt and Drew, if I'd been with them in the war. Together, the three of us were invincible. And maybe I could have saved Mama and Daddy if I'd gone with them to see the gravesites. At the very least, I would have been with them in their final moments.

A hundred miles passed before a sign for Memphis pulled me from my somber reverie.

Marina stirred from her nap and asked, "Is there anything good to eat in Memphis? I'm getting hungry."

"Is there anything good to eat in Memphis? Did you ask if there is anything good to eat in Memphis?"

"Yes, I did." She looked shocked at my sarcasm.

"Well, being on the Mississippi river, right up the river from Louisiana, I'm sure we can find some good seafood or creole cooking. We can probably find some good southern comfort food too. But if you really want to experience Memphis, we should find somewhere to stay for the night, and go have some barbecue."

Marina looked at me and smiled. "I trust you Will Massey, you choose."

"Barbecue it is," I proclaimed.

I drove us into downtown Memphis, looking for a respectable hotel for the night. We parked the car and grabbed our things and headed inside this stately hotel I knew Marina would like.

"I don't know about this place Will, it looks like it might be a little pricey for our budget."

"Don't worry, Marina," I said. "Every once and a while you've got to treat yourself."

"Welcome to the Sheraton Peabody Hotel," said the man from behind the counter, "Need a room for the night?"

I glanced at Marina inquiringly.

"Get one room Will, I feel safer sharing a room."

"Yes sir, one room, two beds if possible." I scanned Marina for her approval. She gave me a smile and a wink, and I was assured of my decision.

After checking us in, the man behind the counter asked, "Would the Missus like a key as well?"

We looked at each other in a moment of embarrassment before both of us giggled and answered together, "Yes."

"The bellhop will escort you to your room. Breakfast begins at seven in the morning. The ducks come in around…"

Marina glared at me, almost questioning if I had heard the same thing.

"Ducks?" she asked.

"Yes ma'am," said the man behind the counter. "We have a small family of ducks who live here at the hotel. They march in at 11am on the dot every day, down from the roof in the elevator and into the fountain over there. In fact, they should be marching back to the elevator and up to the roof here in just a few minutes."

We turned and looked at the beautiful fountain situated in the center of the lobby. People had started to gather. Just then, a man who was dressed from head to toe, like the commander of a mighty armada, entered the room. Exuding confidence and class, he tapped the cane he was holding on the edge of the fountain and five little ducks began to file out one by one. I glanced over at Marina and noticed she was just standing there staring at the ducks with a smile that could light up the room. It was like nothing else in the world existed, except for those ducks. We watched those little feathery creatures waddle their way across the room along the red carpet and into the elevator before the doors were closed by the 'duckmaster'.

Marina turned toward me with a look of awe. "Did you know about this place?"

"I've known about it my entire life, but I've never had the chance to stay here and see it in person. I thought it might be a nice surprise."

"You folks ready to see your room?" The bellhop was patiently waiting for us.

"Yes sir, thank you very much", I answered. We followed him to the elevator.

"I've never seen anything like that," Marina expressed.

"It was pretty amazing," I replied.

As the bellhop pushed the button to the seventh floor, I glanced at Marina. The smile had drained from her face and was now replaced by the look of sheer horror.

I gave her a quick raise of the eyebrows, inquiring if something was wrong. She leaned over close to me and whispered into my ear, "I've never been on an elevator before."

Smiling sympathetically, I placed my arm around her shoulder and pulled her in closer when the elevator began to move.

Marina must have been holding her breath, because when the

elevator door opened, she breathed in heavily like she had been deprived of oxygen.

Entering our room, we noticed two full beds with an elegant chaise sitting in the corner near the window. The room, like the hotel in general, was showing typical signs of age, but through the faded paint, outdated tapestries and worn bathroom fixtures still shined a luxury that was hard to miss. I tipped the bellhop and we both set our bags down. Marina made her way around the room, inspecting every inch.

"Will, are you sure we can afford this?"

"Don't worry about it Mar, it's just for tonight"

Content with my answer, she sprawled out on top of one of the beds.

"It's so beautiful and soft. It's like I've died and gone to heaven."

I smiled at her and watched while she soaked it all in.

"Should we venture out for some dinner?" I asked.

After a brief moment of indulgence, Marina popped up like she was shot out of a cannon. "Let's go."

We headed back out of our room. I let her push the button on the elevator and I watched in delight as she beamed like a child with a new toy.

Exiting the elevator, I made my way over to an older black gentleman who was adorned in a snazzy red bellhop uniform.

"Excuse me sir? We are thinking about heading out for some barbeque. Can you recommend a place?"

He smiled at me, raised his eyebrows and stated in a matter-of-fact manner, "Leonard's Pit BBQ, down off Bellevue and McLemore, just a few miles southeast." He must have read my look of helplessness, because he quickly pulled a pencil and small piece of paper from his coat pocket and jotted down some simple instructions and a crude map for me.

A few turns and a few miles later, we pulled into this happening little joint with some carhops and a small dining area on the inside. After finding a seat, an energetic young lady came up to our table and asked, "What can I get you two lovebirds to drink?"

"We're just two friends travelling together, that's all," I said. "We're not really lovebirds, I mean." I looked at Marina for approval.

Marina bit her lip, smiled and winked at me.

The waitress gawked at me, like I had said something wrong.

"I'll have a cola," I answered, hoping to swiftly move on from the uncomfortable moment.

"I'll have the same," Marina replied.

"And how about to eat?" asked the waitress.

Before Marina could think to reply, I announced to our waitress, "Surprise us."

Marina peered at me with a look of complete astonishment. "Will Massey, am I rubbing off on you?" she asked with a sly grin. Before the waitress could get too far away, Marina shouted out to her in a last second rush, "Oh miss, could you make sure it's not chicken livers?"

We both laughed when the waitress shot back the strangest of looks.

"What should we do tomorrow?" Marina asked.

"I suppose we could drive out through my old neighborhood and I can show you where I grew up, that is if it's still around."

"I'd like that." Marina said with a smile.

I smiled politely back at her. It's hard to explain, but there was an indescribable ease that enveloped me whenever I was around Marina. It was like we had lived our entire lives with the sole purpose of being there, on that journey, at that time. Before I could open my mouth and stick my foot in it, our server arrived with our food.

"Make way. I've got two pork specials, two Cokes and a slice of ice box lemon pie. I'll come back and check on you two in a few." With that, our waitress left us to ourselves.

I couldn't help but smile as I watched Marina delicately pick up the pork sandwich, trying ever so hard not to let the whole thing fall out all over the place. It was a work of art. A soft warm bun piled high with the most succulent slow cooked smoked pork. On top of the pork, they had placed a dollop of the best coleslaw I believe I'd ever had. To the side was a sizeable helping of barbecue-baked beans, with little pieces of bacon and a sweet and tangy taste that was almost like candy. Marina finally decided this would require a more aggressive approach and she took a bite worthy of any man I had ever met. She glanced my way and rolled her eyes and mouthed to me, "This is so good".

It had been a while since I had truly watched a woman eat, and I quickly realized I was staring and stealthily studying with delight.

Around us, the soft murmur of conversations blended with the occasional clatter of dishes, creating a lively yet comfortable backdrop. Marina finished her meal a little before me, and pulled the pie toward her side of the table. Using her fork, she scooped some up to her mouth. A soft cloud of the cream had caught on her lip. I watched as she made short work of cleaning it off with the tip of her tongue. She looked at me and made an unpleasant face.

"What's wrong?" I asked.

"The pie isn't that good. I don't think you will like it, Will Massey," she proclaimed playfully. With that statement, she took another large scoop and slowly moved it toward her mouth. At this point her little ruse had delighted her so, that she giggled and winked at me while pulling the bite of pie from her fork.

"I'll be the judge of that." I stretched across the table with my fork and took a bite.

"I told you that you wouldn't like it!" Marina teased, snickering through her words.

"You're right, that's terrible." I reached across the table again for another bite.

We began to laugh at our little game, as we finished off the rest of the pie.

Not wanting the evening to end, I decided to throw out an idea. "You know, I saw an interesting looking bar down from the hotel. We could go back, park the car, and check it out. What do you think?"

Marina smiled and answered, "Sounds like fun."

We finished up and made our way to the quaint little place. It had the feel of a modern juke joint. Its outdated lighting barely highlighted the old brick walls and worn out wooden floor. It was only about half full, but still bustling with about forty patrons inside. Smoke lofted about, but not too much and there was a distinctive smell of bourbon wafting through the air as well; a truly perfect atmosphere for a night out in Memphis. We made our way to a small round table over on the side and sat down.

"What can I get for you two lovebirds?" We looked up to see a rather round petite black lady with her hair up in a scarf. She had a kind demeanor about her but was noticeably tough enough to handle herself on a street like this.

Before I could correct her misinterpretation of our situation, Marina glanced up at the waitress and stated before turning her playful gaze toward me, "I'm not sure. Honey, what are you going to have?"

Without missing a beat, I answered, "You know sweetheart; I think I'll have a Manhattan tonight."

Marina looked both surprised and a little shocked at my move, but only for a second. "Make that two Manhattan's," she replied with confidence.

"Two Manhattans coming right up," confirmed the waitress.

Marina was about to say something when we heard the voice of a little old man on the stage. He started with a scat, then lifted an old worn-out trumpet up to his lips and began to play. Soon after, he was accompanied by another man playing a snare drum and a cymbal and yet another older gentleman playing a standup bass. I pulled my chair around closer to her so we could both see the stage and enjoy the show. Marina turned her face toward me and our eyes locked on to each other. She gave me a smile, and then turned to face the stage while leaning into me ever so slightly.

Our drinks arrived and I could tell, as Marina choked a little on her first sip, that she had probably never had alcohol before, at least nothing that strong. After a couple of more sips, she looked like a bourbon connoisseur. The band made it through about three songs without either of us realizing it.

"Would you two like another drink?" the waitress asked.

"Yes please!" Marina answered, before I could open my mouth. I watched her fish around the ice and dig the cherry out of the bottom of her glass. Triumphantly, she lifted it by the stem, displaying her prize with a playful flourish before skillfully plucking it from the stem with her teeth and savoring the sweet burst of flavor. Despite being ensconced in this charming little bar, with the soulful strains of blues filling the air and a fine bourbon cocktail warming my hand, it was Marina who captivated my entire attention. Her simple, joyful act illuminated the moment, making the vibrant ambiance and live music fade into the backdrop of her presence. I hadn't been that happy in years. The warmth of her smile and the aura about her was like a drug I began to crave.

We sat there together and enjoyed several more songs and

another round before realizing how late it was getting and how tired we both were.

"You know, we do have more driving to do tomorrow. Maybe we should call it a night?" I suggested.

Marina frowned and sighed, "You're probably right."

We both slipped back into our coats and said goodbye to this unforgettable place. There was a noticeable chill in the air when we came out of the bar.

Marina glanced up at me with a smile. "Thank you, Will Massey."

She looped her left arm inside my right arm and took my hand into hers. "My hands are a little cold," she explained.

I gave a gentle squeeze. I didn't care if she just needed my warmth; I was pleased to have a reason to hold her hand.

Turning the corner toward the hotel, we noticed an older homeless man who was standing against the wall. Everything he owned appeared to be neatly stacked next to him on the sidewalk, and what appeared to be an old military hat was laid out in front of him to collect spare change from passersby. He was playing a small clarinet while keeping time with the tapping of his feet. We stopped to listen to his wonderful rendition of "When the Saints Go Marching In". I pulled a five-dollar bill out of my pocket, handed it to Marina and motioned to his hat. Marina took the money, her eyes wide with surprise. Her shock softened to a smile, and she placed it into the man's hat.

"God bless you, little lady; thank you so much."

Back at the hotel, not a word was said while we each took turns getting ready for a good night's sleep. We slipped into our respective beds and turned off the light. Marina whispered, "Good night, Will, I can't wait for tomorrow."

CHAPTER 7

December 4, 1970

DAWN ARRIVED QUICKLY. The chorus of *'When the Saints Go Marching In'* echoed from the bathroom. Marina's voice, full of warmth, filled the air with an infectious energy that seemed to dance through the room. There was a brief whisper in my mind. A tiny voice urging caution against the overwhelming surge of emotion her singing inspired. Yet, a stronger, more resonant voice within me insisted, 'soak this up.'

After taking my turn, I emerged and found Marina gazing thoughtfully out the window at the streets of Memphis below. Her usually restrained hair cascaded freely down her back, ending midway in a gentle wave that moved subtly with each breath she took. A small headband adorned her head, pushing back stray wisps of hair and framing her thoughtful expression. The light from outside sculpted her figure, highlighting the graceful contours of her silhouette against the backdrop of the city. Her presence provided an air of peacefulness to the room.

"Are you ready to show me where you grew up?"

Her question cut through the tranquil silence of the room, jolting me back into the present. Memories of the previous night's pleasant distractions receded into a familiar mix of anxiety and nervousness. This mingling of apprehension and nostalgia created a poignant tension, as the reality of revisiting my childhood home and all the memories it could bring became more probable.

Turning to face me, she clarified, "That is, if you still want to."

"Oh, no, I mean… uh, yeah, we could do that today."

"And, Will, I need to call Aunt Mildred and let her know we made it to Memphis safely. Maybe while you are checking us out, I will try to find a pay phone."

"That's probably a good idea."

After settling us up with the front desk, I sat in the lobby waiting for Marina to return. Soon enough, the bellhop helped us get our bags to the car and we said goodbye to the magnificent Peabody Hotel.

We decided it might be best if I drove, so I took the keys and we were soon on our way. Heading southwest out of downtown, I started to see landmarks that assured me we were in the right area. A small red-bricked church looked unchanged from when I was a child, although everything appeared much smaller now. So much had changed, yet so much had remained the same. We crossed a multitude of railroad tracks and passed the remnants of the old lumber mill where Dad had worked at for some time. A larger, more modern lumber mill now stood past the old one. I could picture where the old general store used to stand.

"Are we lost?" Marina asked.

"No, I know exactly where we are. Our road is about a quarter of mile up on the left."

As we turned onto an old gravel road, I saw the row of houses that used to be my neighborhood.

"Unbelievable. They are all still here." I was in shock.

"It looks deserted," Marina declared somewhat glum and disappointed.

The entire neighborhood stood abandoned, almost lost in time. A water line about two feet up from the ground was apparent on many of the houses. They all had a similar sign tacked to their front door.

"It's a little eerie," Marina stated.

"Must have flooded a few years ago and nobody came back."

The tires crunched over the gravel road. Clumps of weeds were scattered along the road in several places. The yards were mostly dirt with some dead grass. The few remaining trees were either dead or scraggly hackberry trees. All the other trees had been cut down, leaving only ant infested stumps where they once majestically stood.

"Which house was it?" Marina asked.

I stopped the car in front of the second to last house, staring at it for what felt like forever.

"Let's go check it out." Marina said with excitement.

Crossing the yard and approaching the front door, I noticed an old birdhouse my brother Walt had helped me make for Mama when we were little. It was in bad shape but still nailed to what was left of the small tree in the front yard.

"Be careful Mar," I pleaded as she stepped up onto the dilapidated porch.

"You were right Will. According to this notice, it's all the property of some Southern Land Company now."

Marina grasped the doorknob and before I could object, she realized it wasn't locked and walked right into the house.

"Mar! What are you doing? This is trespassing."

"There you go again, Will Massey. Where is your sense of adventure?"

Under objection, I entered the house that had once been the home to a happy and loving Massey family. With the exception of an old broken hall tree, most of the contents were long gone.

I pointed to the corner of the small living room we were standing in. "Mama and Daddy both had a chair right there in the corner with a small table in between. We had an old radio that sat on a table. Man, there were many nights when my brothers and I would sit on the floor right here while Mama patched up our clothes and Dad would sing along with the radio."

"What kind of work did your parents do?"

"Daddy worked odd jobs, loading and unloading riverboats, farming and some commercial fishing on the river. Mama cleaned houses for the wealthier families around town. We didn't have much, but we always had what we needed."

Marina was obviously proud of herself for this little adventure. "What's in here Will?"

"That's the kitchen." I followed Marina into the small room that once looked so big to me. "I spent many an afternoon sitting on the counter right there while Mama would make dinner for all of us."

The memories were flowing faster than I could keep up. Marina made her way into the next room. "Whose room was this?"

I followed her voice into another room. "This was Mama and Daddy's bedroom. I don't remember much about it. We were never supposed to be in here."

Marina huffed and we made our way to the last room, "Did you share this room with your brothers?"

"Sure did. I can't believe a room so small could so comfortably fit three young boys." I walked over to the window looking out into the back yard. Picturing the three of us throwing a baseball around in the small yard, I rubbed my finger across each of our names that were still visibly carved into the windowsill.

Marina saw the names as well. "Oh wow, that's you and your brother's names."

"Yep… that was one of the worst switching's we ever got. I think it was a week before I could sit down without feeling it." I snickered while remembering the ordeal. "You know, not a single one of us ever admitted who did it."

"So who did it?"

Smiling back at her, I slowly walked over to the small closet. I bent over and whispered under my breath, "I wonder if it's still here?"

"Did you hear me, Will? Who did it?"

Continuing to ignore Marina's question, I knelt down on one knee and checked for a loose baseboard in the corner of the closet. It popped right off, like it did when I was twelve years old. Reaching in, I pulled out the small object.

"Well, I'll be."

"What is it?" asked Marina.

"It's Drew's pocket knife that he gave to me before he and Walt left for the war. I had forgotten all about it. It was so well hidden I guess nobody else ever discovered it either."

Marina took it and studied the knife thoroughly before handing it back to me. "That's amazing Will."

After examining the knife for a few minutes, I choked back a tear before I flipped it in my hand, smiled and slipped it into my pocket.

I ambled around inside the house quietly for a little while longer, remembering my family and my childhood. I've often wondered how someone can be happy and sad at the same time, but this was definitely one of those moments for me. On one hand, I could have gone the rest of my life without ever seeing this house again, but it was fulfilling to be there and to think of all the happy memories residing like ghosts inside that hollow shell of a home.

"Mar, I think I'm ready to go now." I gave Marina a quick smile of satisfaction and we strolled back to the car together.

"I'd like to keep driving for a bit longer, if that's okay." I thought if I focused on driving, it might help occupy my mind enough to prevent it from drifting to more mournful memories.

Marina smiled and nodded in agreement.

My eyes focused on Marina, and I thought about the events which had led me to this place in time.

She looked a little uncomfortable with my gaze. "Is something wrong Will?"

"Nothing at all," I replied. "I'd just like to say thank you for suggesting this. It was good for my soul."

She smiled back. "You're welcome, Will."

After snaking back through Memphis proper and getting back on the highway, we noticed the old bridge.

"Whoa, is that the Mississippi River?" Marina asked with her eyes wide open.

"It sure is. We are now leaving Tennessee. Hello Arkansas. We should be able to make it to Little Rock around mid-afternoon. It's fine if you'd like to take a nap or something."

"I'm okay Will." She seemed to be in a fog, staring out at the partially flooded fields next to the road.

Far from her talkative self, I decided to pry. "What's on your mind?"

Marina looked over at me with a sad smirk and stated, "All of this talk of your family… seeing your home and you remembering your mom and dad sitting with you and your brothers… I guess I'm a little jealous that's all."

"Jealous? Why should you be jealous?"

"I don't know, maybe that's not the right word."

I thought for a second. "So, tell me about your favorite memory from your childhood. You know, before you went to live with Mildred."

"There's really only one that comes to mind. I must have been about five years old. Before my dad's health turned for the worse." She paused, collecting her thoughts. "At the time I didn't know why, but I remember everyone was excited and happy. I found out later, my oldest brother Ray had been accepted into the Army, and it was our last get together as a family before he went to boot camp. My brothers and sisters loaded blankets and stuff into the back of our truck. We rode up into the hills, out in the woods. I'm not sure I even know where or how far we went because I fell asleep. When I woke up, we had arrived near a small lake and we all filed out of the truck. Somebody stacked up some rocks to form a place for a campfire. Dad was dragging limbs, branches and fallen trees up closer to the area we were at." Marina stopped again and smiled. "Ray took me by the hand and led me over to the water. He tried showing me how to skip the rocks across the lake, but I couldn't do it like he could. The lake was like glass, and he could make those rocks skip almost to the other side. He was so strong and kind. I think we camped out there for several nights. I remember falling asleep in my dad's lap while everyone was singing songs around the campfire at night."

Marina's eyes had welled up and she turned her head back toward the window and raised her hand up to dry any tears that might fall.

"I sat up many a night when I was younger trying to remember everyone's names, trying to remember what our home looked like. The older I got, the more I forgot. But you know, thinking of that camping trip, I can remember each and every moment."

I liked the fact that this conversation was bringing Marina some joy, so I prodded, "So tell me about them, we've got plenty of time."

Marina looked at me, contemplating whether this was a good idea or not. Spinning around toward me with her back toward the passenger window and her left knee up in the seat, she began, "So, my dad's name was Thomas. My oldest brother went by Ray. He was tall like my dad, dark hair with a slight curl. It dipped down into his face ever so slightly. I remember him the most. He had to have been around eighteen years old during that trip since he headed off to the Army right after. I had an older sister Estelle. Everyone called her Stella. She was only about a year younger than Ray, and I recall her being shorter with curlier hair like mine. Then there was Arthur. Everyone called him Artie. He was always quiet and played by himself. He was short like Stella and me. Lastly, there was Leona. She was about seven years older than I was, but she was super tall like Ray and Dad. Her dark hair was more flowing than curly."

"Sounds like you remember them well," I stated.

"More from that camping trip than any other time." She turned back toward the window. "We kept up with each other for a little while, mainly through Aunt Mildred. Ray went off to the war before Dad died. I heard he stayed in the military until the war had completely ended, then he came back and started a family back in Florida. He must be about forty-three now. Stella got married right after I went to live with Mildred. Artie and Leona ended up with Stella and her husband for a few years. At one point I thought I would go and live with them, but Aunt Mildred said

Stella's husband was a bad drunk and she'd never let me be subjected to that life. I'm glad she didn't because a few years later we found out Artie and Leona had been put through some serious abuse for the couple of years they lived with them."

"So where are they now?"

"Artie died in a car wreck when he was twenty-two. I think Mildred said he was racing when it happened. Stella has been divorced and married a couple more times. She did come through Hudson to visit about ten years ago, but she didn't stay long. I think she was hoping Aunt Mildred could give her some money. I honestly don't know what happened to Leona. We lost touch with her back after Artie died. She was always a free-spirit, so I wouldn't be surprised if she was part of one of these hippie communes you read about."

A somber, quiet stillness settled over the car as we continued towards Little Rock.

"You know Mar, right before the war started, I remember my mama and daddy taking our family on a camping trip like you described."

"Hmm…" Marina mumbled, continuing to stare out the window.

"It was a place called Devil's Den. Not sure why it's called that, but I remember going through Little Rock to get there."

Marina continued to stare out the window in a dreary and unresponsive state. I hated seeing her in this funk and wanted to try anything to restore her fun and sunny disposition.

"What if we stop in Little Rock, get some supplies, find where this Devil's Den is and go camping for a couple of days?" I waited for Marina's response.

She slowly turned toward me and sincerely replied, "I know what you're trying to do Will. It's not necessary."

"I don't know what you are talking about. Your story about you going camping when you were a child brought back fond memories for me. I think it might be fun."

Glancing at Marina, I could see her rolling her eyes at me.

Reaching over, I turned the radio up, and determined this would be the plan.

We cruised along listening to the radio and eventually entered the outskirts of Little Rock. Noticing we needed gas, I pulled into a service station to fill up the tank and ask for some directions. It was a larger Texaco, with a small general store attached. A spry little man came walking out to the car with his red oil rag tucked inside his belt. "Filler up?" he asked.

"Yes sir."

Marina opened her door and stated, "I'm going to go find the ladies room."

"Hey Mar, do you want to get us a couple of sodas and maybe a snack?" I inquired while holding out some money for her to take.

"Can do," she said with a smile. "Anything in particular?"

"Surprise me."

Marina laughed out loud as she walked toward the building.

"Hey mister, we were thinking about doing a little camping at Devil's Den, can you give me directions?"

The station attendant, peering into the car replied, "Grab the Hammond you have there and I'll show you."

Picking up the road atlas we had brought along with us, I opened it to Arkansas. The old fellow took his pen out of his front pocket and leaned in putting his elbow on my door.

"You're right here." He drew a small 'x' with his pen on the map where we were. "You wanna go on up about ten miles and get on this highway here. Then you go about a hundred miles or so and you'll start to see the signs."

"Thank you," I said. "Is there anywhere close by where we could buy a few items for camping?"

He exhaled and gave me a look that could only be interpreted as meaning '*if you have to ask, you probably shouldn't be camping*'.

"Keep going up this road here for about a mile, and turn right on Blakely. There's a store up there called Discount Center. I think it's about to be turned into a Gibson's, but for now it's Discount Center. They should have most of what you'd need."

Marina came strolling back to the car. "One bottle of Nu-Grape for you, and one for me. They also had a popcorn maker in there like at the circus, so I got us a couple of bags to snack on."

We left the service station and headed straight down the road to the Discount Center. Pulling into the parking lot, Marina asked, "What are we doing here?"

"I'm going to run in and get a few things for the trip."

"Okay?" Marina countered with a slightly confused look.

I gathered up several items, including a couple of sleeping bags, a medium size tent, and various other pieces of camping gear. I also grabbed a bag full of groceries including some canned goods, some coffee, some sodas and a small foam cooler with ice to put some of it in. Approaching the car, I realized Marina was staring a hole right through me.

"You were serious?"

"Of course…"

"Hmm…" I heard her mumble.

After a few minutes of driving, I asked, "So what did you mean back there?"

"What do you mean, 'What did you mean back there?' What are you talking about?"

"Back there, when you questioned my seriousness about going

camping and I answered 'yeah' and you said 'hmmm…' What did you mean by 'hmmm?'

"I don't know what you're talking about Will Massey."

"You don't think we should go camping, do you?" I asked with a grin.

Marina ignored my question and began humming a tune I did not recognize. Soon after, Marina closed her eyes for a short nap. For the next couple of hours, I imagined how great this camping excursion would be and how happy it would make Marina. Confident this would be one of the most memorable parts of the trip, I basked in the awesomeness of my plan.

We approached Devil's Den a little after dusk. The sign at the entrance instructed us to find a campsite and pay in the morning, since the office was already closed. We were circling around looking for a site when we noticed a sign that read, "Beware of rattlesnakes!" Marina glanced at me with a look of concern.

"Will, I need to find a restroom."

"Which tree would you like?" I quipped with slight laugh.

"Not funny, Will Massey, not funny at all."

I noticed a small laundromat up ahead with its lights on. Next to it appeared to be a bathhouse for campers.

"Mar, I bet that bathhouse will serve your purpose."

I stopped the car and Marina jumped out. She made a beeline into the bathhouse. Within seconds I noticed her coming out of the bathhouse and heading into the laundromat. I couldn't tell what she was doing, but after a few minutes she came running back to the car and hopped in.

"Did you find a restroom?"

"Let's go Will," Marina said with haste.

I was a little confused by her reaction.

"Will, go!"

I started driving again, and looked her way. "Was the bath-house clean?"

"I don't know."

"What you mean, you don't know?"

"I don't know," she shot back with a testy look. "The lights wouldn't come on in the bathhouse."

"So, you didn't use the bathroom?" I inquired, not ready to give up on the inquisition.

"I had to use the …." Turning to look back out the window, her voice tailed off.

"You had to use the what? I couldn't make out the last part of what you said."

Marina turned toward me and said quite sternly, "I had to use the bathroom in the trash can; inside the laundromat."

"You did what?" I exclaimed with a look of amazement and utter delight.

"You heard me, I really had to go, and the lights wouldn't come on in the bathhouse and there wasn't anyone in the laundromat."

I tried my best not to laugh, but it was too much for me to hold in. Tears were welling up in my eyes and I began to laugh uncontrollably.

"Ha, ha, ha, laugh it up. Never mind me."

"I'm sorry, but that is one of the funniest things I've ever heard anyone do. Why didn't you just go outside by a tree?"

"Because of the snakes."

"Snakes?"

"SNAKE!" Marina screamed as she pointed at the road in front of us.

I glanced up to see the largest rattlesnake I had ever seen, taking it's time, slithering across the pavement in front of us.

"Run over it, Will!" Marina demanded in a panic.

I drove over the snake, which felt like running over a large rock in the road.

"Did you get it?"

"I don't know, I think so."

"Back up and see."

Stopping the car, I backed up slowly. We both looked anxiously for the snake. There wasn't a trace of it.

"Where did it go?" Marina asked hysterically.

"I don't know. It should be here... I know I ran over it."

"Then where is it?"

"I don't know. That was a huge snake. It doesn't look like we hurt it at all."

We continued around a slight curve before seeing a perfect camp site with a large tree. It was close to the creek and was nice and flat.

"This will do perfectly," I stated.

We began to remove the supplies from the car. Both of us were extremely on edge. We carefully erected the tent and unrolled the sleeping bags. The moon was bright in the night sky as we both settled in. I reached over and turned off the lantern we had been using for a light. Lying there in the dark, I chuckled while thinking about Marina relieving herself in a trash can within the laundromat.

Suddenly, we both heard rustling alongside the edge of the tent.

"What was that?" Marina asked.

"I'm not sure."

We both lay there in the darkness, in complete silence, as still as we could.

"There it is again. Will, did you hear that?"

At this point, I wasn't sure what I was hearing, but I was hearing something.

"Snake!" Marina screamed.

I turned the lantern back on and exclaimed, "Where?"

Marina was now standing on her sleeping bag clutching her pillow to her chest.

"I think I heard a rattle. Will, was that a rattle?"

"I'm not sure."

We were both now completely flustered.

Trying to be helpful, I proclaimed, "We are safe in this tent from any snake. I promise."

Marina squealed again then cried, "Will, you should have killed that snake. You just made him mad. He knows it's us and he's come for his revenge!"

At this point, I was starting to believe her. Every slight wisp or rustle had me imagining a giant rattlesnake was about to eat its way through our tent and end up in my sleeping bag.

"Ok...maybe this wasn't such a good idea after all," I declared.

"Will, can we go find a motel?"

"I thought you'd never ask."

We quickly broke down the tent and packed up all our things in the car and headed back out to the main road. It was quiet in the car for several miles. At some point I glanced over at Marina and she glanced back at me. We both smiled and began laughing like two drunken teenagers as we thought about the folly we had just experienced.

As midnight approached, we pulled into a small motel with a vacancy sign flashing and checked in for the rest of the night.

CHAPTER 8

December 5, 1970

I T WAS AS if the night had barely settled before the pale light of dawn began to creep through the curtains. Marina was not in the room. Curiosity nudged me toward the slightly ajar door. I opened it to find her outside. Wrapped in a blanket against the morning chill, she stood by the motel's railing. Her gaze fixed peacefully towards the east.

"Look at the beautiful sunrise, Will," she whispered, her voice tinged with awe.

Looking back towards Arkansas, the sky was a canvas of hazy blues and soft pinks, with a gentle southern breeze weaving through. The sun itself was not yet visible, but its early light danced gracefully across the distant trees, casting a dreamlike glow. The enticing aroma of bacon drifted over from the nearby truck stop diner, blending with the fresh morning air.

Marina closed her eyes and drew in a deep, slow breath, fully immersing herself in the freshness of the dawn. "Have you ever been to Denver?" she asked. "I've always wanted to go there."

"No. I've never been there, but I wouldn't mind seeing it someday."

She spun around with an inquisitive look on her face. "Do you think we could swing through Denver on our way to the west coast?"

"I'm not sure," I responded. "I don't think it's on our way, and we hadn't planned on going in that direction." I could tell from her body language my answer wasn't what she wanted to hear. It was a look that said, *wrong answer, William!'*

"But I'm sure we can study the map during breakfast and plot a new course that would take us right through Denver," I added.

To my surprise, Marina's face lit up like the morning sun and she flung her arms around me and whispered, "Thank you Will Massey."

We freshened up for the day and loaded the car with our bags. Next stop, 'Jimmy's', a local truck stop diner whose bacon, we hoped, would taste as good as it smelled.

We sat down at a table and the waitress brought us each a cup of coffee and a menu.

"I know what I want," exclaimed Marina. She placed her menu on the edge of the table before announcing, "French toast with bacon and a scrambled egg."

"And I'll have the silver dollar pancakes, sausage patties and two eggs over medium."

When the waitress walked away, Marina jumped up and slid into me on my side of the booth with the road atlas in hand.

"Okay, let's see if we can figure this out."

I could smell the fresh scent of shampoo from her hair and the lotion on her skin. It is amazing how the sense of smell can mark a memory so well.

She continued talking, but I wasn't fully paying attention.

"Will, are you listening to me?"

"Sorry, Mar, what were you saying?"

Letting out a loud huff, she pointed down to the atlas, "I was saying, it looks like we can continue on to Oklahoma City. From there, we can head north toward Wichita, Kansas. If we keep going on to Salina, we can get on Interstate 70, and then it should be a straight shot into Denver. What do you think?"

"Let me see," I pulled the atlas toward me and traced the route she had laid out. "We could go that way, or we could take a more diagonal and direct route through Kansas."

Marina glared at me.

"Or, we can go through Wichita and on to Salina," I stated, with a slight wink of an eye. "Either way, it will take a full day of driving to get from Oklahoma City to Denver, with not much in between."

"Maybe we should shoot for Oklahoma City today and get a good night's rest before heading to Denver," she stated. Beaming with satisfaction, Marina went back to her side of the table as our breakfast was being brought out. A part of me secretly wished she would have stayed next to me in the booth.

We finished our meal and settled ourselves back into the car.

As I drove us along Interstate 40, I glanced over at Marina and noticed her staring intensely at a yellow paper.

"Whatcha got there?"

She looked up at me in deep thought and responded, "It's a flyer I grabbed in the café as we were leaving. I guess this area has a large American Indian population, and this is an announcement of a powwow that is being held today and tomorrow just outside of Oklahoma City."

I could tell she wanted to explain further so I encouraged her a little. "What does it say about the powwow?"

"It says it's a gathering of tribes from around the country and they will celebrate life and honor their culture. Looks like there will be dancing, music, food, and shopping with arts and crafts. Sounds interesting, do you think we could go?"

I was a little puzzled by the request. "But we're not American Indians. Would we be welcome?"

"It says here, it's open to the public, so I guess we can. What do you think?"

I could tell she was intrigued by this and even though my brain wanted to explain we hadn't planned on this little adventure, my mouth chose otherwise, "Sure, it sounds like it might be fun. Oklahoma City is only about three hours away, so we could use something to do anyway."

Marina gave me a quick smile of appreciation and continued to look at the flier and stare out of the window at the landscape around us. She was intently focused on the hills, woodlands, fields and streams as we drove through eastern Oklahoma.

"What's on your mind?" I inquired.

She turned her gaze toward me, apparently amazed I knew she was thinking about something. "I read on this flyer about the Trail of Tears. Have you ever heard about that?"

I crumpled my face in deep thought. "Isn't that when the US government relocated all the American Indian tribes from the east out to the west?"

Marina nodded solemnly and answered, "Yes. I was reading how many of them died during the journey. I think many of them ended up all around here, in Oklahoma. Could you imagine how sad it would be? To be told you have to move and you must walk thousands of miles to an unknown place to live?"

I knew from the moment I met her that she had a tender heart, and I found it respectable that the very thought of the Trail of Tears was making her sad.

"I can almost picture the children playing in that creek we just passed, or some of the men hunting in the meadow back there." I was making my best effort to put a positive spin on a sad thought.

She continued to stare out the window. "You know, I was thinking the same thing. It wouldn't be the same as your home, but I guess you'd eventually make it your home."

We continued along, both of us pointing to different spots where we could imagine children playing together, men hunting, and women gathering berries. It seemed to cheer her up a little and distract her from the sad thoughts around the trek so many were forced to make a little over a hundred years before.

Once we were within about fifty miles of Oklahoma City, Marina began giving me detailed instructions on where to exit the interstate and how to get to the small fairgrounds where the powwow was being held. I can't recall the town where this gathering was, but I do remember pulling up to the venue and noticing the number of cars, trailers, tents, etc.... We appeared to be more the minority than the majority at this event from the looks of things. Many were dressed in their native attire and if they weren't, then they had some type of hand-crafted accessory either in their hair, on their head or about their bodies. I hesitated before getting out of the car, not sure if I was ready for the awkwardness. Marina rapped on my driver's side window.

"Come on Will, we've probably missed a lot already."

As we walked toward the action, immediately our attention turned toward the sound of drums. We soon realized the event had just begun.

It was a magnificent scene. There was a large arena in the center where we noticed throughout our time there was where the dancers would gather and dance. A smaller circular area was off to the side with a covering where several drums and drummers would sit. Outside of the arena was a spattering of tents and trailers with different food offerings, handmade blankets, artisans and merchants selling clothing and creations.

We watched them honor their tribal veterans and military members, some of whom could not attend due to the ongoing war in Vietnam. They announced the tribes and nations represented at the event and the host drum, which seemed to play a vital role in the ceremony, given its position in the center of all the other drums that would come and go.

We took a seat in the spectator area and watched in silence and amazement. The beauty and respect of this sacred tradition unfolded before us like a masterpiece. The mesmerizing beat of the drums aligned with the voices of those singing in a language we could not understand. The movements of the dancers' bodies, their feet, their hands and their heads played the role of a great storyteller with a passion that had been unbridled.

Marina shielded the sun from her eyes while smiling at me. "Will, it's beautiful, absolutely beautiful."

I looked out and noticed a small girl, seemingly around five years of age. She entered the group of dancers from the area where family and participants were gathered. She had a buckskin dress on with tall moccasin boots. Her hair was dark and wavy. It was pulled back from her eyes by a woven headband adorned with turquoise, silver, and small feathers. She moved around the arena with the composure of a grown woman, smiling occasionally when she wasn't focused on not making a mistake. Her innocence and beauty reminded me of Marina. She was full of power and grace but innocent and naïve at the same time. My mind wandered in reflection.

I must have been smiling as I watched this small child dance freely around the arena, because Marina nudged me with her elbow and whispered, "You would make a great father, Will Massey."

I wasn't sure how to respond, so I gave a quick smile back at her and returned to watching the dancers and drummers.

We sat and enjoyed the music and dancing for over an hour. The smells of the food were drifting about and making us both hungry.

"What do you say we walk around a bit and find something to eat?" I asked.

"I would love to."

We made our way out to the area around the arena where all of the vendors and artisans had set up. We noticed an older man who was hovering over a small fire box and something frying in a hot skillet.

"That looks wonderful! What do you call it?" Marina asked the old man.

"Fry bread", he replied.

"Is this considered Native American food?" she inquired.

"It has been a staple of my people, the Navajo, for many years. It represents the hard times my nation faced in Arizona when they were placed upon reservation lands during the last century."

Marina was fascinated by the passion within his answer but quickly pivoted her questioning to keep the conversation from becoming too bitter and sad. "So what is it exactly?"

"I take the flour, salt, sugar, water and lard, and I make dough. I take some of the dough and flatten it out to the size of a small plate and I fry it in the fat until it is golden", the man explained.

"And then you just eat it like that?" I asked. My stomach was now tired of the talking and ready for the trying.

"Some eat it with honey or sugar upon it. I serve it with meat, beans, lettuce and cheese"

"Like a taco?" Marina asked.

"Yes ma'am, like a taco." He smiled as he acknowledged her question.

"We'll take two of them and two lemonades also." She looked my way to ensure no disapproval.

I winked, giving my acceptance to her order.

We found a small picnic table to sit with our fry bread tacos and our lemonades. They were delicious, but again I realized I was enjoying the company as much as the food.

We finished off this newfound delicacy and sat sipping our lemonades watching the world pass by around us. Although we were surrounded by noise and chaos, there was a peacefulness to that moment that is hard to describe.

"You know, we probably shouldn't stay out here all day. We still need to make it to Oklahoma City and find a room for the night," I opined.

Marina looked surprised by my statement but understood. "Will, can we at least check out some of the tents where they are selling things they've made before we leave?"

"Sounds like a good idea, Mar."

It was amazing; there were tents full of hand-crafted blankets made by the people selling them. Another small tent was full of soapstone carvings. Little bears, eagles, buffalo and several depicting Native American men and women. The artist was actually behind a table carving his latest masterpiece. We stopped and watched for several minutes while he meticulously and delicately demonstrated his abilities for anyone who would watch. Marina had picked up a small turtle figurine with a smiling face and held it out to me.

"What do you think Will, isn't he cute? It kind of reminds me of you."

I wasn't sure if it was a compliment or not, but I could see it made her happy, and I did like that feeling.

"How much for the turtle?" I asked.

"Four," the man replied as he continued to work on his project.

"Would you take three for it?"

The man exhaled noticeably. "Sure."

I handed Marina a five dollar bill which she gladly handed to the man after he had set his tools down.

"Keep the change," she exclaimed, turning away with her turtle.

I glanced her way only to receive the most eyebrow raising reprimand a woman could deliver without saying a word.

I followed Marina into a much bigger tent. It was full of baskets, blankets, jewelry, moccasins, dresses, purses, dream catchers, dolls, carvings, you name it and they had it. While wandering around the tables, I noticed the tent was operated by an older woman, a younger man and a younger woman sitting behind a checkout table. With every movement I made, they watched me closely and carefully, sometimes whispering to each other. We slowly made our way towards them to look at the fine handcrafted jewelry that was in a display case where they sat.

"Excuse me." The young man had risen from his seat and was addressing me. "What nation are you a member of?"

"Me?" I pointed at myself.

"Yes," he replied.

"I'm not aware that I am. I was always told when I was a child that our family had ancestors that might have been of Choctaw decent, but that's about it."

At this point, the older woman tugged on the young man's sleeve to pull him near and whispered something to him. I could see her eyes filling with tears, although they had yet to fall.

"I'm sorry to have bothered you sir, but my mother thought you were her other son she hasn't seen or heard from for a long time. My brother left fifteen years ago after a disagreement and we have longed for his return ever since. When we saw you walk in, we all thought he had returned to us."

I could see the disappointment in all of their eyes, but I was at a loss for what to say. As I stepped closer to the table to purchase a small bag of jerky I had been carrying around, the older woman came from behind the table to take a closer look at me. I offered her a hug. She instantly buried her head into my chest, released her emotions and began crying into me. After a long embrace, she pulled herself away from me, stared up into my eyes and returned to her seat behind the table.

I paid for my purchase and the young man offered me his hand and we shook. "You have no idea how much that meant to her, thank you."

We turned and left the tent and made our way to the car. Soon we were back on the interstate. After a few minutes of silence, Marina blurted out, "So that was strange."

"What was strange?"

"The older woman thinking you were her long-lost son."

"I suppose."

"I noticed you said something to her when she was hugging you and crying. What did you say to her?"

"I told her that her son loves her and misses her very much."

With that answer, Marina smiled before going silent and gazing out the window for a while.

Dusk was upon us as we entered the outskirts of Oklahoma City. I found an exit with a few motels and chose a newer looking travel motel for the night.

Hopping out, I stepped into the office to get us a room while Marina stayed in the car. When I came back out with the key, she was in a strangely serene mood. We parked in front of our room, unloaded our bags, and made our way inside.

"Will, can we go out tonight? I'm not sure I want this day to end yet."

"Funny you ask," I replied. "I told the front desk manager we were passing through and asked if he had anywhere he'd recommend we try tonight. He told me about a place down the road called the Diamond Ballroom. He said it has live music, dancing, drinks and some food options."

Marina smiled. "Sounds perfect. I'm going to freshen up, if that's okay."

I propped my back up against the headboard of one of the full size beds and closed my eyes. I must have dozed off, because the next thing I remembered was Marina touching my foot and announcing, "Wake up sleepy head."

I opened my eyes to what seemed like a vision of an angel. Her hair was perfectly styled, freshly blow-dried and brushed to a soft sheen. She had applied just enough makeup to complement her natural beauty. Her green eyes sparkled, and her dimples emerged as she smiled warmly at me. "You aren't planning to sleep all night, are you?"

After doing my best to freshen up, I announced, "Well I've done about all I can do to look good, and it doesn't seem to be working."

Marina chuckled at my attempt at humor. "You look very nice Will."

After a brief drive, we reached the Diamond Ballroom. The parking lot was teeming with cars and streams of people were flowing into the bustling venue. Stepping inside, the vibrant energy was palpable. A country western band was live on stage, their music filled the air, which was thick with the scents of beer and cigarette smoke. We navigated through crowds of people clad in jeans, boots, and cowboy hats. Feeling a little out of place, I momentarily longed for the comfort of the powwow we had left behind, but I reminded myself, *this was just another chapter in my unfolding adventure.*

We found a small table close to the dance floor and pulled up two chairs. The band was playing some lively tune and couples were dancing in harmony in a counterclockwise pattern around the dance floor. A waitress made her way over to our table and asked, "Can I get you two a beer?"

"Yes please," I replied.

We sat, somewhat mesmerized, taking in the scene around us. The dance floor was a melting pot —older couples gliding gracefully and younger couples with energetic steps. The bar was just as diverse; groups laughing together and singles mingling casually. Everyone was enjoying the night; drinking, socializing and dancing. A couple to our right, clearly infatuated, were more interested in kissing than anything else. Noticing this, Marina gave me a knowing grin, arching her eyebrows and biting her lip to hold back her amusement.

After a few minutes, the waitress returned with our beers, "Here you go."

"Thank you," I replied, "Do you serve any food?"

"Sorry, only liquid nourishment, honey."

Marina smiled and shrugged and held her bottle out for a quick 'cheers' before turning it up.

"You know," I stated, "we have a full day of driving ahead of us tomorrow. If we are going to make it to Denver by evening, we might need to watch the clock and not stay out too late tonight."

Marina acknowledged my comment with a smile, a nod and a tilt of the bottle before taking another drink.

We sat there listening to the music and people watching. Neither of us had experienced anything like this before.

After about our third beer, Marina looked my way and asked,

"You wanna give it a try?" She motioned her head towards the dance floor and stood up from her chair.

Every ounce of my being was saying, *hell no, I don't want to try that*, but again my mouth had other plans. "Sure!" I replied.

Marina gave me a shocked look, took my hand and lead me onto the crowded floor. We realized if you don't start moving at the same pace and in the same direction with the crowd, you will literally get run over. Trying to emulate others, I timidly placed my right hand on her lower back while taking her right hand into my left. We began to step clumsily to the music as we improvised our way through. After a couple of songs, we started to get the hang of the quick stepping motion even though I am certain we looked like two goldfish that had just leapt from the fish bowl. As the dance floor paused between songs, she looked up at me trying to catch her breath. "Will, this is so much fun!"

At that moment, the lead singer of the band asked his wife to join him on stage and the band began to play a slower ballad. Feeling a little awkwardness between us, I started to pull away and lead us back to the table when I realized Marina had squeezed my hand tighter and pulled me back towards her. The singer began to sing, and we had transitioned into more of a slow dance stance with each other. Both of my arms were gently around her upper back, while her hands were slightly around my lower back. There was still a small gap between us as I was careful not to make this too uncomfortable.

I hadn't realized until that moment how a country music song can tell a story and touch your soul to its core. As the male singer with the smokiest voice sang of his woman, and how she was the reason he was alive, I felt my heart melt for *this* woman in my arms. I swore I wouldn't allow this to happen, but the bond between us felt like it had been arranged from above. How could I feel this way toward someone who I had known for less than a week? My mind was trying to rationalize and suppress my feelings in hopes of protecting me from emotional pain that was almost certainly a guarantee.

Then a woman's voice joined in, singing that she had never felt this way before and she could feel it in her soul. Marina broke the invisible barrier we had created between us, sinking into me completely as she exhaled deeply in submission.

We held each other tightly, swaying to the soft rhythm and melody of the music, completely enveloped in the warmth of our embrace. Our bodies melded together, moving as one, her breath and the gentle thud of her heartbeat pulsing through me. As the final notes of the song faded away, we clung to each other, unwilling to let go, almost forgetting the world around us. When we finally, reluctantly, stepped apart, our eyes locked, reflecting a deep, unspoken yearning that lingered inside us.

"Excuse me, may I cut in?"

Standing next to us was a striking young man, dressed in polished boots and a cowboy hat. His shirt was neatly pressed and a hint of cologne surrounded him. He was clearly closer in age to Marina, and I could see a spark of excitement in her eyes as she realized this young man wanted to dance with her. She glanced my way, searching for a reaction. Inside, I felt a tug of reluctance at the thought of her dancing with someone else, especially after what we had just experienced, yet I didn't want to curtail her freedom. A twinge of jealousy washed over me; a poignant reminder of the deepening feelings I had already developed for Marina.

"You don't need my permission," I said with a half-hearted smile. "I will go order us a couple more beers."

She smiled at me and I turned and walked back over to our little table.

I sat and drank not only my beer but the beer I had ordered for her as well. Watching the two of them dance, I smiled and gave a quick acknowledgement wave to Marina each time she would look my way. After about half an hour she finally made her way back to the table. I noticed he was right behind her like a puppy following its new owner.

"William, this is Toby. Toby this is William. I was telling him that you and I were travelling together out to California and just passing through. Toby comes here a lot. He knows all the moves."

"I'm sure he does," I replied acridly.

"I thought you were going to get me a beer, William?"

"I guess I forgot, Marina."

"That's okay, I'll go get us both a beer," interrupted Toby.

As he departed toward the bar, I leaned over toward her. "We should probably get going, remember we have a full day of driving ahead of us tomorrow."

Marina's expression shifted to annoyance. "You don't want to dance anymore? Aren't you having fun?"

Before Toby had shown up, I was completely sold on the idea of dancing the night away with Marina. However, seeing her bask in the attention Toby was giving her, a dull ache settled in my chest. Deep down, festered doubts about her interest in me, especially when compared to how I felt about her.

Masking my true feelings, I mustered a smile. "Sure, I'm having fun, but I think we might need some rest if we're going to be on the road all day tomorrow."

"If you want to go back to the room and get some rest, I can see if Toby will bring me back in a little while. You could drive the first leg tomorrow so I can rest, then I'll drive the second leg and let you rest."

I didn't know how to respond. If I pointed out I was worried about her safety, it wouldn't end well. If I told her she didn't even know this guy, it would probably end up worse. After all, she barely knew me. Toby walked back up to the table with two bottles of beer. "Here you go, pretty lady!"

"Thank you, Toby. Hey, could you take me back to our motel in a little while? William wants to leave and go get some rest. That way I can stay and you can show me a few more dance moves."

"Why yes ma'am, I'd be happy to deliver you safe and sound. Don't you worry about nothing, Mr. William, I'll get her back to you with no problems," Toby proclaimed.

Before leaving, I pulled Marina into a gentle embrace. "Be careful, Mar," I pleaded. Her face flickered for a second with a look of concern. However, her expression softened into a reassuring smile. Heading toward the door, I watched the two of them giggling as they made their way back onto the dance floor.

The drive back to the motel lasted forever. Unable to sleep, I spent nearly two hours wrestling with the sheets, agitated and racked with unease. The image of Marina, alone in the bustling honkytonk a thousand miles from her home, played on a loop in my mind. Every few minutes I would look at the alarm clock on the nightstand to see what time it was. *I should have never left her there*, I thought.

Overwhelmed with worry, I hurried out of the motel and sped back to the bar. Along the way, I scrutinized every passing car, hoping to spot them. The bar's parking lot, while less crowded than before, still had a significant number of vehicles. Inside, I scanned the dance floor and the surrounding area for any sign of them, weaving through the tables and drunks under the smoky haze.

By the time I reached the women's restroom, my nerves were frayed, and I was in disarray. With a mix of guilt and fear,

I called into the open restroom door, "Marina! Are you in there?"
No answer.

After completing a full circle of the bar without any sign of her or Toby, I wondered if perhaps they had returned to the motel without me noticing.

Exiting the building, a full panic attack set in. A deep, unsettling feeling told me she was in trouble, and I felt utterly powerless. I swept my gaze across the parking lot, my heart pounding fiercely. My eyes landed on a figure seated on a railroad tie at the building's edge. Approaching cautiously, I realized it was her.

"Marina?"

She slowly raised her head, her eyes red from crying. As she stood, I wrapped my arms around her, and she leaned into me. "Are you okay? Are you hurt?"

She shook her head.

"I thought I had lost you."

Hearing this, Marina stepped back slightly, and looked into my eyes with a faint smile. She opened her mouth to speak but instead doubled over and began retching into the grass.

I helped her back to the car and we rushed to the motel. Over the next hour, she barely left the bathroom floor, battling waves of sickness. I held her hair back and applied a cool washcloth to her face and forehead, doing my best to comfort her. It wasn't until around 1:30 AM when she finally fell asleep. I stayed awake a bit longer to ensure she was alright before drifting off myself.

CHAPTER 9

December 6, 1970

I STIRRED FROM MY sleepless night at six o'clock in the morning; brushed my teeth, shaved, showered, and prepared for the long drive ahead. Exiting the bathroom, I noticed Marina was still sleeping.

I reached down, shook her bed, and announced, "It's time to get up and get going." I grabbed my bag, headed out the door to the car, and placed it into the trunk. Walking next door to a small store, I bought a bag of powdered donuts and a large coffee for both of us.

"Good morning, Will," she stated softly as I returned to the room.

"Good morning, Marina." I replied coldly. The events from the night before had soured my mood and I wasn't sure how to process it all.

We exited the motel and continued our drive. For the stretch of Interstate 35 between Oklahoma City and Wichita, Kansas, not a sound was made in the car other than the radio. I pulled over for gas in Wichita.

Marina got out of the car and went to the restroom. I stared blankly out across the horizon while the attendant cleaned our windshield and checked our oil. Soon we were back onto Highway 81, headed toward Salina. The road was a little rough due to construction; Interstate 35 had yet to be completed between Wichita and Salina.

"Will, I guess we should have gone the way you had originally recommended and we would've avoided all of this."

I remained silent, sinking deeper into my quiet funk. Throughout my life, I'd been told I had a tendency to shut down and isolate when faced with trouble or trauma. Clearly, this was one of those times. After another hour and a half on this road, she didn't look well.

"Will… Can we find another gas station? I need to use the restroom again."

I pulled into the next gas station and Marina went in to ask for the key to the restroom. Although I was still upset about the events at the Diamond Ballroom, at this point, I was starting to get concerned about her.

After pulling onto Interstate 70 and driving a few miles we both noticed a sign that read *Denver 425 miles.*

It was about that time that she turned the radio off and announced, "I have my question for you today."

"Okay."

Marina positioned her body toward me with her back against the passenger door. "What's wrong? You've hardly said a word. Are you mad at me?"

I stared straight ahead, down the road. "I shut down sometimes; when I'm really upset."

Marina gave me a concerning look. "At me?" she asked fragilely.

I hesitated to answer, then began, "Do you want to know why I ordered an ice water to go at Mildred's?"

She gave me a befuddled look and nodded tenderly.

I took a deep breath, exhaled, and proceeded.

"It was the fall of 1949. I was a junior at Wharton School of Finance and Commerce at the University of Pennsylvania in Philadelphia. Her name was Susan Jane Ruggles, from Akron, Ohio. She was a freshman. I was working part-time at a local deli to support my studies. That's where I first met her. She walked in one afternoon for a late lunch, and I was captivated as she approached the counter. Her deep blue eyes and long, flowing blond hair, neatly pulled back with a pink bow, left a lasting impression. I made her a hoagie—with lettuce and tomato, no mayo. I barely managed a word during our first encounter, but she soon became a frequent visitor, stopping by three or four times a week."

"As her visits became routine, we gradually started talking and developed a friendship. I looked forward to our chats during my afternoon breaks, where we'd discuss a variety of topics. Eventually, I gathered enough courage to ask her out. We went on several dates, where I was the consummate gentleman and she, the epitome of grace and class."

I glanced over and noticed Marina was intently hanging on every word I was saying.

"A year later, I graduated with my degree in management. I wasn't a risk taker, so it was Susan who encouraged me to stretch my boundaries and aim higher. We aligned our careers to work alongside each other. By 1952, we made the decision to get married. We both devoted ourselves to our work, and spent all of our time together, but not really doing anything together other than working. Susan dreamed of starting a family and traveling the world, whereas I preferred to wait and save money. Despite our differences, she was the source of my joy. She was my everything."

I tried valiantly to keep my voice from breaking.

"In June of 1961, we were finishing up a late workday, I noticed Susan stagger. She later mentioned she had blacked out. I managed to somewhat cushion her fall, but not before she struck her head hard against the desk. I rushed her to the hospital. After several weeks of tests, the doctors diagnosed her with a type of cancer known as lymphoma. For the next two years, I stood by her while she bravely fought the disease. The doctors employed a range of treatments, including some newer methods combining radiation and chemotherapy. They frequently left her nauseous. Initially, I would hold her hair back while she would get sick into the toilet, placing a cold washcloth on her forehead and neck to ease her discomfort. Eventually, she lost her hair, and her body grew weak and frail from the ongoing treatments."

I paused, took a deep breath and regained my composure before continuing.

"After months of this painful cycle, I started to notice a slight change. Somehow, by the grace of God she began to add weight back on and regain some strength. By November of '63 the doctors declared her in 'remission'. By the next summer her hair, although darker than before, had grown back to just below her shoulders."

At this point, tears were trickling down my cheeks and Marina's eyes were ready to erupt.

"Like fools, we kept working. I think because it allowed me to spend every waking second with her and she wanted me to be happy."

"It was June of 1965; she came up behind me one morning and put her hands over my eyes. She leaned in and whispered in my ear, 'congratulations, Daddy!' I was both elated and terrified at the same time. I turned to her and before I could say a negative word, I saw the woman I loved exuding the most radiant glow I had ever seen. You know, I thought I had made her happy for those fifteen years, but this was an all-new kind of happy I had never seen before in Susan."

I paused long enough to force a smile and take a deep breath.

"I felt guilty I had kept her from being this happy for so long. So much so, that when I wasn't distracted with work or worry, I was consumed with this guilt. She filled all of my free time with converting our guest room into a nursery and going on shopping sprees for supplies we would need. After fighting it for a while, I finally allowed myself to be happy and enjoy the miracles of both her victory over cancer and the fact that I was going to be a daddy."

"A few months later, we travelled from our home in Philadelphia and celebrated Thanksgiving with her family in Ohio. On Sunday, we were preparing to leave and I was loading the car with our luggage. Susan came out of the house with her mom and sister. I turned and saw her from the driveway; she appeared so full of life and radiant. She looked right at me and smiled. Then, it was as if someone flipped a switch and all of the energy drained from her body. Susan crumpled like a rag doll and fell forward down the porch steps onto her back… I followed the ambulance to the hospital and after waiting a couple of hours, they called me back. The doctor informed me the cancer had returned and had spread into her blood. She experienced a stillbirth and we lost our baby girl on that day. I sat beside her in the hospital room for two days waiting for her to regain consciousness. On December 1, 1965, she opened her eyes and looked at me."

"'William, look at me,' she demanded. 'Did we lose our child?' I couldn't hold back the tears as I nodded. 'Is the cancer back?' she asked me."

"I nodded again. 'I thought as much', she muttered. 'I don't feel good at all William, I can feel my heartbeat and it doesn't feel right this time.'"

"I leaned forward and took her hand in mine and reassured her, 'Susan, you are going to get through this, we are going to get through this.'"

"She tugged slightly on my hand and whispered, 'Come here William, I would like a kiss.'"

"I crouched over her and gave her a kiss on the lips. I remember thinking that her mouth felt cold."

"She shared her final words with me, and she closed her eyes and passed away."

I stared at the road ahead trying hard not to break down.

"I buried her and our daughter in her family's cemetery outside of Hudson. After their deaths, I moved to Cleveland to be closer to them. Every year on December 1st, I make a trip to their graves and place flowers on them and I sit there from early morning until the sun goes down."

Marina was softly crying at this point and trying to keep her eyes dry with a handkerchief.

"This year was the five-year anniversary of their deaths. You know, I had passed Mildred's Diner every year for five years, but never stopped. I made my way out to the cemetery this year, with flowers and a full bottle of sleeping pills. I wanted the pain to stop. But I couldn't even do that right because I forgot to take anything with me to wash down those damn pills. That's when I remembered Mildred's and decided to go back into town and have 'Ohio's Best Fried Pie' and get a glass of ice water to take back to the cemetery with me. I'm not sure what forces might have brought me to the diner, but I can tell you, the last words Susan said to me were, 'William, stop thinking and start doing. Be free, take risks, live life, for me.'"

I inhaled deeply and looked at Marina. "When I overheard your decision to just leave, take off, without a plan, a little voice inside my head said, *be free, take risks, live life*."

I paused for a second, wiped my eyes on my sleeve, and then continued with my confession.

"In the past five days, I have bonded with you more than you can know. I count you as my only friend at this time in my life, and I have felt no more alive than I did dancing with you at the Diamond Ballroom. When I returned to the motel room last night without you, I felt something deep within warning me you were in trouble. When I searched the Diamond Ballroom for you and you weren't there, I thought I had lost you forever. When I took care of you last night while you were sick, a thousand negative thoughts rushed back into my mind. I held this silver locket, which contains a picture of Susan, tightly in my hand and I thought about that bottle of pills. When I thought I had lost you, I felt the loneliness and emptiness I had felt every day for the last five years until Tuesday of this past week when I met you. I never wanted to feel that again, but I did and now I don't know what to do."

With that, I glanced over at Marina. Her face was dripping wet from a steady stream of tears. She turned back to stare out the passenger window of the car.

For miles we drove across the flat farm land of Kansas, no radio, no talking, only silence.

After a while, without turning toward me, she began to speak. "You know, yesterday was one of the greatest days of my life, until it wasn't. You didn't object when Toby cut in, although I'm not sure how I would have taken it if you had. I danced with him for another hour and a half and then I asked him to drive me back to the motel. Instead, he insisted we should go to his place. All I could think about was you, and how I wished you were there."

I felt an even bigger burden of guilt for leaving her, but before I could apologize, she continued. "He tried to force me into his truck, but I slapped him. He got mad, struck me in my stomach and I doubled over. He just laughed at me, called me a tease and then jumped in his truck and sped away." She paused at this point and took a deep breath before continuing, "I was so alone and afraid and I didn't feel great either. I'm sorry Will. I'd like to forget about last night, except for our dance."

At this point, my blood was boiling inside, and my heart rate and blood pressure was surely spiking. I was angry for letting Toby cut in and I felt guilty when I thought of the danger Marina was in.

"I should've knocked his lights out when he asked to cut in!"

She flinched at my outburst, then bit her lip and as she suppressed a reactive grin.

I peered out of the corner of my eye at her and replied, "You're not alone. We're in this together. I am truly sorry I left you there last night. I should have never done that to you. Are you okay?"

With that, Marina wiped her eyes, nodded, then smiled tenderly and placed her head on her pillow and stared quietly out the window.

CHAPTER 10

Present Day

"DAD LEFT YOU in a honkytonk with a total stranger, halfway across the country? What was he thinking?" Mother was livid as she confronted Grandma.

Grandma shifted uncomfortably in her chair before responding calmly, "It wasn't like that, dear. I know how it sounds, but at the time, it didn't seem wrong."

"You could have been kidnapped, raped, or killed!" Mother's voice escalated with each word, her anger palpable. I was somewhat taken aback by the story, but I also admired the way Pawpaw respected her freedom.

"You have to understand, we were practically strangers ourselves. We had only met four days earlier," she explained, trying to provide some context.

Mother continued to shake her head in disbelief, her irritation evident. "I don't care if he had just met you, Daddy should have known better than that. It doesn't make any sense."

Feeling compelled to add my opinion; I chimed in, "It was a different time back then, I guess."

Mother turned her glare towards me. "What do you know about 1970?"

"I would say I know as much about it as you do," I retorted, my heart pounding faster with the tension in the room, even though my mind reminded me this had all happened fifty-four years ago.

"Please, Susan... Izzy Bee... let's put an end to this bickering," Grandma pleaded, her voice a blend of weariness and sincerity. "What happened, happened. It was as much my decision as it was William's. I was very independent-minded back then, though admittedly still a bit naive about the world."

Mother's voice crescendoed, "What were you thinking?"

Grandma paused, reflecting on the past with a faraway look in her eyes. "To be honest, I was just enjoying myself for the night. I had spent my entire life waitressing in a small town, watching the rest of the world pass me by. That night, I wanted to be part of it... to feel alive and unbound." Her voice softened with the weight of the memories, a mix of nostalgia and a hint of regret.

Mother exhaled sharply, her frustration apparent. She stood up from the couch and announced, "I need a bathroom break. Don't start reading again without me."

Grandma and I exchanged glances, both of us surprised yet managing to suppress any visible reaction. She grimaced in apparent discomfort, shifting her position once more in her chair.

Realizing Grandma was experiencing some pain, I asked, "Are you alright?"

"I'm fine Izzy."

Although I wasn't convinced, I knew better than to question Grandma against her word.

As Mother disappeared down the hallway, I picked up

Pawpaw's pocket knife and examined it more closely. "I can't believe he carved his name into the window sill," I remarked, amused by the revelation.

Her face lit up with a fond smile. "Oh, I can believe it. Your Pawpaw wasn't as innocent as he might have presented. I've heard plenty of stories about the mischief he got into when he was a child." Her eyes twinkled. "I saw flashes of his mischievous spirit during our wonderful life together."

I grinned and chuckled softly, envisioning a young version of Pawpaw—mischievous and lively—getting into all sorts of harmless trouble. Imagining him as a boy, full of energy and curiosity, brought a warm feeling of connection to the grandfather I knew and loved.

Mother reentered the room, carrying the coffee pot with a sense of purpose. She gracefully poured more coffee into Grandma's cup before settling back into her seat.

I continued with my line of questioning. "What were you thinking when he explained why he wanted the ice water?"

Grandma paused, taking a slow sip of her coffee. She glanced at both of us. "I was shocked, but not surprised," she confessed. "Even Aunt Mildred had mentioned she thought he looked 'broken, but not beyond repair.' I suppose that's exactly what we were sensing from the second he walked into the diner."

Leaning forward, she set her cup down on the coffee table with a gentle clink. She pulled a tissue from the box, dabbed at her nose, and held the tissue delicately in her lap.

"He was in so much pain, emotionally," she continued, her voice softening, her expression turning tender. "You could see it in his eyes, the way he carried himself—it was as if he was holding onto a burden too heavy to bear alone." Her face was a canvas of heartfelt sympathy as she remembered the visible struggles of a man trying to find peace in a bottle of pills and a cup of ice water.

Mother's face was etched with disbelief. "I can't believe he shared all of that with you so soon. You barely knew each other."

"It was probably because of the question game," I interjected. "That was a pretty clever idea, Grandma."

"I can't take all the credit for it," she replied, her voice soft and reflective. "When I was a teenager, after one of her failed relationships, Aunt Mildred sat me down and shared some valuable advice. She told me men often use silence as a way to control situations, to keep from saying too much. She emphasized how important open communication is for building trust." Grandma paused, her gaze intensifying with the weight of the memory. "And she always said every successful relationship has to be built on trust."

As we sat together, I noticed Mother looking at Grandma with an expression of sudden curiosity, as if a realization had dawned on her. "Mom, did you already know before this trip started?" she asked.

"Know what?" I inquired.

Grandma offered Mother a weary, half-hearted smile and nodded subtly. The transformation in Mother's expression was immediate; her look of curiosity shifted to one of understanding mingled with sadness, like she suddenly grasped the gravity of what was to come.

"Know what?" I repeated, my irritation growing as I sensed secrets being kept from me.

"Let's keep reading, Izzy." Grandma gave me a reassuring smile suggesting everything would eventually make sense. Trusting her, I turned back to the stack of papers, flipped to the page where I had left off, and resumed reading, the mysteries of our conversation hanging in the air, promising to unfold with the turn of each page.

CHAPTER 11

December 6, 1970

I T WAS NOW approaching 4 o'clock on Sunday afternoon; Marina had fallen asleep with her head against the passenger window. There wasn't much to look at after miles and miles and many hours of flat open land. A stray patch of dry corn stalks were about the only thing breaking up the scenery. Coming over a slight rise in road, I could barely make out the silhouette of what at first looked like low clouds on the horizon. I realized we were approaching Denver and the Rocky Mountains would soon be clearly in sight.

"Mar, wake up, you don't want to miss this." I reached over gently and nudged Marina enough to stir her from her nap.

"What is it Will?" she asked in a sleepy daze.

"Look straight ahead."

Marina rubbed her eyes and squinted. There in front of us, jutting out of the landscape, were the Rocky Mountains. Jagged and majestic, their tops were covered with the whitest snow on a backdrop of an orange, pink and blue sky as the sun was starting to reach the horizon behind them. Her mouth gaped open as she looked south then north at the full range that was in sight. Her gawk changed to a smile and then a loud laugh. "Have you ever seen anything so beautiful?"

"I suppose not," I replied with a hint of sarcasm, as I soaked up the glow on her face. She was oblivious to my answer.

The taller more grandiose peaks of the Rocky Mountains began to tuck themselves behind the less formidable foothills the closer we came into downtown Denver. We were quickly losing daylight. "What's the plan?"

Marina gave me a look conveying that the word *plan* wasn't in her vocabulary. "I don't have one, but I am getting a little hungry."

I contemplated what to do for all of five minutes. "I like your idea, Mar, we'll find a spot to eat dinner and we can figure out where to stay once our stomachs are full."

I followed the signs to downtown Denver and exited the interstate. We headed down one street before turning back up another, looking for an acceptable place to eat. Denver was an older looking city with a new vibe to it. Many of the downtown streets were one way and alternated directions for each block we would pass. Broadway was the main road through downtown and we crossed it several times. Most of the shops and windows of the buildings were decorated for Christmas and there was a certain feeling in the air that the holiday season was upon us. We were on Curtis Street when we noticed a red and white striped awning. It was a quaint little place with a warm and inviting glow emanating from inside. I located a small lot and we parked the car and headed inside.

"Welcome, have a seat anywhere." The greeting came from an older man, clean, well groomed, with glasses, wearing a black tie and white apron. The warm family atmosphere was a welcome sight after being on the road for so long.

We settled into a booth. I had been in many Coney Island style diners in my lifetime, especially on trips to Michigan and northeastern Pennsylvania. This place brought back some fond memories.

A younger man approached our table with his smooth baby face and his Pepsi Cola hat, "Can I get you something to drink?"

Marina answered, "I'll have a coffee with cream and sugar, please."

The young waiter turned his attention to me, "Sir?"

"I'll have a Pepsi."

As he walked back to the counter, Marina continued to study her menu.

"So…. This is Denver, huh?" I asked.

"I guess so," she stated without looking up from her menu.

My thoughts were adrift, lost in concern and confusion when the fatherly like man who greeted us approached the table and asked, "You two from around here?"

"No" I responded, "we are travelling out to California, from Ohio."

"Welcome to Denver, where are you folks staying?"

We both glanced at each other almost as though one of us would have an answer.

"We just arrived and need to find a place after we eat," Marina replied in her most innocent pleading voice possible.

"Hmmm…," pondered the older man. "How long you staying for?"

"Not sure," I answered.

"Maybe a couple of days," Marina stated.

"Looking for cheap, clean or upscale?" he asked.

I was too busy trying to discern what was going on with Marina. I had never seen her like this in our short time together, almost businesslike in her demeanor. She was engaging with others, but not so much with me.

She shrugged her shoulders as if to say she was at a loss for words.

My mind quickly processed the situation. I felt impelled to cheer her up.

"Something nice," I replied. "Maybe a place with some Christmas decorations and a bar, you know, since we are staying for a few nights."

"If you can afford it, I'd recommend the Brown Palace Hotel. It's down a few blocks on 17th street at Tremont." The old man winked at me and added, "You won't be disappointed!"

As he walked away, the young waiter came back with our drinks and asked, "Are we ready to order?"

"I'd like two eggs over easy, with bacon and buttered toast. Oh, and a side of hash browned potatoes please," Marina added with a smile.

I set my menu down. "I'll take a coney with mustard, chili and cheese. And a small bowl of your red chili with some of those oyster crackers if you have them."

We sat without saying a word to each other. She was holding her coffee cup in the palms of both of her hands while staring quietly out the front window at the lights dancing on the sidewalk.

"Mar, are you okay?"

"I'm fine, Will. A little tired, that's all."

Our food arrived at the table and I watched as Marina prepped her meal for eating. She gently used her fork and knife to cut up her eggs. She shook the peppershaker over them and picked up the saltshaker. Rather than shake the salt over her eggs, she gathered a small amount of salt into her left hand and proceeded to pinch it with her thumb and index finger on her right hand and rub them together over the top of her eggs. I must have been a little obvious with my gawking.

"Your chili is going to get cold." Marina raised her eyebrows as she flashed a reserved smile my way.

I took the crackers and placed them into my chili. It was warm and comforting. We both ate our meal without much discussion, just a few friendly glances across the table to each other and a chuckle or two.

As we sat there, almost ready to leave and make our way to the car, I reached my hand out to Marina across the table and took her hand from her coffee cup and into mine. "You know Mar; I haven't thanked you for letting me come along with you on your journey. Thank you."

She sighed with a tender smile as her eyes watered. "Oh Will. I should be thanking you. I'm not sure I would've made it this far without you. Even if I did, I know I wouldn't have had as much fun. Thank you."

I squeezed her hand and whispered, "Shall we go check out the Brown Palace?"

"Are you sure we can afford it?"

"It will be fine," I reassured.

Stepping into the lobby was like stepping into another world. There were balconies stretching above the atrium. The second floor had arches standing guard from above and each archway was adorned with white Christmas lights and boughs of fresh evergreen branches. Dark red ribbons and bows were positioned throughout. In the center of the lobby was a magnificent Christmas tree adorned with hand blown crystal balls. A grand multitude of sparkling lights were strung carefully from limb to limb and the finest ribbon flowed down and around the tree like a magical waterfall.

Marina approached the tree and stood there with her head tilted upward gazing at the star on its peak.

"Look at the ceiling, Will."

Above the seven floors was a beautiful stained-glass ceiling that echoed the Christmas lights from below onto the dark backdrop of the night sky.

"I'll go see if I can get us a room, okay?" I proposed.

She held out her hand and softly nodded as if to say, 'go right ahead'.

"May I help you?" asked the lady at the front desk.

"Yes ma'am, my friend and I need a room for a few nights. Do you have anything available?"

"Let me check." She flipped through her records, and glanced back up with a smile, "I do have some availability. How many nights will you need?"

"I'm thinking three nights might do, for now at least."

"Would you like a king or two full beds?"

"Two full beds would be nice, but we can make a king work if necessary."

"I have a nice room in the annex, the Brown Palace West, will that work?" she asked.

"The annex?"

"It's across the street, the larger tower; there is a sky bridge connecting the two buildings. It's our economical option." She must have sensed my disappointment in her assumption that I was looking for a budget option. "Or, I do have a room in the main atrium here, but it's more expensive," she explained.

Without hesitation, I said, "I'll take it."

She processed the paperwork and handed me two keys. "Enjoy your stay Mr. Massey."

"Thank you," I replied.

After scanning the lobby twice, I finally located Marina sitting in a large comfortable leather chair, watching everyone passing by and taking it all in.

"We're all set," I declared. "I booked us a room for three nights. We can extend it for more, but I thought a few nights might give us a chance to rest before we continue on."

She looked up with an expression of gratitude. "Thank you Will, I'm exhausted."

After grabbing our bags, we headed up to our room on the fifth floor. It was a wonderful room with two full beds fitted with down comforters, an antique settee and a bathroom fit for king. We both prepared for a much-needed night of sleep. I slipped into my bed and Marina slipped into hers. I reached over and turned the light off.

I lay there in the dark staring at the window, knowing I needed some rest, but truly anxious about the secrets I had revealed earlier in the day and how they might affect the remainder of this trip. After about thirty minutes of this, I heard her soft voice whisper, "Will, are you awake?" I considered ignoring her so that she might just drift off to sleep, but relented, "Yes Mar, I'm still awake."

"Would you tell me more about Susan? That is, if it's not too difficult."

I contemplated the question, then answered, "I'm not sure how much more I can tell. It worries me that every time I think of her now, I can only remember what the cancer did to her."

Marina apologized, "I'm sorry Will, I didn't mean to cause you pain."

"It's okay, Mar," I reassured. It had been a long time since I had spoken to anyone about Susan Jane. Most people avoid talking to you about a loved one that you've lost for fear that it might stir some painful emotions. I guess it could, but somehow it felt liberating to remember her and talk about her.

"I remember her eyes more than anything. She had the most beautiful blue eyes. I suppose that's why, along with her middle name being Jane, that her family nicknamed her 'Blue Jay'. You know, when I was sitting at the table in Mildred's Diner listening to you discuss your plans with Mildred; I saw the most magnificent blue jay on the lamppost outside. I guess a little part of me thought it was possibly a message from Susan."

"Maybe it was," whispered Marina.

"She would have loved this trip. She would have admired your free-spirit and you two would have probably been great friends."

"Did she suffer much?"

Her question struck me as odd and uncommon, although I had thought about it myself for the past five years.

"If you mean, 'did she experience discomfort and pain?', then I'd have to say yes, but that wasn't the sole source of her suffering I suppose."

My eyes had adjusted to the relative darkness of the room and I could tell Marina was staring at me on edge, waiting for me to continue.

"The more I've thought about it, the more I believe we all face a certain amount of physical pain and discomfort in our lives, but the worst kind of suffering has to be the complete loss of hope. I'm not sure Susan ever truly lost hope until the end, when she knew her body was failing. Even then, she didn't show how much it was hurting her."

"Sounds like she was a strong woman," Marina whispered.

"Yeah, she was," I agreed, still in deep thought. "Have you ever considered how it's the one's left behind who have to replay all the memories and cry all the tears?"

"Or smile all the smiles," Marina replied.

"Yeah, that too." I was beginning to notice how Marina would always have a positive spin on things that would lift my spirits.

She must have realized I was getting emotional talking about Susan. "Get some sleep, Will Massey, tomorrow is a new day."

With that statement, we both gave in to our physical and emotional exhaustion.

CHAPTER 12

December 7, 1970

AFTER A PEACEFUL night of rest, I rose the next morning and realized Marina was still sleeping soundly, even after I had awakened and gotten ready for the day.

Instead of rousing her, I located a notepad and pen in the small desk within the room and wrote her a note.

'Mar,

You were resting so peacefully that I didn't want to wake you. I am going down to the lobby to see if I can gather some suggestions on what we might do over the next couple of days. Feel free to order room service or venture down to the hotel restaurant, have some breakfast, and charge it to the room. I've got this, so don't worry about the cost. I'll be back in a little while.

Sincerely, Will'

I folded the note, left it on the pillow of my bed for her to find, and headed out the door and down to the lobby.

"Good morning sir, did you sleep well?"

I turned and smiled at a hotel employee as she straightened some boughs of evergreen.

"Yes I did."

"If there is anything we can do for you, just ask."

"Actually, can you give me some ideas about what my friend and I can do while we are staying here in Denver?"

Immediately the woman replied, "Of course sir, if you'll check with our concierge desk, they can give you plenty of ideas and maybe a few discounts too."

I navigated my way through the lobby. The sounds and smells of the season were in the air. An instrumental version of 'White Christmas' was playing from speakers discreetly placed throughout the hotel. Aromatic hints of cinnamon and pine mingled with the inviting smell of fresh coffee, created a warm, holiday atmosphere. My attention was drawn to a small desk labeled 'Concierge' where a friendly-looking man stood. He greeted me with a broad smile, "Good morning Mr. Massey, beautiful day, isn't it?"

I had no idea how he knew my name, but I thought, *what a nice touch.*

"So far, so good," I replied. "I heard you might be able to help me."

"I will certainly do my best. What's on your mind?"

"My friend and I are traveling from Ohio to California, via the scenic route. We are only here in Denver for a few days and we have no clue what we should do or where we should try to go while we are here."

"I've got you covered sir. Do you want history, nature, indoors or outdoors?"

I hadn't given it much thought, and my lack of planning was a little embarrassing. Yet, channeling my best impression of Marina, I replied, "Surprise me."

"A man of spontaneity, huh?" he responded.

If only he knew. I couldn't help but chuckle inside.

"We have the Denver Zoo; it's one of the best in the country; the Natural Museum; a great way to learn about the state of Colorado and all of our animals and regions. There is also a great planetarium over there, if you like the stars. They are all nestled right together."

"Sounds great, but what about the mountains and the snow. We really expected to see some snow in Denver."

"For the next week or so, you'll need to go out past the foothills to see some snow. We tend to have some nice days in the winter that offset the cold ones. You happened to arrive during one of those spells right now."

"Where would you recommend we stop, in the mountains, once we leave Denver?"

"Are you travelling on Interstate 70?"

"Yes, I think that's the plan."

"Did you want to stop real quick in the mountains or were you wanting to stay a night or two?"

I had no clue, since Marina had banned me from planning out the trip and looking ahead, but I would never admit that to another human being. "I would say we might stay a couple of nights, somewhere."

"There are several places that are beautiful, but my favorite, if you don't mind the detour, is Aspen. I've never experienced anything like it. It's absolutely breathtaking, like much of the Rocky Mountains, but you also have the celebrities and the hippies right now. Makes for a great experience if you ask me… and you did." He smiled with his last comment.

"Sounds like a great place. What would you recommend as far as shopping around here and maybe some places for lunch or dinner?"

He thought about it with his pencil to his lips and grabbed a small map of the downtown area from under the counter. "There are plenty of small boutique shops in all directions around us. You could stay within three blocks and find clothes, trinkets, furniture, food, antiques, pretty much anything you might want. I'll circle a few restaurants I believe are required for anyone wanting to get the real experience."

"Thank you so much. I'm hoping to surprise my friend with some great experiences."

He glanced up toward the ceiling with a look of contemplation. "You know, if you are planning to travel on Interstate 70, Buffalo Bill Cody himself is buried out there on Lookout Mountain. You can visit his grave and look down on all of Denver from up there. Down below in Golden is the Coors beer manufacturing facility. They give tours out there, if that interests you at all."

"Can I borrow your pencil?" I asked, knowing if I didn't write this down, I was sure to miss something when talking with Marina.

"Sure thing," he handed me the pencil from his hand. From its wetness and roughness, I could tell it had been in his mouth most of the morning. "You can keep it if you'd like, it's a Brown Palace pencil."

"Thanks," I hesitantly accepted his gift and proceeded to jot down a few notes, *Coors brewery, Buffalo Bill and Aspen.*

I reached into my pocket and pulled out a couple of dollars and handed it to the concierge, "You have been extremely helpful, thank you sir."

He politely accepted and responded, "If you need me to arrange anything for you, let me know, my name is Jeffrey."

I headed out the front door of the hotel and onto the sidewalk outside. It was still early, but the downtown scene was already bustling. I ambled along the street, peeking inside each storefront and diner. After walking about two blocks, I began to feel guilty I was enjoying this early morning stroll without Marina. Passing by a small shop full of sundries, I noticed a sign stating 'cameras sold here'. I thought, *a camera would be nice*. I stepped inside and with help from the salesperson, selected a small camera that seemed to be perfect for the rest of our trip. After paying for my new toy, I headed back.

Reaching the hotel entrance and entering the lobby, I noticed a small table with a sign that read 'Complimentary Mulled Cider'. Making my way over to it, I poured two small cups, and hastened into the elevator and up to our room.

As I entered, the warmth of steam and the clean smell of soap hit me like a down pillow. From the bathroom, I could hear the faint strains of Marina joyfully singing her own version of 'Jingle Bells'. I approached the bathroom door and gave a gentle knock.

"Don't come in here!" Her voice rang out in alarm.

"It's me Mar. I brought you some hot apple cider."

"I thought you were going for a walk or something?"

"I did, but I started feeling guilty about leaving you behind." I could hear the splashing of water. "Are you taking a bath?"

There was a brief pause before she responded, "Yes, I am! So, don't you come in here, Will Massey."

I couldn't help but snicker at her feisty reaction. "I'll leave your hot cider by the bathroom door if you want it. You take your time and enjoy your soak. I'll head back down to the lobby to wait for you."

She remained silent.

"Is that okay, Mar?" I asked playfully.

"That's fine, Will. Just leave it by the door. I'll come meet you in a little while."

"Yes, ma'am."

I returned to the lobby and poured a fresh cup of hot cider. Picking up a copy of the local newspaper, I settled into a cozy chair in the atrium. A pianist took his seat at the baby grand in the lobby and started playing one Christmas favorite after another. As the melodies filled the air, I became completely engrossed and lost track of time. Suddenly, I felt a gentle tap on my shoulder; I looked up to see Marina smiling down at me.

"Excuse me, sir, is this seat taken?" She was standing there with a playful smile, twirling her hair around her fingers.

I returned her smile warmly and replied, "Yes, ma'am, that seat is taken... by you."

As Marina took her seat, I watched her eyes dart around the room, eager to absorb every detail. She turned to me, curiosity sparkling in her gaze. "What do you have planned for us today, Will?"

"Funny you should ask; I hope you like animals." I folded the newspaper and set it down on the table, then stood up and reached out my hand to Marina, "Shall we?"

She sneered at me and asked, "Animals?"

We made our way out to the portico where our car was waiting for us. I tipped the valet, took the keys and settled into the driver's seat with the crude directions Jeffery had given me. After a few minutes in the car, we stopped at an intersection preparing to turn when she noticed the sign, *Denver Zoo*.

"The zoo?" Squealing with excitement, Marina leaned over and gave me a peck on the cheek. "I've always wanted to go to a zoo."

I was astonished to learn she had never been to a zoo.

It was a perfect day for it. The sky was a clear, vibrant blue, and every now and again, a gentle breeze would brush across our faces. The air was crisp enough to warrant a light jacket. Together, we entered through the gates and stepped onto the zoo grounds.

Marina beamed with excitement as we meandered from exhibit to exhibit. At times, she would hurry ahead like a young child who couldn't contain her excitement, then she'd stop and stare forever at another.

We stopped in the Feline House where several lions and tigers were on display behind large glass walls. Each had its own outdoor enclosure and a large moat surrounded the area to keep the big cats in without the feeling too much like a large cage. I noticed her staring blankly at the majestic creatures.

"Will, do you think they feel trapped?"

"I don't know, Mar. They have each other and they are taken care of, but I suppose they could miss the freedom that is probably inherent in their bones."

She nodded in silent agreement.

"Why don't we go find the Monkey House," I suggested.

Marina glanced back at me with a goofy look and asked, "Do you think they will sing for us?" It didn't hit me at first but once she began to sing, I caught on quickly.

I joined in with Marina and crooned along to the chorus of 'Daydream Believer'. Giggling hysterically at our crazy rendition, we decided to stop momentarily at a concession booth for some hot cocoa and a short break.

"You know, if you get tired of the zoo, we can make our way over to the Denver Museum of Natural History. I went ahead and had the concierge at the hotel get us tickets for that too."

She smiled and looped her left arm under my right arm. "So, what's in the Museum of Natural History?"

"The concierge said they have these life-sized models of things from animal habitats to people from around the world. They're called dioramas."

Marina giggled at the sound of the word diorama, then pronounced it herself a few times while laughing, "Diorama… dior-ama… di-or-rama…"

I interrupted her silly soliloquy and stated, "He also mentioned they have a planetarium there."

"What's a planetarium?" she asked with heightened curiosity.

"It's a dark room with a dome-shaped ceiling. It has chairs that recline back, allowing you to comfortably face upward. Once they turn off all the lights, a projector illuminates the dome with images of stars, galaxies, and the vastness of outer space. It's supposed to be more captivating than gazing directly into the night sky."

The idea of a planetarium triggered something within her. She stopped in her tracks and demanded, "Will, let's go do that!"

"You don't want to see the monkeys?"

"Maybe another time?" she asked.

I nodded in concession and we began our walk to the planetarium.

"I love the stars. When I was around eight years old, Aunt Mildred and I got into an argument. I don't even remember what the argument was about. I stormed outside to get away. Mildred had recently paid a couple of men to come out and fix a leak on her roof and they had left her tall ladder leaning against the house. I'm not sure what got into me, but I climbed up the ladder and onto the roof. It was a clear night, not a cloud in the sky. I sat up there for over an hour or so."

"Did Mildred catch you?"

"No. Why does that matter?" Marina was frustrated by my question. "That's not the point of my story, Will."

I knew that was my cue to stop asking questions and simply listen.

"From that point on until probably two weeks ago, any time I needed to get away, and the night sky was clear, I would set the ladder back up. Climbing up on the roof, I'd spread a blanket out and prop my head on a pillow. I would just lie there facing the heavens." Marina drifted off into her own little world.

"Sounds like a great way to spend an evening. I could've benefited from that many times."

She peered up at me and smiled, "You know, I don't think I've ever told anyone about climbing up on that roof."

I found a small amount of satisfaction in knowing Marina had let me in on her secret ritual.

As we entered the Museum of Natural History, she looked on the map and plotted the most direct route to the planetarium. "Will, did I tell you that I know all the constellations?"

"No, you didn't." I was completely entertained by Marina's passion and excitement.

"Well, almost all of them," backing off ever so slightly from her claim.

As we approached the doors to the Gates Planetarium our mood changed from excitement to dejection. A sign was positioned in front of the doors that read *TEMPORARILY CLOSED FOR MUCH NEEDED UPDATES AND REPAIRS.*

Marina suddenly halted. I could tell she was disappointed. After fixating on the sign, she turned to me, her voice cracking, and said, "It's okay; it probably wasn't that great anyway. Let's check out the rest of the museum."

We continued our exploration, pausing at each diorama and

exhibit. Despite my efforts to lift her spirits, the most I could elicit was a couple of forced smiles. After another hour, with a gentle tone, she whispered to me, "Will, I'm ready to go when you are."

I searched for any anything I could think of that might cheer her up. "You know, we could go back and just enjoy the hotel. Maybe have a drink and relax and take in the sights and sounds."

She smiled at me. "I think that's a great idea."

During the drive back to the hotel, Marina gazed out the window in a silent daze. Entering the lobby, we were enveloped in Christmas music again. A man seated at the piano in the lobby skillfully played the classics. Marina stood there with her eyes closed allowing the ambiance to surround her.

"Mar, can I get you something to drink?"

She opened her eyes and responded, "That would be awesome Will. Can you get me a Manheim, like we had in Memphis?"

"One Manhattan coming right up." I winked at her only to receive a confused look in return.

"I'll get us a seat," Marina stated as she headed toward a couple of high back chairs at a small cocktail table.

Returning with our drinks, I observed how beautiful her silhouette was as the Christmas lights twinkled behind her. It was like she was mesmerized, staring at something, but not really. Her eyes were watering and a small tear trickled down her right cheek.

"Is everything okay?"

My question startled her. She stammered a reply while wiping her cheek. "I'm okay Will, really I am."

I shook my head gently in concerned disagreement. "Mar, what's wrong?"

She gave me a half-hearted smile. "I'm emotional right now Will, that's all."

Marina noticed the extra cherries in her glass and began to twirl them with her finger.

I pressed again, "Penny for your thoughts?"

She slowly made eye contact with me and her look of concerned morphed into a caring smile, "Did Susan Jane like Christmas?"

Her question was not what I was expecting. I took a long sip of my old fashioned then took a deep breath and nodded. "Yeah, she did. I'd say it was her favorite time of the year."

We continued to listen to the sounds of the holidays around us, both clutching our drinks like some sort of security blanket.

Marina broke the silence first, "Do you think those who have died are up there in the stars? Looking down on us?"

What a strange thing to contemplate, I thought. "I like to think they are, but I don't know. Maybe."

She smiled, appearing to find solace in my answer. Then she quickly changed the subject. "I'm starting to get a little hungry."

I finished the last drops of my drink and stood up. "I'll go see if Jeffrey has any recommendations for dinner. Are you okay sitting here?"

She smiled at me and nodded approvingly.

I made my way back across the lobby to the concierge desk. Jeffrey glanced up from a notepad and placed his pencil down. "Mr. Massey, what can I do for you?"

"I know I said I would see you tomorrow, but I need some guidance tonight."

He nodded in total understanding. "No problem, how can I be of assistance?"

"We had a long day at the zoo and disappointing ending at the planetarium, so I think we need a nice restaurant for dinner."

Jeffrey responded with a concerned glance, "What happened?"

"I don't know. I guess we both expected to see some snow

in Denver and maybe we had a false idea that Denver was in the mountains. Then I was hoping to surprise Marina with a trip to the planetarium, which she was really excited about, but it was closed for maintenance."

"I see. Well first, let's take care of dinner. May I suggest the Buckhorn Exchange? It's been in Denver since 1893 and has great history, like the Brown Palace herself. I believe it was founded by a close acquaintance of 'Buffalo Bill' Cody, and they have some of the best steaks around." He glanced at me, pausing momentarily to gauge my reaction.

"Sounds great," I replied.

"I can give them a call and have them reserve a table for you at, say seven tonight?"

"Perfect. Thank you, Jeffrey."

I felt a sense of relief that I at least had a plan for dinner.

"Now, let's tackle the other issues," Jeffrey proclaimed. "If you want mountains, snow and stars, have I got the place for you. Remember how I mentioned Aspen? It's on your way to California and I have a friend who works at the Hotel Jerome up there. She told me yesterday they have several inches of fresh snow and the skies are projected to be clear for the next several days. There is a little restaurant up there on the mountain that would be the perfect setting for an intimate dinner with views of the snow. Shall I make a call and get you guys in?"

I thought about it for all of a one second. "Can you book us for tomorrow night?"

"Consider it done, and you are also all set for your dinner tonight at seven."

He pulled a small map out, traced the route to the restaurant from our hotel, and handed it to me.

"Thank you for all your help, you are a Godsend." Looking

down at the map, I thought about it, and then handed it back to him, "Do you think you could arrange a cab for us to the restaurant tonight?"

"Most certainly sir," he replied.

I shook Jeffrey's hand, turned, and made my way back to Marina.

"I think we have a plan," I declared as I approached the table.

Marina looked flippantly shocked with my exclamation.

"The concierge is getting us a table at a local restaurant that's been around for a while. Sounds like it will be a memorable place to visit."

She continued to be entertained by my enthusiasm. "I guess I should go get ready for dinner then."

Making our way back to the room, I smiled as I realized how relaxed we had both gotten with each other. It was a comforting feeling that I had been yearning for since losing Susan Jane.

"Mar, I have an idea for tonight," I announced from the bathroom as we both prepared for our evening out.

"What idea?"

"I was thinking that maybe, just for fun, we order for each other tonight."

"So, you want to order for me, and you want me to order for you?"

I stepped out of the bathroom to explain, "I thought it might add an element of surprise and fun to the evening. I wouldn't order anything I didn't already believe you would like."

"No chicken livers?" she quipped with a look of genuine concern.

"No chicken livers," I replied with a huge smile.

She considered it for a minute before answering. "I'm up for it."

We collected our jackets and made our way down through

the lobby. I held the door open for Marina, catching a hint of her perfume as she stepped inside. Slipping into the taxi beside her, I felt the quiet hum of the city fade outside the closing door. I was completely entranced by her appearance. Her hair was freshly brushed, falling in dark waves past her shoulders. She wore very little makeup, allowing her face to radiate a natural warmth and glow. She gazed out the window, her eyes absorbing every sight and landmark we passed.

Soon we arrived at the Buckhorn Exchange. It was an older two-story structure with a white washed brick façade. It sat like a monolith where the street took a decidedly ninety-degree turn. Across the road was a myriad of train tracks and an old station. After paying the driver, I raced to the restaurant door and held it open.

As my eyes drifted from Marina's face to the inside of the restaurant, I froze in disbelief. There were animal heads and bodies mounted on almost every square inch of the restaurant. There were birds, mountain lions, raccoons, I felt like we were back at the zoo.

I turned in a panic toward Marina, "I'm sorry. I didn't know this place would be like this."

She gave me a confused look. "You mean all of these beautiful animals?"

"Ye...ess," I stammered.

"Will, this doesn't bother me. In fact, whatever reason these animals were killed, they would have died anyway. This allowed them to be forever remembered and memorialized. They're beautiful creatures."

I was both perplexed and amazed at her response.

"Welcome, do you have a reservation?" the host interrupted.

"We should have a table for two under Massey," I answered.

"Yes sir, I have you down right here. If you'll follow me, I will show you to your table."

We made our way to a small table near the back. Her eyes were scanning all around the building, taking it all in. "Will, this is an amazing place. I wonder how old some of these things are."

The waiter must have overheard Marina's exuberant plea. "Most of the animals in here date back to before World War I. In fact, several of them were reportedly bagged by Teddy Roosevelt himself, including the African Cape Buffalo over there on that wall."

She turned in excitement, "You mean a President of the United States has eaten here?"

"Not only him, Eisenhower and Kennedy both ate here as well."

"JFK ate here?" Marina looked like a school girl who had received a letter from Elvis.

"Yes ma'am, even asked for some bones for his dogs."

"Wow!" she exclaimed.

"I'm guessing the two of you have never been here before? Here are some menus for you to look at, take your time. In the meantime, can I get you something to drink?"

"I'll have water." Marina answered. She glanced at me, curious of what I would order.

"Me too," I responded.

As the waiter walked away, Marina glanced over the top of her menu giddy with excitement and asked, "So how do we do this? Are you going to go to the restroom first while I order for you?"

At first, I was confused and then I remembered the proposal I had made at the hotel. I glanced down at the menu and quickly found something I knew Marina would like. "I'll step away first to go wash my hands while you order for me."

I made my way to the men's room and proceeded to wash my

hands. Looking into the mirror and at the silver locket around my neck, I thought, *Susan would have liked this place.* After escaping briefly into that thought, I headed back to the table. Marina was speaking with the waiter when she saw me and waved me over.

"Okay, I've ordered for you, now it's your turn Will."

She hopped up from her seat and headed toward the ladies room. I turned to the waiter who was smiling with delight at the playfulness he was witnessing. "I will order the buffalo tenderloin for my, …" I stuttered, "my girlfriend. Medium well, with a baked potato and uh… what kind of soup do you have?"

"I would recommend the bean soup, it's wonderful with the cooler weather outside and we are kind of famous for it."

"Sounds delicious," I replied.

Marina came strolling back to the table with a giant smile upon her face. "Will, this place is incredible."

"I'm glad you like it."

Sitting back down, she placed her linen back in her lap, and again began to gaze at all the sights within this little restaurant.

"So what do you think about Denver?" I inquired.

"It's okay,"

Her answer took me a little by surprise, "Just okay, is something wrong?"

She raised her eyebrows at me and smirked with a reply, "It's very nice Will, but I guess I've always pictured Denver in the mountains, cold, and with tons of snow on the ground."

"I had a great time today," I countered, "but I was thinking maybe we get back on the road tomorrow."

Her smile turned to a frown, "Will, I didn't mean to offend you or anything. I'm having the most wonderful time of my life."

"No offense taken Mar, I have a surprise planned for you for tomorrow, elsewhere."

Marina tilted her head at me and inquired, "What surprise?"

"Well, if I told you then it wouldn't be a surprise anymore, now would it?"

Before she could deliver a witty response, our waiter arrived, placing our soup on the table

"A cup of our famous bean soup for you ma'am and a cup of our French onion soup for you sir. Enjoy"

Marina looked at her cup of bean soup before shyly glancing my way. I stopped my spoon before I could get it to my lips. "What's wrong Mar?"

She hesitated cautiously, and replied, "I bet this is a great cup of soup and I appreciate you picking it for me, but…"

I could tell she was struggling to find the words she wanted to say.

"But?"

"Will, I'm not sure I want to eat beans and then be in a car with you all day tomorrow. It might not be very, lady like, if you know what I mean."

I graciously pushed my French onion soup toward her and went to pull her cup of bean soup toward me.

"No," Marina protested. She placed her hand on mine to stop me from pulling her bean soup towards me. "I don't think you should eat it either."

I grinned, if only to keep from laughing out loud before nodding in agreement to her conclusion. At that moment, the waiter reappeared with our meals. "I'm sorry, but the kitchen got a little ahead of itself tonight."

"That's quite alright," I responded.

The grand reveal was at hand and both of us were curious like children on Christmas morning, eager to see what the other had ordered.

"For the lady, I have an American buffalo tenderloin, medium well with a baked potato."

Marina smiled and mouthed 'Thank you' to me from across the table.

"And for you sir, I have an order of our famous Rocky Mountain Oysters with a baked potato as well."

I looked down at a pile of the most unusual fried oysters I had ever seen. "These look amazing!" I announced.

As soon as the waiter had stepped away, we both began to enjoy the food laid out in front of us.

"How is your buffalo steak?" I asked.

"It's so good. It has a leaner texture than beef, but I can't believe how it melts in my mouth. It's so tender I can pull it apart with my fingers. How are your oysters?"

"They are crispy on the outside, but chewier and denser than any oysters I've ever had. The flavor is amazing, but they do have kind of an aftertaste that I can't quite put my finger on."

We sat there enjoying our meal, making small talk. Our plates began to empty when the waiter came by to check on us.

"How is your meal, is there anything else I can get for you two?"

I noticed Marina had a mouthful of food so I replied, "Oh, I have eaten about all I can. Those oysters were delicious. Can they make them Rockefeller style?"

The waiter gave me a confused look.

"You called them Rocky Mountain oysters? I've never heard of them. Are they freshwater oysters? Do they get them from mountain lakes or streams or something?"

Marina was continuing to eat while listening to my conversation with the waiter.

"Sir, I don't think you understand."

At this point I was a little confused. "What do I not understand?"

"Rocky Mountain oysters are bull testicles," the waiter explained.

Marina spewed part of a chewed potato and a sip of water across the table.

I felt a bit nauseous.

"What did you say?" Marina asked after wiping her mouth with her napkin.

"They are sliced and fried bull testicles."

At this point I was in a daze as Marina began to laugh hysterically.

Flustered by this revelation, I spoke in a squeaking, panicky voice, "Why would anyone do that?"

The waiter wasn't sure what to say and Marina had tears streaming down her face from laughing so hard.

"They've been serving them here since the place opened in the 1890's," the waiter replied.

I was starting to feel a little clammy. "I think I need to go to the men's room," I replied through my labored breathing, stumbling from my chair.

"Are you okay Will, you look a little pale," Marina stated while biting her lip to hold back more snickering.

I made a beeline to the men's room. I splashed cold water on my face and rinsed out my mouth. They didn't taste bad, in fact they were very good, but finding out what I had eaten after already eating it wasn't the right order of things. I dried my face and made my way back to the table. As I passed each animal within the restaurant, it felt like every one of them were now staring at me and laughing. Marina was eyeing me the entire way, trying hard not to smile and especially not to laugh. I was more embarrassed at this point than anything else.

Reaching the table, I turned to the mounted bison head on the wall directly behind me. "Sorry, buddy."

I paid for our meal and we stepped out onto the sidewalk to

wait for our cab. It felt good to take a deep breath of the crisp night air.

Marina squeezed my hand in comfort and confided, "You know, you really took the bull by the horns back there." With that comment she began to laugh uncontrollably again.

"Haha, very funny. I think you planned that from the start."

"Will Massey, I did not! I swear, I thought Rocky Mountain oysters were real oysters."

The ride back to the hotel was quiet. Marina laid her head against my shoulder. "I had a wonderful time Will. Thank you."

I leaned back into her and replied, "I did too, Mar."

Once we arrived back at the Brown Palace, we slowly made our way back to the room. As I fumbled for the key and opened the door, Marina leaned in close to my face, "Will?" she whispered seductively.

"Yes, Mar?"

"You ate bull balls," she replied as she began to laugh again hysterically, running into the room and away from me.

CHAPTER 13

December 8, 1970

IT FELT LIKE my eyes had only been closed for an instant, when I was awakened by Marina's beautiful voice. "Will, wake-up bully boy, time to get the day started." She was still glowing with amusement, milking every ounce of enjoyment out of the previous night's dinner at my expense.

"What time is it?"

"It's time to get the day going so I can find out my surprise."

Although I was exhausted, I found it delightfully irritating that Marina was in such a great mood. I was acutely aware of her emotional funk for the last couple of days and was beginning to worry I had overshared when talking about my life with Susan.

"I'm assuming we will see some snow today?" she asked, while placing her bag near the door of the room.

I nodded in agreement, as I sat up in the bed and rubbed my face and eyes.

"I think I'll meet you downstairs, I want to call Aunt Mildred.

If we have time, I'd also like to enjoy a cup of coffee or cider in the lobby before we leave."

She headed downstairs and I was left in the silence of the room.

I stepped into the shower; the hot water felt amazing. Standing there in a comfortable daze, I struggled to convince myself that this was real. I finished getting dressed and called down to Jeffrey to check on the arrangements, and ask if our car could be brought up for us.

After a final pass through the room to ensure we were leaving nothing behind, I headed down. Stepping into the lobby, I noticed Marina had gotten comfortable in one of the soft leather chairs. She was sipping a hot cider and 'people watching' while listening to Christmas music in front of the magnificently decorated Christmas tree.

I stopped briefly to pick up some notes and directions for our Aspen stay.

Marina was holding her cup of hot cider in the palms of both of her hands when I walked up. The steam rose in misty clouds from the cup as she closed her eyes and breathed it in slowly.

"You look cozy."

"I am cozy. This place is incredible."

"Too cozy to join me for the rest of our adventure?"

"Never," Marina responded, setting her cup down and standing up to join me.

We navigated through the maze of streets and pulled away from downtown Denver.

"I'm going to miss this place," Marina confessed.

We headed west into the foothills. Both of us were too captivated by the scenery to speak. Finally, Marina broke the silence, her voice tinged with excitement, "Will, look at the ice waterfalls."

Large icicles protruded from the cut hillside, resembling miniature waterfalls that had suddenly frozen in time.

"Is that a mine shaft?" I pointed at a massive manmade hole in the side of the mountain with a small wooden structure attached to it.

"Wow," she exclaimed "I wonder what they mine out here."

"I would think gold and silver for the most part, maybe some diamonds or other gemstones." I had no clue, but Marina was just nodding and taking me at my word.

"My ears keep popping. Are your ears popping, Will?"

"Yeah, they will probably do that the higher we climb."

Approaching the eastern slope of the Rocky Mountains, we started to notice more and more construction trucks and crews. Trying to impress her, I explained, "I read in the newspaper at the hotel that they have been working on a large tunnel in this area that would allow you to drive straight through the mountain."

I glanced over and noticed a definite look of concern on her face.

"But it's not finished yet, so we will be going over the mountain," I reassured. Marina breathed a sigh of relief.

We came around a curve in the road and started up another steady incline when we saw the continental divide up ahead. There were large meadows of snow coming down and small bench-like seats connected to cables going up and down the mountain.

Marina squinted while she studied the hillside, "Is that a ski resort?"

"I think so, and those are chair lifts that take people up to the top so they can ski back down."

She shook her head in disbelief, "Amazing… truly amazing."

We began a very steep ascent up the mountain. The road curled back and forth, like a massive snake, as we made our way up the patchy snow-covered road. At this point, I would have been happy with a tunnel through the mountain. Every twist and turn had me imagining the car careening off the road and down the steep slope.

My concern must have been obvious, because Marina reached over with her hand and touched my right shoulder. "You're doing fine, Will."

With that simple gesture, I felt my worries ebbing away. But as we reached the summit of the pass, the car windows began to fog up. I frantically tried the windshield wipers, but they were ineffective—the fog was on the inside. Marina quickly switched on the defroster, but for some reason, it failed to clear the fog. She then grabbed a small shawl from the back seat and began wiping the windshield the best that she could.

With snow plows having built up walls of snow on either side of the road, pulling over wasn't an option. I continued driving, straining to see through a small clear patch on the windshield. After a flurry of panicked efforts to maintain visibility, I finally rolled down my window and stuck my head out. For what felt like miles, I drove with my head exposed to the biting cold, my face becoming chapped by the wind. Marina found humor at the sight of me hanging my head out of the window. She closed her eyes and bit her upper lip to refrain her laughter.

Eventually, the fog began to dissipate from the windshield, and I pulled my head back inside. I turned the heat down, and glanced at my reflection in the rearview mirror. "Well, that's lovely." I turned my attention toward Marina. "And all you could do is laugh and make jokes?"

She tried to hold back more laughter, smiling innocently at me. "I've always wanted a dog who would hang his head out of the window. Who needs a dog, when I have you, Will Massey?" With that comment, Marina winked at me and grinned. I returned the

favor with squinting eyes, a crinkled nose and a smile that hope-
fully conveyed I would get her back.

Continuing down the interstate with that fearful episode
behind us, I realized the car had gone silent again.

"My turn, right?" I asked.

"I think so."

"What is the real reason you were leaving Hudson and
Mildred's Diner?"

Marina tensed up. She turned to look out the window. Her
mood grew cooler than the frigid mountain air. I obviously struck
a nerve with my question.

"I told you why. I was tired of little Hudson, Ohio. I needed
a change."

I shook my head and pushed a little harder, "I'm not buying it.
There's something you're not telling me. I can almost sense something else is bothering you."

"I would rather not answer that right now, Will. Can you ask
me something else?"

Frustrated by the stonewall response, I huffed and quickly
changed my tune to one of more lightheartedness, "Okay, what do
want to be when you grow up?"

With that question, you could literally cut the tension in the
car with a knife. I knew my second question was poorly worded so
I interjected, "Not saying you are not grown up, I meant in a few
years, you know?"

"It's okay Will, your question was fine, I really don't feel like
playing right now. I think I'd like to take in the scenery."

I conceded, so we listened to a radio station that kept fading
in and out on us as we continued our trek into the small town
of Aspen.

Marina pulled out the road atlas and asked me curiously, "Where are we staying and what street is it on?"

I took the folded piece of paper that Jeffrey had given me and handed it to her.

"The Hotel Jerome, East Main Street," she read aloud. "It should be on this road, up here on the left."

After a few more blocks, we arrived at the hotel. It was a large, square shaped structure, three stories tall. The building was painted white with light blue trim. It had a worn look about it, but majestic none the less.

Entering the lobby, we could sense the history of this beautiful building. Much of the hotel appeared to have been recently remodeled and refurbished; although some of it was still in need of repair.

"How long are we staying here?" Marina asked.

"I think we stay for tonight and see what we feel like tomorrow."

She nodded in agreement.

I approached the front desk with some apprehension. "Excuse me; I think we have a reservation."

"What's your name?" asked the front desk attendant.

"William Massey," I replied.

"Oh yes, you're Jeffrey's friend. I'm Celeste. Jeffrey's such a cool dude. What can I do for you?"

I was a little puzzled by her question but decided to give it another try, "I think Jeffrey called and made a reservation for me?"

"Yeah man, I've got you down, but check-in isn't until like 3 o'clock."

"Oh, okay. We'll go and check out the town and come back then."

Celeste nodded, agreeing with my plan, "Sounds cool. We've got the J-Bar, if you want to check it out."

I turned to Marina who had witnessed the exchange. "Do you want to check out the J-Bar?" I asked.

"Sure."

As we opened the door and stepped into the bar, we were immediately struck by its historic charm. The interior was beautifully appointed with wood paneling and trim stretching from wall to wall. Old leather chairs and weathered tables filled the space. Along the outer wall, a series of windows overlooked the snow-covered street, framing the wintry scene outside.

Approaching the bar, a voice from a shadowed corner called out, "Emerson once said, 'Never lose an opportunity of seeing anything beautiful, for beauty is God's handwriting.'" We turned toward the sound to see a young man, about Marina's age, seated alone at a corner table. He sported amber-hued aviator sunglasses and a bucket hat. The table was completely covered with papers and magazines, a half-finished pint of beer and a partially eaten hamburger.

"You know, if I weren't a happily married family man," he began, his gaze lingering on Marina.

"But you are?" Marina shot back sharply.

This prompted a slight hesitation from the young man, followed by a broad, delighted smile. "I'm Hunter, and you are?"

Feeling the need to step in, and not wanting a repeat of Oklahoma City, I stated, "I'm Will, and this is…"

"Marina," she cut in, giving me a look that suggested I might be acting a bit too protective.

"Nice to meet you two, welcome to my town. What brings you to Fat City?"

I was about to ask him about the Fat City reference, when Marina piped in, "We're on a road trip from Ohio to the beaches of California."

"Nice," replied Hunter as he nodded. "Honeymoon?"

Marina embarrassingly smiled as big as I had witnessed up to this point and glanced my way. "No, we met a few days ago, even though it feels like a wonderful lifetime together."

The next few comments are a little fuzzy to me since I was completely lost in her comment.

"Where are you headed next? Las Vegas?"

"No," Marina answered, "San Diego."

Let me get this straight," Hunter continued, "you two just met and decided to trek across the country in a car together? Far out man, that's so real. I applaud you two." He raised his glass to toast us with his support.

Marina nodded down at the cluttered table, "Do you live at this hotel?"

"Oh," Hunter smiled, "no man, this is my office, I work here. I ran for sheriff, but I was screwed by the jackals and greedheads. No worries though, I am a writer and as Bulwer-Lytton so adequately stated – 'The pen is mightier than the sword.'"

As the young man thought about his defeat, he shook his head in disgust, and inquired, "Did you pass through Kentucky?"

"Yes. We left Hudson, Ohio and drove down through Louisville to Nashville and on to Memphis," I answered.

The young man drifted into a daze, like he took a quick trip down memory lane. He smiled, took a long drag on his cigarette and exhaled in delight, "I should probably get back to work. It has warmed my soul meeting the two of you today. I hope you enjoy my town and make it gloriously to your final destination."

He stood up from his seat and offered his hand in friendship. We shook his hand and turned to walk away.

"Mar, why don't we take a walk around town and give him some peace and quiet to work?"

She smiled in agreement, and we stepped outside and onto the sidewalk.

It was early afternoon and any snow left on the road had now turned into a muddy, slushy mess. I reached into my pocket and retrieved the instructions for our stay that Jeffrey had given me.

"It looks like we need to follow these directions and be at the restaurant for dinner at 6 PM. We could walk around for a little while, then come back and check into the hotel. I think that would leave us with enough time to get ready and drive to this place for dinner."

Marina smirked at me.

"What?" I asked.

"Nothing"

"No, not nothing, what was that smirk for? You think I'm planning again don't you?"

"It's okay, Will. Sometimes a little planning is a good thing."

I didn't have a comeback for that, but I was trying my best to think of one when she reached down and grabbed my hand.

"My hands are a little cold," she explained.

We walked along the sidewalk, taking in the sights; Long-haired hippy types wrapped in blankets and singing songs; a different dog on every stoop of every shop, and wealthy types adorned with the latest ski apparel and carrying their skis and poles over their shoulder. If there ever was a melting pot of culture, we had definitely stumbled into it.

"Where did all these dogs come from and who do they belong to?" I wondered aloud.

"I'm not sure, but nobody appears to mind them."

"They look so cold and hungry."

"I'm sure their owners feel like their freedom is more important than chaining them up or locking them away inside a house," Marina replied.

As we passed by a small park, Marina noticed a small area on the other side of the sidewalk that was smooth and pristine with a nice undisturbed layer of snow. "Let's make a snowman, Will."

She excitedly stepped off the sidewalk as she tried to navigate her way to the spot. At that moment, a clump of snow fell from the branches of an evergreen above and startled her. As she stepped backwards, I realized she was backing into a snowdrift that was disguising a deep ditch that separated the park from the street and sidewalk. It all happened so fast, but felt as though it was in slow motion. Marina fell backwards into the snowdrift and literally disappeared into the snow.

"Will! Help me. I can't get out."

I couldn't restrain my laughter. I leapt into the snowdrift and reached down to grab her arm. When I pulled her out, she appeared to be in frozen shock.

"Well, you managed to make a snowman, or snowwoman," I quipped through my snickers.

"Not funny, Will Massey!"

Marina, with a mischievous grin, then managed to shove me backward into the snowdrift, and thus began our spontaneous snowball fight. It wasn't a traditional snowball fight since neither of us took the time to meticulously form snowballs; instead, we scooped up handfuls of snow and playfully tossed clouds of it at each other. For several minutes, we were immersed in laughter, high-pitched shrieks, and beaming smiles, creating what would become one of my most cherished memories.

"Truce!" she called out; her hands raised in surrender.

She was a delightful sight, covered in snow—her hair, face, ears, and shoulders all dusted white. We stood there, face to face, panting from the exertion and lost in each other's eyes. Carefully, I brushed the snow from Marina's shoulders, her silky hair, her eyebrows, and her chin. She returned the gesture, gently clearing the snow from my shoulders, coat, hair, and ears. For a few lingering seconds, we stood there, breathing heavily while still facing each other. I felt an overwhelming desire to kiss her, but I hesitated, fearing it might disrupt the perfect moment we were sharing.

She smiled at me. "What a mess we are now, Will Massey"

"Shall we?" I offered her my arm. She looped her arm in mine and we headed back down the sidewalk toward the hotel.

Crossing over, we walked along another street lined with shops and restaurants.

"Oh, look Will." Marina stopped at a man sitting on a stool at the edge of a small alley. He was painting a snow-filled scene of the street with the mountain behind it. His palette was well worked and he had several paintings hanging on the wall of the building for all to see.

"These are incredible," I stated, inspecting each one closely.

"I like this one," Marina declared, her voice filled with admiration. She pointed to a painting, roughly the size of a placemat that captured a serene winter scene. It depicted a quaint little stone church situated at the end of a snow-covered street, bathed in the soft, warm glow of the setting sun. The artist had skillfully rendered a young couple, arms interlocked, strolling toward the church, their figures infused with a sense of peaceful togetherness. Behind them, the majestic Aspen Mountain loomed, its slopes blanketed in pristine snow, adding a breathtaking backdrop to the idyllic setting.

"How much for this piece?" I inquired to Marina's surprise.

He looked up from his current project and stated, "Ten dollars?" His response seemed to ask me if I was willing to pay that.

I reached into my pocket and pulled out a twenty-dollar bill and handed it to him. "Will you take twenty for it?"

The man smiled at me and nodded in appreciation.

I took the painting and handed it to Marina. "For you."

Her face beamed as she stood there smiling from ear to ear. Then she stepped towards me, wrapping her arms around me in a huge bear hug. "Thank you, Will. I'll cherish this forever."

After an interesting check-in process with Celeste, we headed up to our room. Marina was unusually quiet while we took turns getting ready for dinner. When our eyes did meet, she gave me a smile that was genuine and reassuring.

I wonder if she knows how deeply her smile touches my soul, I thought.

Marina stepped out of the bathroom and proclaimed, "I'm ready, I think."

I looked up from my thoughts and gazed at her. She had a glow about her that took my breath away. "You look perfect," I stated.

"Thank you Will," she responded with a bashful grin.

We headed down the stairs and into the lobby, past some folks smoking something I had never smelled before. I opened the car door for her and confirmed that her jacket was safely inside before closing it. I handed her the directions from Jeffrey. "You get to be the navigator."

She looked at me nervously and whispered, "That's reassuring."

We made our way out of downtown Aspen and back toward the road we came in on.

"Turn on this next road… I think," Marina directed. I peaked over at her hoping for more confidence in her navigation skills.

We seemed to be leaving civilization and heading into the wilderness.

"It should be up ahead on the right," she advised.

We came upon a small gravel parking lot with a few cars in it. There was a split rail fence surrounding the perimeter of the lot. It was becoming more difficult to see because the sun had disappeared beyond the mountains and nighttime was descending upon us quickly.

"I don't see a restaurant Will."

"I don't either," I responded with growing concern.

Standing next to an opening in the fence was a man with a flashlight. There were several skiers not far from the fence. *Why would someone want to ski cross-country at night?* I mused.

"Will, let's pull in and ask that man if there's a restaurant out here somewhere. I know I followed the directions word for word."

"It's okay, Mar. I'll park and go ask."

Pulling into the parking lot, I parked and left the car running as I walked over to the man.

"Excuse me sir, we may be lost. We have dinner reservations at a restaurant out here, but we may have taken a wrong turn."

The man looked up at me and tugged his scarf down from his face, "You are in the right place, are you the Massey's?"

I glanced over my shoulder, checking to see if Marina was still in the car or not. "Yes, Will and Marina Massey," I answered confidently.

"You are in the right place. If you will get the missus and wait right here, we will be on our way shortly."

I was still a little confused, but I walked back to the car and opened the door for Marina, "Go ahead and turn the car off and get the keys. He says we are in the right place."

She gave me a confused look. I shrugged my shoulders in response. We walked across the parking lot towards the man. "I'm not sure what Jeffery set up for us, so I am as in the dark as you are. No pun intended."

With that comment, Marina smiled and chirped, "That's not like you at all Will Massey… It's nice."

No sooner than joining the man next to the fence, we noticed the group of skiers began to trek into the darkness of the night. Guided only by their headlamps and the moonlight from above, they headed off on their skis into the woods.

"Where are they going?" Marina asked.

"I have no clue," I answered while buttoning up my jacket.

Through the wintery silence, we heard the sound of metal bells rhythmically ringing in a pulsating, steady tempo as a beautiful sleigh, pulled by two majestic looking horses came to a stop next to the fence. The man pulled down a step from the side of the sleigh and offered Marina his hand. She smiled with a look of amazement as he helped her onto the sleigh, "Watch your step ma'am."

He then gestured for me to follow her, so I pulled up into the sleigh and onto the seat next to Marina. The sleigh appeared straight out of a Christmas fairy tale, but the inside was more rustic and crude. We sat on a bench seat made of wood with no cushion. I noticed it was worn smooth by the numerous riders before us. The walls of the sleigh were simply a wood veneer stretched around a wooden frame with a thick layer of waterproofing stain to protect it from the elements. Once we had settled ourselves on the cold wooden bench, the driver made one last check of the reservation list with his parking lot compatriot then turned to us with only his eyes and upper cheeks visible through his face covering and stated, "You folks are the only ones who chose to ride tonight. Enjoy the privacy and your dinner."

He flicked the reins; shouted 'get up!' and the two brown shires with their feathery white legs began their rhythmic march forward, pulling the sleigh across the snow.

"First time?" the driver inquired.

"Yes," we both responded in unison.

"I'm guessing you didn't bring a heavy coat?" the driver inquired facetiously. "Here take this." He stretched his arm out and offered us what appeared to be an extra horse blanket. It was coarse and smelled like the woods, but it was a welcome layer of warmth when we pulled it across both of us.

Although the horses marched forward heavily, the sleigh sailed across the snow, like a scull gliding across the top of a placid lake. The warm breath of the shires plumed out from their faces like white clouds of smoke, while the constant jingling of the bells soon became part of the beautiful backdrop.

"Up ahead is an old mining camp. Hasn't been in operation for years, but you can see the log cabins and other out buildings that the miners once used. Nowadays, the cross-country skiers use it to take a break and catch their breath from the cold while they trek across the mountain side."

Frozen in time was this amazing little ghost town, once a bustling little community for miners on this mountain. We were speechless, gazing in awe at the site.

We meandered our way through a stretch of woods and up a steeper trail before coming out on a larger snow-covered meadow. The sheer face of the snow-covered mountain was to our left. Sharp gray boulders and slabs would peek through the snow in the moonlight and were an amazing contrast to the pureness of the snow.

Marina nudged me with her elbow. She had slumped down in the seat, and had tilted her head back and was facing the night sky with her mouth gaping open. It was a clear night and therefore a very cold night, but even more importantly, there wasn't a cloud in the sky. We were very high in elevation and there wasn't a town or manmade light anywhere around. When I looked up, I realized why she was silent and fixated on the heavens above. It was unlike anything I had ever experienced or have ever experienced since. There were billions of stars visible on that night. Not just the normal stars that I was accustomed to seeing, but galaxies were even visible.

"There's Perseus," Marina pointed up in sheer delight.

I nodded like I knew what she was pointing at.

She continued like a child overcome with excitement, "Oh Will, that's Andromeda there!" Her eyes were watering with joy. "This is so amazing! You can almost picture her outstretched arms to Perseus, longing for him to save her. Can you see it Will?"

"I sure can." It truly was the most spectacular sky full of stars I had ever experienced. Trying desperately to participate in the conversation, I added, "Look over there, it's the Three Kings."

She wrinkled her face awkwardly and stared in the direction I was pointing. "You mean, the Three Sisters?"

"Those three stars in a row," I replied, "they're the Three Kings, right?"

She scowled playfully at me. "Let's just agree to call it Orion's Belt."

"Agreed," I answered, winking playfully at Marina in a friendly compromise.

"Will, we can see galaxies tonight," she whispered.

The stars looked close enough to touch.

I couldn't help but fixate on the starlight as it outlined her face. "You really do know all the constellations, huh?"

Marina smiled at me, her eyes sparkling from the reflection of the evening sky.

As we pulled around the edge of the mountain, I looked ahead and saw the soft yellow glow of lights from a beautiful log cabin up on the rise ahead of us.

"Look Mar." Making our final turn, I pointed to the cabin off in the distance.

The sleigh pulled up to the cabin and came to a stop. It was a rustic little structure with snow piled up around the outside. The roof was clear of snow, cleansed from the warmth radiating from within. Rays of light emanated through the curtains on the windows and out onto the winter wonderland surrounding it.

A man approached the sleigh and held out his hand. I gratefully accepted his help and made my way onto the snow-packed ground. I turned back and extended my hand to Marina. She placed her hand in mine, her fingers cold but her grip firm. She stepped down gracefully beside me, her shoes crunching softly in the fresh snow.

As we approached the door, we noticed the group of skiers who had left before us were drawing near from a different path.

"I'd rather ride," Marina scoffed quietly.

We were seated at our table, next to a wood burning stove that was warming the dining area. We had the most romantic candlelit dinner with great food and good wine and unforgettable surroundings. Celebrating the day and the trip to this point, we laughed about the experiences we had already shared together. When we had finished our meal, I pulled the camera out of my pocket and asked our waiter if he would mind taking a photo of us.

"Is that a camera? Where did you get that?"

"I bought it in Denver while you were soaking in the tub. It's a Kodak, the lady at the store said it's a good one." Marina inspected the camera with delight, and then proceeded to take a few pictures of her own.

When it was time to leave, we braced ourselves against the chill and climbed back into the sleigh. We draped the musty, itchy horse blanket over our laps once again. With the sleigh gradually picking up speed, I glanced back to see the soft lights of the restaurant fade into the distance. A thin veil of clouds had drifted over, slightly warming the air. Marina rested her head on my shoulder and intertwined her arm with mine. The rhythmic trot of the horses and the gentle jingle of the sleigh bells, combined with the nighttime luminescence on the surrounding snow, created a scene that was as close to peace on earth as I could ever imagine.

We exited the sleigh at the parking lot and watched as it departed for the evening. Finding ourselves momentarily alone in the darkness, Marina took my hands into hers, drawing me close. She leaned in and placed a gentle kiss on my cheek. Then, bringing her lips close to my ear, she whispered tenderly, "Will, no matter what happens in your life, promise me you will never order another ice water to go, ever again."

CHAPTER 14

December 9, 1970

MORNING CAME FAR too soon. I stumbled out of my bed and made my way into the shower. When I came out of the bathroom, I paused to watch Marina sleeping. I didn't want to wake her yet, so again I wrote her a note and left it on the table between the beds.

'Mar: I went to find us something for breakfast. Back soon. — Will'

I stepped out of the lobby and onto the sidewalk. The evening had delivered a fresh inch or two of snow and everything glistened in the early morning light.

I remembered seeing a donut shop when we arrived the day before, so I made my way down the street a couple of blocks to where I thought it was. After entering the little shop to the smell of freshly made coffee and sugary sweet donuts, I stood there frozen. There were dozens of breakfast confections. Crème filled, jelly filled, cake, chocolate… my heart raced. It was a silly thing to stress about, but I didn't know what she would like. A wave of embarrassment crashed over me. I'd driven half-way across the country and didn't know her donut of choice. I barely knew this woman at all.

Then it hit me. You do know her. *What would Marina order?*

"I'll take a dozen assorted donuts, you choose for me. I'll also take two coffees and a milk."

After doctoring up both of our coffees, I gathered it all up in my arms and headed back down the street to the hotel. Marina was sitting up in her bed with her back against the headboard smiling at me when I entered the room.

"What did you bring me?"

I walked over to her bed and set the donuts down. "I honestly do not know. A dozen assorted donuts, baker's choice."

"Living on the edge, Will Massey?" She smiled and winked at me to let me know that her remark wasn't an insult at all.

We sat on her bed and ate our donuts. I watched in delight as she would go from the milk to the coffee and back again. I was again proud of my final decision.

"So, what's the plan?" she inquired, wiping some icing and milk from the corner of her mouth with a napkin.

I swallowed my current mouthful of donut and chased it with some coffee. "I was thinking that we check out of the hotel and get back on the road."

"I'm good with that, then what?"

"For someone who doesn't like planning, you seem to be asking me for a plan," I teased.

"Just checking," she fired back with a smile.

"I was thinking that maybe we keep our swimsuits within reach. I saw a sign when we were coming here that advertised some hot springs in Glenwood Springs. Maybe we could stop there and give it a try, if you're open to it that is."

Marina stopped mid chew and realized that she needed to swallow before replying to my comment, but I interjected, "You did bring a swimsuit, didn't you? I mean, we are headed to the beach, right?"

By this time, she had finished her bite, washed it down, and was waiting to respond with attitude, "Of course I brought my swimsuit, and don't even question my spontaneity!"

I winked at her playfully as I finished my donut and rose from the bed, "Come on slowpoke, are you going to stay in bed all day?"

Marina threw a pillow at me as I turned to walk toward the door. "Give me fifteen minutes?"

"You got it," I replied. "I am going down to the J-Bar and see if they have any coffee, I think I need one more cup."

After a short time, I returned to the room with my coffee in hand. Marina had just finished getting ready and handed me her bag as I walked in the door.

"Let's go," she ordered.

"Yes ma'am."

She was quiet for the first thirty minutes of our drive as she studied the road atlas, flipping pages back and forth and taking some notes and making some calculations.

"What are you working on?"

Peering up from the road atlas with a serious look on her face, she proclaimed, "If my calculations are right, we have about a thousand more miles to go. Maybe something like twenty-four hours of total drive time remaining?"

"That sounds about right."

She continued, "We could be on the beach in three days, unless we choose to stop a couple of more times. Either way, we surely will be on the beach in five days."

The more that I thought about her timeline, the more anxiety

I felt. I didn't want to think about it ending. She put the atlas away and became very quiet. I wondered if they same thought had entered her mind.

After a few more miles, I felt like I needed to break the silence. "We just passed a sign that said ten miles to Glenwood Springs, you still feel like a swim?"

Marina turned slowly toward me, smiled and affirmed, "Yes, I do."

Glenwood Springs was right on the interstate and seemed to be a rather old town that never lost its appeal. I remember reading once, how people with tuberculosis used to come to Glenwood Springs to soak in its healing waters, but I had no idea what to expect.

We pulled into the Glenwood Hot Springs parking lot and made our way to the large sandstone building. I purchased a pass for both of us and handed Marina hers.

"I guess we go change and then I will meet you at the pool?" I asked.

"See you there."

The bathhouse was rustic, yet charming. There weren't many people there on this day; in fact, we practically had the place to ourselves. After changing into my swimsuit, I grabbed a towel and headed out to the pool. The air had a definite chill about it. Steam rose from the pool and formed a fog around the water. Snow was still standing on the roof and around the outer areas of the pool. The water was dark, yet clean, much like the rivers and lakes that I had grown up with.

As I surveyed the pool and the surrounding grounds, a familiar voice came from behind me, "Is it hot?"

I turned and suddenly realized that this was the first time I had seen Marina in anything but pajamas or clothes. My reaction must have been quite apparent.

"Is something wrong, Will?" she asked, her gaze falling over herself, checking for something out of place.

"Uh, no, not at all, it's a…" I was stumbling over my words, trying to articulate my thoughts. Deciding to be as honest as possible, I explained genuinely and sincerely, "You are as beautiful on the outside as you are on the inside. That's all."

Marina fell silent, smiling bashfully, her eyes shifting around as she searched for something else to focus on. "Why don't we get in? I'm going to freeze to death standing here."

We both waded in up to our waist. The water was very warm, and it felt good on our tired bodies. It seems that traveling in a car for hours at a time can make your body ache more than hard labor. She took a deep breath, ducked under water, and then sank down to allow only her head to remain above the water line. I decided to follow her lead and we ended up side by side near the edge of the pool.

"This feels amazing," I said. "Don't you think so?"

Marina had a strange look on her face.

"What's wrong?"

She continued to contort her face, and then whispered, "What's that smell? Is this water clean?"

"It's the sulfur in the hot springs."

"It smells really bad, Will. Are you sure this isn't some sort of dirty water?"

That comment really caught me off guard along with the continued facial expressions that she was making. I began to laugh. "Your nose will get used to it after a few minutes. You won't even be able to smell it anymore."

She closed her eyes and laid her head against the concrete lip of the pool. I joined her in this little ritual and felt more relaxed than I had for some time. I opened my eyes and glanced at Marina. Her eyes were closed, her mouth was full of air, her cheeks were puffed out, and she was pinching her nose to keep from smelling the sulfur. I began to laugh again.

"Mar, could you have ever imagined when you set out from Hudson that you'd get to soak in natural hot springs in Colorado?"

"To be honest, I never imagined any of this," she admitted, gazing upwards at the steam clouds wafting from the water of the pool.

"Really?"

"I must admit, Will, when I stepped into the diner and I didn't see you, my heart sank into the pit of my stomach." Marina paused, before allowing herself to open up more. "I was a nervous wreck the closer this trip came, but I could never let Aunt Mildred know that. When you offered to go with me, it was almost like a prayer had been answered." She paused again and seemed to be second guessing her willingness to share.

"I know what you mean."

"I didn't sleep much that night; not because I was nervous about the trip, but more so because I couldn't wait to talk with you some more. Isn't that strange?" She continued to stare up towards the sky, avoiding eye contact at all cost.

I knew exactly what she meant. The ability to just sit and talk with another human being is underrated. We almost need it, we crave it. Yet I had avoided it completely for five years.

There was an awkward silence. Both of us were lost in our own thoughts.

Marina was the first to break. "I can't believe that Aunt Mildred knew you were there and didn't say a word. In fact, I think she enjoyed knowing that you were there and that I was affected by it."

"I noticed that too."

"She's always been good about letting me be me. The fact that she toyed with both of us like that means that she approved."

"Approved?"

Marina turned her head and looked at me for the first time since we sank into the pool. "Of you," she stated with a smile.

I wasn't sure how to reply to that statement without being awkward. Luckily Marina decided to help me out.

"Will, my swimsuit is going to stink now. People at the beach will think that I smell funky."

"Just think, Mar, thousands of people; even famous people have soaked in this pool."

"It smells like it!" she quipped.

"As much as I am enjoying this, do we need to leave?"

Marina looked at me and grinned, "Not yet. It does feel good, and I already smell awful, so maybe just for a little while longer."

I placed my head back against the side and stared up to the sky. I stayed like that for a few minutes.

Marina broke through the silence again as she slowly twirled her fingers along the top of the warm water. "I'd love to know what you are thinking right now."

I continued resting my head and staring up at the sky. "It's not really what I am thinking, but how I'm feeling. I feel happy, but at the same time, I feel guilty."

"What do you mean?" Marina asked.

I contemplated how to word my thoughts. "Mama, Daddy, Walt, Drew, and Susan Jane, none of them got to experience what I am getting to experience. It doesn't seem fair."

Marina thought about my comment for a minute before interjecting. "I see what you mean, but don't you think that they'd want you to experience it just the same? Don't you think they would want you to be happy?"

"I suppose you're right." We both closed our eyes.

"Although I'm not sure how envious they would be if they could smell this sulfur water," Marina quipped.

I began to smile and laugh at her attempt to lighten the conversation. "I take it that you've had enough? Are your ready to get back on the road?"

"Only if you are."

"Okay, Mar, let's go."

We waded back over to the bathhouse side and climbed out of the pool. The chill of the cold air was a shock as it contrasted with the heat that we had felt in the pool.

"I'm going to take a shower and try to rinse this off." Wrapping herself in the towel, Marina raced back into the bathhouse.

I just shook my head in delight, before drying off and heading into the bathhouse as well.

It didn't take me long to shower off and get dressed. While waiting for Marina, I chuckled as I thought of her reaction to the pool. About thirty minutes later she emerged from the ladies locker room refreshed and ready to go.

"That hot shower and the soap they had was just what I needed," she said.

I leaned in and sniffed her hair, "Are you sure that you used enough shampoo?"

"What?"

"I'm just kidding, Mar, you smell wonderful."

"I better," she replied. "The last thing I want is to be in the car smelling like a rotten egg. In fact, I feel revived. I can drive for a while."

"Are you sure?"

"You can take a break, Will, I'll drive."

We left Glenwood Springs and headed west. Curious to know where we were headed, I opened the road atlas and noticed that Marina had used her pencil to trace the route on the atlas that she wanted to take. I must have been smiling noticeably, because she asked, "What's so funny?"

I looked over at her and thought about my reply first. "Nothing, I just noticed that you have been very meticulous in planning out the rest of our journey. I'm impressed."

Trying to keep her eyes on the road and determine her excuse, Marina fidgeted and then responded, "We don't have to go that way. I was just looking at our options."

She continued, "Since we are headed for San Diego, we need to take a more southern route sooner or later. I've always wanted to see the large red rock formations of Monument Valley that are in almost all the western movies. When I looked at the road atlas, it looked like we can either go into Utah then down to Flagstaff, Arizona passing right through that area, or we can go down through Colorado first, but the mountain passes might be covered in snow. I just decided the safer route might be through Utah."

I smiled and nodded my head in total agreement. "Am I rubbing off on you Mar?"

She rolled her eyes. "You can be my navigator and tell me when we need to turn in order to follow my plan." She then smiled with commanding delight.

We listened to the radio for a while, but soon we were both getting restless.

Looking at the road atlas again, I advised, "When we get to Crescent Junction, we need to take highway 160 south to Moab."

"Okay. Thanks, Will." She then reached and turned down the volume on the radio, "I guess it's my turn?"

"Awe man, I thought we were done with this game?" I teased.

Marina gave me a scowl, "No, we are not done with this 'game' as you call it, until the trip is over.

"I was just teasing."

"Hmmmm..." Marina thought for a minute, "What's the most difficult thing you've had to learn in your life?"

"Wow," I replied. "That's a tough one. Let me think about that."

She interceded, "But don't say anything dumb like college math or something. I want your honest opinion."

"The most difficult thing I've had to learn?" I repeated. Hesitating until I realized that Marina was getting antsy. "Unfortunately, it's that everyone I ever love, dies."

My response clearly unsettled her. Her eyes widened noticeably, and her shoulders drooped in a telltale sign of discomfort. She nibbled nervously on her lower lip before responding. "That's a very dark statement. You don't think you're to blame, do you?"

"No... that's not what I meant. You know; my mama, my daddy, my brothers and then Susan Jane... I understand that everyone dies, but they all seemed to die way too soon."

I noticed that Marina was avoiding eye contact again. "I'm sorry for asking that, Will. I wasn't thinking."

"It's okay, Mar, you don't have to apologize."

"Can I ask you a different question, just to make up for that one?" she proposed, clearly trying to steer the conversation in a lighter direction.

I smiled at her effort to shift the mood. "Sure,"

"How many times have you been 'in love'?"

"Twice," I immediately replied.

"Ooh... Let me guess," she interjected. "One would have been Susan Jane, correct?"

I nodded nervously, realizing I may have answered too hastily.

Honestly, Susan had been my only love until now. But, I was falling for Marina. Our relationship had blossomed more naturally than any before. I had doubted these feelings at first, labeling them as convenient or even rebound. But this was a deeper connection that I was struggling to reconcile with.

Now, I had created a predicament. I had to choose: be honest about my growing feelings or keep avoiding the subject. If her feelings weren't mutual, I risked offending Marina or driving her away.

She piped in again, "The other would have been your mother, am I right?"

In one fell swoop, she had let me off the hook without realizing it.

I smiled with relief. "Good guess."

She seemed proud of herself, grinning and raising her eyebrows at my compliment.

"What was your mom like?"

I hadn't thought about Mama for a while now. Pausing, while I unlocked those memories, I began, "Mama was a tough little woman. She had dark hair and her skin was fairly pale. She wasn't very tall, maybe a little over five feet, but that didn't stop her from enforcing her will when she had to."

I chuckled before continuing. "She had a temper. Not as bad as Daddy's, but she definitely had a temper. She had the gift of empathy too. No matter what was going on with someone, if it was joy or sadness, worry or fear, she could relate at your level. That didn't mean that she agreed with you or felt any pity or sympathy for you, especially if your actions or bad decisions were the cause, but she could definitely feel what you were feeling."

I paused again for a minute or two as thoughts raced through my mind.

"I sure could have used her when Susan Jane passed away," I whispered.

"Sounds like a special lady."

"You don't know the half of it," I explained. "She could cuss like a sailor when she felt the need, and did. But she could also kneel by your bed when you were sick and deliver the most eloquent prayer that you've ever heard."

I peered over at Marina as she continued to drive and listen to my story.

"This one time, Walt, Drew and I were in the back yard throwing a ball around. I couldn't have been older than eight. Anyhow, I went to catch the ball and it jammed my ring finger on my right hand. I yelled out 'DAMN IT!' None of us realized that Mama had raised the windows but left the curtains down. I immediately heard her yell from inside the house, 'William Riley Massey, what did you just say?' I had to think fast, so I responded 'I jammed it!' that's what I said Mama!"

Marina was shaking her head in disbelief while smiling from ear to ear.

"Mama just yelled back, you better watch your mouth young man or I will have to tell your daddy when he gets home!"

I smiled and laughed, thinking of how much I loved her and missed her.

"There was this other time, when I was about six years old. One of our neighbors had gotten themselves a beagle to go hunting with. It would wander around at night just looking for trouble. This one night, it got down below freezing and we were all curled up under the blankets in our beds. That dog showed up under Mama and Daddy's window and started baying like it had treed a raccoon or something. Daddy jumped up out of bed, madder than a stirred-up hornets' nest. He was cussing at the top of his lungs as he put his feet into his slippers. He grabbed the old broom Mama kept in the closet and out the back door he went."

I was laughing at this point, so was Marina, as we both pictured this scene in our minds.

"We all gathered around the back door. Mama was yelling at him to come back in and leave that dog alone, but he just ignored her. He ran around our back yard chasing that dog with that broom in nothing but a t-shirt, his white briefs and his slippers."

"We had never seen Daddy move that fast. That dog thought it was a game and he kept him moving for probably twenty minutes. But there was this spot where our sink and Mama's washing machine emptied out into the yard. It stayed wet most of the year, and on that night, it was a sheet of clear ice. Daddy hit that patch of ice and went flying through the air; landing right on his back."

"Mama went running out into the yard while the three of us boys ran back to bed knowing that we couldn't stop laughing and if Daddy saw us laughing, there's no telling what he would've done to us."

I smiled, replaying it all in my mind.

"She stayed up the rest of the night with Daddy, rubbing his back and putting some ice on it. She never really said anything disparaging about his foolishness or how funny it was, she just supported him and told him that he almost caught that dog and had it not been for the ice, she thinks that he would've."

I stared out the window while more memories flooded into my mind. I noticed we had passed through Moab and Monticello, Utah.

"You know, come to think of it, when they told me that Walt and Drew had been killed in action, I cried all night long. Mama laid there in the bed with me and stroked my hair and tried to reassure me that everything would be alright and the hurt would eventually go away." I took a deep breath and wiped my eyes. "I'm sure she cried a river over my brothers, but I don't think she ever let me see her cry about it."

I paused again and stared out the window, watching the landscape whip by like the memories of my childhood.

"What else do you remember about your mom?"

"She was a great cook," I responded. "We never had much, but Mama did so much with what we did have. Everything she cooked was delicious. She would make biscuits and I would just sit and lather them with jelly."

"So what was your favorite thing that she would cook?"

I pondered on that question for a minute. There were so many meals and dishes that Mama made that I had to really debate in my mind over which was the best.

"She made the best chicken and dumplings. I could have a bad day and come home to the smell of that in the house and all my worries would disappear. It would warm you to your core."

Marina smiled at my stories.

"You know, back at the powwow, when the older lady thought I was her son? And then I hugged her and told her that her son loves her very much? I think we both needed that. I never got the chance to hug my mom again and tell her I loved her, and she never got the chance to hug her son again and hear him say it."

I stopped again and gazed out at the rock formations that were casting shadows and silhouettes as the sun was starting to set. "We should probably find a motel. Not sure it would be smart to drive at night out here with so few towns on our route."

Marina nodded. "I think I saw a sign a few miles back that we are coming up on a town called Bluff. Maybe there is a place to stay there."

Entering the town, we stumbled upon a motel with a restaurant next door. The sign out front read 'VACANCY', so I jumped out of the car and went inside the office to get us a room. The man behind the front desk was watching a small television while eating a sandwich and drinking a beer. He let me stand there a moment before finally wiping his mouth with a rag and then standing up to offer his services, "Yep?" he said.

"I'd like to get a room for the night. Preferably a double, if you have one."

Without acknowledging me, he spun around to board with room numbers and keys hanging on it, grabbed a key, then turn back around to me, "Room number five," he proclaimed. "Best room in the house." He smiled at his own inside joke. "That will be fifteen dollars."

It seemed a little high for the location and quality, but I wasn't in the mood to haggle and I didn't want to risk losing a room in such a remote location, so I paid the man and signed us in. Near the door was a display stand with several tourist brochures and fliers for attractions in the area. I grabbed a sampling of them before exiting the office.

"Check out is at ten. No exceptions!"

I just raised my hand to acknowledge him and then proceeded back to the car. We parked in front of our room and headed in with our bags. It was clean, with two beds, a small bathroom, and a small television.

Marina chose the bed on the left, which was closest to the bathroom and furthest from the window and door. She set her bags down and then sprawled herself out on her bed to 'try it out'.

"Driving in a car for hours at a time can make your body hurt," she declared.

"That's why I thought the soak in the hot springs would have been a welcomed break."

"It did feel good once my nose got accustomed to the smell."

I noticed Marina had closed her eyes, waiting for my teasing response. Instead, I set my bags down, sat down on my bed and lay back. I stretched out and at that very instant, the left side of my bed gave way and crashed to the ground. Marina sat up, realized what had just happened and began laughing at my predicament with her hand over her mouth.

"What the he….," before I could finish my statement, the other side of the bed collapsed as well, jolting me onto my side.

Marina completely lost it, laughing so hard that tears streamed down her face. Suddenly, she rocked back and tumbled off her bed onto the floor. Her fall only intensified our laughter, sending us into another bout of giggles for a few more minutes. Eventually, the room fell silent as we lay there, catching our breath in the quiet.

"We should go find something to eat," Marina suggested.

"I agree."

As we both stood up, Marina asked, "What should we do about your bed?"

"Leave it," I answered. "I wouldn't want to try and fix it only to have it fall in the middle of the night."

Marina smiled and nodded in agreement.

We decided to walk to the little steakhouse next door. It was just a local establishment with plenty of smokers and lots of beer. Everything in the place seemed to be made of wood or of stone. The walls were covered in Southwestern décor.

The owner met us at the door, "Welcome to Canyon Ranch Steakhouse, just two of you tonight?"

"Yes sir," Marina confirmed.

"Right this way." The restaurant wasn't that busy, but yet he seated us within ten feet of all the other patrons. "Your waitress will be with you in just a minute."

A cloud of smoke filled the air around our table. We seem to be the only people in the place who didn't have a cigarette in our hand.

"Why do they always do this?" I observed.

"Do what?"

"Seat us so close to everyone. Look at all the empty tables in here and yet we might as well be sitting at the same table with everyone else."

Marina smiled and explained, "It's easier to wait on the tables if the customers aren't all spread out. I don't mind it. Try not to focus on them."

I realized that I was complaining and quickly buried my head in the menu.

A buxom older waitress with very blonde hair approached our table, "What can I get you two lovebirds to drink?"

I looked at Marina, suggesting that she go first.

"I'll take water and a beer," she replied.

"I'll have the same."

"What are you getting, Will?"

"I think I'll get the sirloin with a baked potato and the ranch beans. It says that all steaks come with a side salad."

Marina nodded. "Sounds good to me."

The waitress returned with our drinks. "You two know what you want to eat?"

"Go ahead Will," Marina insisted.

"I'll have the sirloin steak, medium, with a baked potato and your ranch beans. What kind of dressing do you have for the salad?"

"Our salad comes with green goddess dressing only," answered the waitress.

"That's fine," I replied.

Marina spoke up, "I'll have the same thing."

"That's easy enough," stated the waitress.

We both took a sip of our beer before Marina spoke up, "I think we are about four hours from Flagstaff. There might be a couple of detours that would be worth stopping for, but if we could limit those to two to three hours, then we could still make it comfortably to Flagstaff before the sun goes down tomorrow."

Marina's plan sounded solid to me, but I wondered, *has this beautiful, fireball of spontaneity somehow turned into a detail oriented planner.* It was both fascinating and amusing at the same time.

The waitress dropped off our salads and without saying a word, we both began to eat.

After a minute or two of devouring our salads, I suggested, "Why don't we enjoy our dinner, go back to the room and look through the brochures and fliers that I snagged in the motel office. Then maybe pick a few spots that are on the route where we might want to stop and visit. We can get up early in the morning and head towards Flagstaff and just play it by ear. If we decide to stop somewhere, we do it. If we decide to not stop, then we don't."

She gave me a strange look. "Who are you and what have you done with my Will?"

I rolled my eyes and smiled at her, "Haha, very funny." Truth is, I was extremely elated to hear Marina refer to me as 'her Will'. Not sure why, but every action and every word that came from her was now being sorted, filtered and analyzed by my brain for any evidence that she might be feeling the same way about me that I was about her.

She was just about to say something even wittier, but the waitress arrived with our plates.

"This looks delicious," said Marina as though she was expecting something much worse.

We both began cutting into our steaks. I mechanically went

through the motions while sneaking glances at Marina. She handled her meal with meticulous care, fork in her left hand and knife in her right. Each slice of steak was carefully topped with a small dab of potato, which she then lifted to her mouth with the back of the fork facing upwards. In contrast, I simply cut my steak, stabbed a piece with my fork, and brought it to my mouth with the tines facing up. Curiously, I attempted to emulate her technique for a bite, but the piece of steak clumsily fell off the fork and luckily landed back on my plate.

She realized what I was doing. "Will, don't feel like you have to change the way you eat for me. Just keep eating the way you know how, even if it's all wrong," she teased, taking another bite and suppressing a laugh with her mouth full.

"What do you mean, 'wrong'? You're the one who eats strangely. Who taught you to press food to the back of the fork? A fork is meant for stabbing and scooping."

She looked surprised at my quick retort. "Hold up now. I was taught by Aunt Mildred to eat like a lady. A lady never stabs or scoops her food."

We resumed eating in silence, the tension slowly dissipating. After a few minutes, she broke the quietness. "Will, I love the way you eat; it's not wrong, it's just your way. I'm sorry I said it was wrong."

Now I felt bad. "I'm sorry I snapped, Mar. You're not the first person to tell me that I eat all wrong. Susan tried to teach me proper etiquette using my fork and knife, several times. It just seems illogical to me."

Marina took another bite then responded, "You know, I bet a farmer wouldn't try to put hay on the back of a pitchfork."

"Exactly," I said.

"Can I make a suggestion? When you cut your steak, just make sure that your knife isn't right up against the tines. I used to do that and my food would always fall off the fork when I would raise it to my mouth."

I stuck my fork into the steak, placed my knife just a little to the right of the tines and cut. I then lifted it to my mouth with the fork facing down.

"Bravo, young Massey," she teased with a flirtatious smile.

I winked in appreciation for the advice, "Thanks Mar."

After eating, we returned to our room. Marina gathered the pamphlets and spread them in front of her on her bed. "Come join me Will," She patted the spot next to her.

I sat beside her and we both began to pick up the materials and go through them. Tediously we would look at sites and attractions and find them on the road atlas to determine their proximity to our route.

"I would like to see the Grand Canyon, Will. Maybe we can do that once we are in Flagstaff tomorrow?"

"That's probably a good plan, since it seems to be just north of Flagstaff, but not really on our way tomorrow. Looks like the same would apply to the meteor crater, the Petrified Forest and the Painted Desert."

Marina continued to study several of the brochures related to some of the named red rock formations. "I wonder if most of these can be seen from the main highway that we will be on. If so, then maybe we can just pull off for a few of them if we want to stretch our legs."

"We definitely need to stop in Monument Valley," I declared. "I think that's where John Wayne filmed a few westerns."

Marina seemed to be off in a different world, smiling and staring blankly at one of the pages.

"Are you okay?" I asked.

"I was just thinking that maybe we can stay more than just one night in Flagstaff, so we can make a few more memories before moving on."

I began to stack all of the papers and pamphlets together along with the road atlas. Marina stepped into the bathroom to get ready for bed.

"Are we going to just go to bed?" I yelled out.

"I don't know," she yelled back. "Maybe there is something on the television?"

The television was an older model that didn't have a remote. I bent over next to it and began to turn the dial channel by channel. Most of the stations that tried to come in were fuzzy, at best. Marina sat back on her bed applying some lotion to her hands. "Do you know how to play backgammon, Will?"

I switched the television off and turned to face her. "I do."

She leaned over, stuck her hand into one of her bags, pulled out a small travel backgammon case, and placed it in front of her on her bed. She then motioned to the spot next to her, inviting me to return.

"Give me one second?" I asked.

I retrieved pajamas from my bag and darted into the bathroom to change. I brushed my teeth and washed my face, then stepped back into the room. As I turned to say something to Marina, I noticed that she had slumped back and to the side. Her head was on the stacked pillow and she had fallen asleep. I took the backgammon game and gently placed it on the dresser. I drew the blanket up and covered Marina with it and gave her a gentle kiss on the forehead.

"Goodnight, Mar," I whispered.

CHAPTER 15

December 10, 1970

WE STARTED THE day early after a restless night. Neither of us slept well. Pulling into a gas station, I had the attendant fill up the tank. I went inside and got us both a cup of coffee and some cinnamon sugar covered pastries that they were selling at the counter. When I came back to the car, Marina had moved into the driver's seat behind the wheel.

"I'll drive again today," she decreed.

"Are you sure?" I asked. "We will probably pass several rock formations that you might want to watch for, rather than driving."

"You've been driving so much; it's only fair that you get to look today. Besides, if I see something I really want to gaze at, I'll just pull off the road."

"Fair enough," I conceded.

It was a chilly, overcast day. Signs of intermittent snowfall from the night before were evident, leaving a light dusting across the landscape and a fine layer of snow blowing on the road. We began to notice majestic red rock formations rising to our right, off the road. They jutted up from the horizon, standing boldly like God had positioned them there for all to marvel at.

As we came into Mexican Hat, Utah we began to see signs that directed us to the Mexican Hat rock formation. Marina turned off to get a better view. We stopped and marveled at this rock for a few minutes, wondering how it stayed so balanced without tipping over.

"Amazing," she exclaimed. "This is better than looking at pictures."

Both of us searched tirelessly for another beautiful formation. A sign ahead read – 'Monument Valley Next Left'.

We turned onto the road and couldn't help but notice that the clouds had dispersed enough to allow rays of sunshine to flood down on the large sandstone formations. Their shadows danced across the mesa as the clouds moved above. It was truly a sight to behold. Pulling the car off onto an overlook, we stepped out for a few minutes and took in the magnificent nature of these massive red structures that stood like soldiers on an expansive battlefield.

"Will, do you think the Native Americans that live here appreciate the beauty of these formations since they see them all the time?"

"I think they probably appreciate them more than you or I could ever imagine. This is their land, their ancestors' land. I would guess that this is sacred to them.

The whole experience seemed almost spiritual to both of us as we marveled at the natural beauty.

We were starting to get cold since the clouds had returned to block the sun. Daylight was also waning, so hesitantly we climbed back into the car and took our seats.

"It's much easier to believe in God when you see something like this in person," she proclaimed.

"I know what you mean."

We continued to follow the road as it looped around the magnificent formations. After several minutes, it brought us back to the point where we had started and we turned back onto the main highway headed for Flagstaff.

"I can't believe how big they are," declared Marina. "It's like an artist placed them in perfect position to each other. I'm so glad I got to see this."

I sat there peering out the window at the vastness of the landscape, realizing that this trip had progressed from the unknown, to something trivial, to an experience that was really deep and meaningful. I turned my gaze towards Marina and realized how grateful I was for her.

My curiosity had gotten the best of me, so I decided to pry, "Describe a man that you have known in your life that you were in love with or could have been in love with."

She stayed quiet.

"Well?" I pleaded.

"Give me a minute, I'm thinking,"

A light snow began to fall again and the sky had darkened even more.

I noticed Marina smiling peculiarly before she glanced at me and began to speak. "His name was George. He was tall, with dark brown hair. He was strong but gentle. He treated me with respect and kindness and always put me first."

I nodded my head in approval.

"He had a kind voice, and a kind soul. His presence filled me with warmth and his absence left me with a chill." She prolonged her glance at me, smiling from within.

"Wolf!" I screamed.

Marina snapped her gaze back to the road just in time to spot a gray wolf standing directly in our path. She jerked the steering wheel to the right. Our front right tire left the edge of the road. In a panic, she overcorrected.

We skidded back onto the highway with a harsh, scraping crunch. The car swerved wildly, going perpendicular to the road. We lifted off the ground and rolled violently through the darkness. The physical turmoil of the car flipping over and over was excruciating.

When I regained consciousness, the car had come to a stop, overturned. I was doubled over on the ceiling, my seat looming above me. Marina was suspended upside down, secured by her lap belt. Her head was beginning to swell visibly, her face marred by cuts and strewn with shards of glass. Blood streamed from her nose and ear. Her beautiful hair was now a matted mess soaked with blood and dust. Steam hissed into the cabin from the damaged engine, and the car's horn blared a continuous, desperate cry for help. Overwhelmed, I slipped back into unconsciousness.

When I woke, I was on a gurney in an emergency room with a bevy of nurses and hospital staff hovering over me.

"Mr. Massey, can you hear me?" asked the doctor.

I was confused at first. *Was this a dream? a nightmare? I just need to wake up*, I thought.

"Mr. Massey, if you can hear me, can you please nod your head."

I nodded my head in response.

"That's good, Mr. Massey. You've been in a car wreck and we are going to roll you down the hall and take some x-rays. Okay?"

I nodded my head and they began to rush me from the room and into the hallway.

"Mr. Massey, are you having any unbearable pain anywhere on your body?"

I shook my head.

"That's a good sign. Can I get you to raise your left arm? Now your right arm? Can you lift your left leg a little? Now your right leg? Again, does anything hurt really bad?"

"No," I whispered.

It was now all coming back to me vividly, like a home movie in my mind that was being replayed just for me. The wolf, the car rolling and Marina…

"Marina? Is she okay?" My voice cracked.

"Your wife? She is going into surgery right now, sir. She got banged up pretty bad and we may have to reduce some of the swelling on her brain, but she's alive and in good hands. Do you understand?"

I nodded my head and began to cry.

They wheeled me into the x-ray room and began to take images of every place on my body. When they brought me to my room, our bags and clothes were all stacked in the corner along with the painting from Aspen. I had an IV in my right arm and a blood pressure cuff on my left arm. I lay there propped up with just the sound of a beeping machine behind me.

The door to my room opened and a young woman appeared. "Mr. Massey, I'm Nurse Penny and I am going to be taking care of you. Do you have any questions?"

"How's Marina?" I groggily inquired.

"I don't know, sir, but Dr. Gray should be in any moment to check on you and give you an update, okay?"

I nodded in acknowledgement.

Nurse Penny left the room and I lay there, replaying the wreck in my mind, and wondering what I could have done to prevent it.

You should have been driving, I began judging myself. *Marina is hurt because of you.* Tears filled my eyes again.

The door flew open again. A tall, older gentleman in a white coat strode in. The doctor's name, embroidered near the right lapel in dark thread, was Dr. Gray. Ironically, his flowing hair and thick mustache matched his name.

"William, I'm Dr. Gray, and I am your attending physician." He paused, waiting for a response, but I only nodded.

Dr. Gray continued, "You are a living miracle. Not a single broken bone, no damage to internal organs, just a few scratches and a mild traumatic brain injury, that's all."

"A mild traumatic brain injury?" I muttered. "That sounds bad."

"Oh, sorry, that's doctor speak for 'you have suffered a mild concussion'," he explained. "I would like to keep you overnight for observation, if that's okay?"

I nodded in agreement, if for no other reason than to get him to move along with the conversation.

"How's Marina?"

"Ms. Payne?" Dr. Gray asked.

"Yes, Marina Payne," I acknowledged, "how is she doing?"

"Your fiancé, I presume?" he asked. "She's still not out of the woods yet. We have given her some medicine to try and reduce the swelling and pressure on her brain. The human body is incredibly resilient. It has ways of healing itself."

"Is she going to be okay?"

"She's still unconscious, Mr. Massey. We'll know more in twenty four to forty eight hours."

"Can I see her?"

He nodded his head. "In due time, okay? She's on the other end of the hall in the intensive care unit, room 1010. You should get some rest Mr. Massey; she'll be out of it for at least the next twenty-four hours. I will check in on you in the morning."

With those parting words, the good doctor left me in the

silence of that sterile hospital room. I tried to close my eyes and get some rest, but my efforts were futile.

My mind was racing. Having no answers and no control was not a comfortable place for me. After an hour or so of this torture, I decided to take the blood pressure cuff off of my arm and see if I could find Marina. I reached for the handle of the door. It swung open and I was standing face to face with Nurse Penny.

"And just where do you think you are going?" she asked dryly.

"Oh… me? I just thought it would feel good to stretch my legs. That's all…"

She stood there with one hand on her hip and raised eyebrows, assessing the situation, shaking her head from side to side. "Okay Mr. Massey, but don't go far, you could still pass out or have side effects from your concussion."

"I won't, I promise." I hurriedly slipped past her through the doorway and headed into the hallway.

"ICU is the other way Mr. Massey," Nurse Penny pointed out with a slight smile.

I stopped in my tracks, performed an about face and tried my best not to make eye contact with her as I began my march toward the other end of the hall.

Entering the ICU, I located Marina's room. I froze in place at the sight of her lying there. A nurse was standing by the bed, checking her vitals. Marina was connected to a monitor that droned on with a familiar but eerie beeping cadence. There was a tube entering her nose and an IV connected to her arm. Her head was wrapped in a bandage and her face was cut and bruised. My mind recalled how Susan Jane looked as she lay dying in her hospital bed and I immediately welled up in fear and sadness at the sight of Marina in this state.

The nurse turned back toward me, "Hello, you must be William?"

"Yes ma'am, William Massey," I replied softly.

"So, you two are engaged I hear?"

I thought for a second. "No, we're actually just close friends travelling together."

"Oh, okay," she acknowledged somewhat confused. "Do you know if she has any relatives or close family that we could contact?"

"No… I mean… yes. She has an aunt that raised her back in Hudson, Ohio. Mildred is her name."

The nurse seemed pleased with my answer. "Good. We found a card in her purse that had the name Mildred Hale, and a phone number, but we weren't clear on whether that was an emergency contact or not. We will reach out to her and find out her medical history."

I slowly made my way over to the bed. "Is she going to be alright?"

The nurse grimaced before responding with a serious frown. "It's still a little early to tell, but we should know more in the next twenty-four hours."

I nodded appreciatively.

"I have a few ground rules, if you don't mind," she announced.

Again, I nodded.

"First, this is an intensive care unit and only one visitor is allowed at a time, no exceptions; two, do not touch any of the equipment, hoses, cables, bandages… nothing; three, clean up after yourself, I'm here for her, not for you. Are we good?"

"Yes ma'am," I responded.

"Do you have any questions for me?"

"Can I get a copy of her aunt's information; I think she would like to know what happened from me. Maybe you can let her know that I will be calling her, if you talk to her?"

She nodded in agreement, "That would be good." She copied the information from the card and handed it to me.

I pulled the chair that was in the room over next to the bed and took Marina's hand in mine. This was all too familiar territory for me and a thousand memories began to rush into my brain, none of which were good.

I fought sleep as long as I could; dozing off at times, only to be awakened by the nurses coming into the room to check Marina's vitals. At some point during the evening, I fell asleep, exhausted from the events that had unfolded that day.

CHAPTER 16

December 11, 1970

STIRRING FROM MY slumber, I realized that someone had placed a small pillow behind my head and draped a soft blanket over my body.

The nurse came into the room to perform her periodic check and greeted me with a soft and soothing voice, "Good morning, Mr. Massey. How are you feeling this morning?"

"I'm a little stiff and sore, but nothing that I should complain about. Thank you for asking. Any change in Marina's condition?"

"I'm afraid not. Best-case scenario is that she continues to rest and maybe wakes up by tonight. At least, that's what I am praying for."

I nodded.

"You should step out and get some fresh air and maybe some breakfast. I've got this covered here for a while." I realized that this was her nice way of asking me to leave.

I reluctantly arose from the chair, leaned down, gave Marina a soft kiss on the forehead, and whispered, "I'll be back soon, Mar."

Slipping back into my room and into the bed, I had started placing the blood pressure cuff back on my arm when Nurse Penny came strolling through the door.

"Why are you putting that back on your arm?" she asked. "It obviously hasn't been on all night."

Busted… I was at a loss for words.

"It's okay," she explained. "I found you early this morning and had the ICU nurses keep an eye on you."

"I'm sorry if I caused a panic."

"Mr. Massey, I knew where you were headed the second you walked out that door last night." Nurse Penny was enjoying this way too much, but I figured that she deserved this moment given the number of unruly and stubborn patients she probably had to deal with each day.

"I suppose you did," I conceded with a slight smile.

"All of your paperwork is drawn up for you at the admin office. You are free to go. Just take it easy and make sure you have some Tylenol or Excedrin if you start experiencing any mild headaches."

I thanked Nurse Penny before replacing the hospital gown with some of my own clothes and freshening up a bit. I grabbed our bags and belongings and headed out of the room.

Drifting through the hallway and over to the office, my body was present, but my mind was still busy processing everything that had happened. I had to refocus; my mind was always my constant, so I began to reflect internally, *what would the old Will do?*

I decided to be positive. *Once Marina gets well, we will need to continue our trip; we need a car.*

I settled my account with the hospital and made my way to the lobby. Stepping out onto the sidewalk, I hailed a taxicab that was nearby. "Take me to the nearest bank."

"Yes, sir."

We pulled up to the Arizona Bank just a few blocks away. "Can you wait for me here?" I asked as I handed him a few extra dollars.

"You got it," he answered.

Entering the bank, I approached a young man sitting at a desk. I explained my situation and gave him some of my information and my license. After a few minutes, he returned with an envelope.

"Mr. Massey, here are the funds you requested from your bank, if you can just sign this receipt for me. We hope that your friend recovers soon. Please come back if you need anything else."

Luckily, my taxi was still idling outside, so I asked him to take me to a reliable used car lot.

As we pulled in, I saw exactly what I was hoping to find: a Ford Mustang. It was a year newer and wasn't the same turquoise color of Marina's now-demolished car, but the light silver blue finish was close enough for me.

I settled with the cab driver and tipped him graciously for his service and made my way over to the Mustang. The closer that I got to the car, the faster the salesman walked to try and meet me.

"She's a real beauty," he proclaimed.

I pretended not to hear him while I peered inside at the deluxe trim package and immaculate condition of the car.

"Low miles," he added.

I opened the door and reached for the hood release. He handed me the keys, "Feel free to fire her up."

I took the keys from him and started the engine. It really was a nice car, very well taken care of and the perfect car for Marina. While the engine continued to run, I stepped out of the car and examined the tires, the body and trim.

"I have cash and not much time. What's your best price?"

His eyes doubled in size before he stuttered in his reply, "I'd take, uh… uh, let me see, can you…"

"I'll give you seventeen hundred, cash, no more."

"Well, let me see, what about…" he stammered.

I pulled the envelope out and looked at him, "Cash, no more." I motioned my head over toward the waiting cab.

He smiled, "Yes sir that sounds fair."

We went inside and filled out the paperwork. I then hopped in the car and headed back into town. A few blocks from the hospital, I found a nice hotel and booked a room. I tried to relax in the room and coral my thoughts, but it was to no avail.

It was early afternoon when I walked back into Marina's hospital room. The nurse and doctor were standing by her bed discussing her chart.

"Excuse me; any updates?" I asked.

"You must be William?" the doctor posited. "I'm Dr. Phillips, the attending neurologist."

"Nice to meet you, Dr. Phillips. Is Marina going to be okay?"

The good doctor gave me a genuine smile of concern before beginning his update.

"Marina sustained trauma to her head during the accident, causing her brain to shake violently within her skull. That trauma caused some blood vessels to burst, like a bruise, and resulted in fluid building in that area around the brain. Initially, we considered performing a craniotomy to relieve the mounting pressure from the swelling. However, after careful evaluation of her condition, I opted against immediate surgery. Instead, we decided to closely monitor the pressure and the extent of the swelling."

"Oh no," I responded with a shaky voice. I bowed my head in disbelief, unable to wrap my head around this evolving situation.

"It's okay, Mr. Massey." Dr. Phillips placed his hand on my shoulder. "This is the best thing for Marina. We have just placed her into a deep sleep so that it will reduce the stress on her brain and allow the swelling to decrease. A comatose brain needs less oxygen than an awake brain. I am very confident that this will get the swelling down."

I raised my head and looked him in the eyes, "What are the chances that she doesn't wake up?"

He gave me a comforting smile. "We will diminish the sedation and wake her up over the next couple of days when the swelling has subsided. That's how this works."

I wiped the tears from my cheeks and took a deep breath. He began to speak again.

"Mr. Massey, can I ask you a question?"

"Sure, anything doc."

"Why hasn't Marina had any treatments?"

His question took me by surprise and I was confused as to what he was talking about.

"Treatments for what?"

"Her cancer," he responded. "We spoke with Ms. Payne's aunt who then directed us to their family physician. We had noticed some abnormal findings in her blood work and when we reached out to her doctor, he confirmed that she was diagnosed with cancer earlier this year. But she has yet to get any treatments."

I hesitated before answering, "I see, I will make sure to, uh, … I'll talk to her about that when she recovers from this wreck."

Dr. Phillips befuddled expression let me know that he realized this was the first time that I had heard about the cancer. "Mr. Massey, pray for your friend. If all goes well, she'll be awake in a couple of days and then she needs to face this bigger demon."

I shook his hand, and then he and the nurse left me alone in the room with Marina. After peering out the window for a while, I decided that I needed some answers.

As I stepped into the hallway, I must have looked confused and lost. A young nurse approached me cautiously, "Excuse me sir, may I help you with something?"

"Can you tell me where I can find a pay phone?"

She smiled and responded, "Down the hall, to the left, near the cafeteria."

Standing in that phone booth for what seemed like hours, I tried to determine what I would say to Marina's aunt. Finally, I pulled out the note with Mildred's number on it and dialed.

The phone rang three times before a familiar voice picked up and announced, "Mildred's Diner, this is Mildred."

I hesitated for a second, "Yes, ma'am. This is William Massey, … uh, the man who is travelling with Marina."

"Oh my God, Mr. Massey!" Mildred replied in a now concerned voice. "How is she?"

"With a trembling voice, I informed Mildred, 'She's in a coma.' I could hear the concern in her silence, so I tried to offer some reassurance. 'The doctors have deliberately sedated her to give her brain the rest it desperately needs and to reduce the pressure building inside her skull. They've assured me that this is a temporary measure, and they're planning to gradually bring her out of it within the next day or so.'"

There was a silence on the other end of the line.

"Mildred, are you still there?"

Mildred exhaled deeply. "I spoke with the staff there at the hospital, but all they told me is that she was in a wreck. What happened Mr. Massey?"

"Marina was driving along a stretch of highway in Arizona as we made our way to Flagstaff. The day had been calm, the road stretching out ahead of us under the wide desert sky. But then, everything changed in an instant. A wolf suddenly appeared, stepping out from the brush and onto the road. Instinctively, Marina swerved to avoid it, but she lost control of the car. Before I knew it we were being tossed about as the car tumbled down the highway."

"Oh my," Mildred mumbled. "Are you okay?"

"Yes, ma'am, thank you for asking. I have a small concussion, but I was very lucky. No broken bones, just a little soreness."

"That's good to hear," Mildred replied before pausing again. "Mr. Massey, I need to know the truth, is Mar going to be okay?"

I tried to collect my thoughts on what to say, and how to say it. "The doctors seem to believe that she will recover from the wreck, although they won't give me a guarantee or a time frame to work with."

Mildred began to cry into the phone before collecting her composure again, "Mr. Massey, I don't think that I can afford to come visit her."

"That's okay…"

"I'm not finished," she interrupted tenderly. "I know you barely know Marina, and this isn't your problem, but I need to ask, will you stay with her until she gets well enough to return home?"

I smiled into the phone then reassured, "I will, I promise."

"Thank you, William."

"Mildred, did you know that Marina is sick?" I inquired. "Did you know that she has cancer?"

She paused again on the other end of the line before exhaling. "She found out earlier this year. Early stages, that's what they told her."

"The doctor said that she hasn't had any treatments?"

Mildred sighed again, "She looked into it, but… she… we, couldn't afford it."

"Doesn't she realize that it will kill her if she doesn't get treatment? Cancer doesn't just go away on its own."

"William, she knows that, we all do, but there really wasn't a way for her to get the treatments. It's one of the reasons that she decided to take off and drive to California. I guess that was one of her ways of dealing with it."

"Dealing with it?" I asked in frustration.

"William, what options does she have?"

I didn't respond. Mildred was right. What options does a waitress in a small town have? I exhaled forcefully in frustration.

"William, will you please keep in touch, regardless of what happens? And tell Marina I love her."

"Yes ma'am, you have my word," I reassured before hanging up the phone.

I made my way back up to Marina's room. Standing at the foot of her bed and observing her condition, I could feel the uneasiness in my stomach growing. My heart was breaking as I watched her breath in and out. How did I end up here, I pondered poignantly?

Pulling the chair closer to her bedside, I took her hand in mine and whispered under my breath, "Cancer, huh?"

I took a deep breath and closed my eyes.

In my mind I returned to October of 1961; Susan Jane had just completed her second cycle of treatments. I'm not sure if it was the radiation or new chemotherapy treatments that caused it, but I began to notice her hair in our bed, on her pillow and in our bathroom sink. Not just strands, but actual clumps. Anytime that I would see it, I would frantically scoop it up and bury it deep within the trash can. I'm not sure why, but a part of me didn't want her to see it. She knew more than anyone else that it was falling out. It was just one of many ways that I tried to protect her.

Although cancer chose her, I always felt a tremendous amount of guilt for not being able to fix it. I would sneak out to our garage sometime at night after she had gone to sleep and sit in my car with all of the windows up. Sometimes I would cry uncontrollably, other times I would scream and cuss like a sailor.

The treatments and medicine frequently left Susan feeling ill. She'd manage only a small dinner with me before retreating to the bathroom, where she'd curl up on the cold tile next to the toilet. There, she'd endure the painful aftermath of her meals. Following these harrowing episodes, I would sit by her bed, holding her hand for hours, silently making endless bargains with God. I pleaded with Him to take the cancer from her and pass it along to me. It didn't work then, but that didn't stop me from trying again this time.

God, please help Marina. I know I don't talk to You much, and I know that I don't understand why You do what You do, but please help me understand what You want me to do. If it's Your will, then just take this cancer from Marina and give it to me instead. Let me deal with it. Please. Amen."

CHAPTER 17

December 11, 1970 (Evening)

DESPITE MY EXHAUSTION, I just couldn't sleep. I would drift off briefly, only to awaken with my thoughts spinning wildly. It was well past midnight when I decided to take a walk to clear my mind. The hospital corridors were mostly silent, aside from the occasional sounds drifting from the emergency room area.

As I roamed the halls, I noticed a young girl, alone and obviously in some labor pains. Her arms laden with bags, she was visibly struggling to make it through the door and head toward the elevator. A look of defeat washed over her face as she dropped a bag, spilling its contents. I quickly bent down, gathered the fallen items, and returned them to her bag, hoping to ease her burden even a little. "Where're you headed?"

Startled a bit by my question she responded, "I'm going up to the second floor; my contractions have been getting closer."

"Let me help you," I offered while holding the elevator door open and taking another bag from her hands.

As the door closed, she explained, "I'm Mary Beth, my husband is over in Vietnam, that's why I am alone."

I smiled and nodded, "Then this is the least that I can do to help. Nice to meet you Mary Beth, my name is William."

We walked to the nurses' station so that she could check in. I set her bags down and placed my hand gently on her shoulder, "You take care of yourself, and don't worry at all. Everything will be just fine and you'll be a mommy soon."

She smiled gratefully. The nurse began to ask her questions and check her in.

I strolled down the corridor, remembering Susan Jane and the radiant glow she had during her pregnancy. These reflections gently transitioned to thoughts of Marina. I pictured her smiling joyfully, a soft yellow summer dress fluttering in a warm July breeze. Her figure marked by the beautiful fullness of impending motherhood. The image brought a smile to my face.

My trance was interrupted when a man standing against a wall of windows caught my attention. His face was pressed close to the glass, peering intently into the maternity ward. Inside, a newborn baby girl was undergoing her first routine check—being gently poked, prodded, measured, and weighed by the attending nurses.

"Is that your little girl?"

He nodded and smiled nervously, turning his face toward me. His eyes were red and watering, but his smile let me know that they were from joy, not from pain.

"She's beautiful," I said.

"She looks like her mother," he confirmed, continuing to stare at this new blessing in his life.

"You're a lucky man."

He turned back toward me and asked, "Do you have any kids?"

Struggling with the memory of losing my unborn daughter

and the hope that I might one day be a dad, I responded, "Not yet, maybe one day."

"Yeah, maybe one day," he reassured. "Hey listen, nice to meet you, I gotta go see my wife. They said that they'd bring my little girl into the room so that we can hold her."

Alone by the window, I gazed at the newborns in the nursery, each with their own unique features, looks, and shapes. I contemplated the appearance of their parents. The thought of these diverse origins and traits coming together in such tiny, perfect forms was fascinating—a truly captivating reflection.

Morning crept up on me unnoticed. I wandered back to the first floor and through the hallways, coming across a small chapel. Inside were a few pews and a cross mounted on the wall. The tranquility of the space reminded me of the solemn time I spent alone in the funeral home before others arrived for Susan Jane's service. A heavy thought crossed my mind: did I have the strength to endure this kind of pain again?

I took a seat in the front pew and bowed my head, lost in thought. While I kept my prayer private, I prayed with a depth and intensity that surpassed any previous moments of supplication time in my life.

After finishing my prayer, I wiped away a few tears, walked to the car, and drove away.

CHAPTER 18

Present Day

"DAD DIDN'T LEAVE you there in Flagstaff alone, did he?" asked Mother.

We had been sitting in the parlor for almost five hours now, completely enthralled in Pawpaw's story, when Mother decided to interrupt.

The initial impact of her question seemed to catch Grandma by surprise.

"No, he didn't, although I'm not certain that it didn't cross his mind," she answered while forcing a smile.

I could tell that this part of Pawpaw's story was not easy for Grandma to relive, but this was a facet of their lives that I had never heard, and was eager to know more.

"Was he there by your side when you woke up?" I inquired.

She smiled appreciatively at my inquiry, then responded, "No... not initially."

Mother scowled, but before she could interrupt, Grandma continued, "As the doctors began to reduce the dosage of sedatives they were giving me, I began to stir from my deep slumber. I was groggy and confused, and I remember glancing around the room. I slowly opened and closed my heavy eyes and at first, I thought, *am I in a hospital room?*"

I watched as Grandma stopped and stared affectionately at the picture of Pawpaw that she was holding.

"There was a tube coming out of my arm, and this annoying equipment kept beeping behind me. My head felt heavy and throbbed, so I reached up and placed my left hand on my head and felt the bandage that was wrapped from my forehead back to the base of my neck."

At this point, she was fidgeting and I could hear her voice breaking slightly while remembering that event.

"I thought, *what happened?* as I lay there in a half-awake, nightmarish state trying to get my bearings about me. *I was driving in the car, it was getting darker outside and snow flurries were falling,* then I remembered *a wolf.*"

Grandma winced then lifted her left hand up to her temple.

"Mom, are you okay?" Mother inquired. Both of us were unsure if reliving this event was making Grandma uncomfortable in some way or if her head was actually hurting.

She continued without hesitation. "As I lay there in the hospital bed, I began to remember the car flipping. The pain of my head smashing against the driver side window, and the smell of electrical wires burning and tires dragging across the pavement."

She looked up and made eye contact with both of us. "It was complete chaos and destruction that lasted for seconds but seemed like forever. I fought to open my eyes, and I could feel my heart racing and my breathing becoming more difficult the more that I recalled the wreck. All I could think about was how I was hanging upside down and William was crumpled up in a contorted mass, blood coming from his nose and mouth. I cried out to him, but he wouldn't respond."

At this point, I had closed Pawpaw's story while keeping my finger in between the pages where I had stopped reading. Mother and I were hanging on every detail and every word while Grandma continued to describe the moment she awoke in the hospital. She began to stare across the room, not really focusing on anything. Memories flooded into her head like waves crashing against a rocky coastline.

"I opened my eyes and sat straight up in bed and screamed, 'WILL!' The nurse had already made her way back into my room, and was doing everything she could to calm me down. I continued to scan the room hysterically screaming and crying out, 'Will? No, no, no, no, he can't be…. No, no, no, no!'"

"The nurse pleaded with me to calm down, but I just kept screaming and crying, 'Where's Will? Where's Will? What happened to Will?'"

Grandma hesitated while staring quietly and compassionately at Pawpaw's photo again. "I thought that he was dead," she whispered as her lips quivered. Her frail fingers outlined his image in the frame.

"It took several nurses and orderlies to hold me down while they gave me more sedatives to try and calm me. At some point, I must've fallen back asleep."

Mother and I sat there in silence waiting for more details. She just continued to intensely stare at the photo of Pawpaw as we both looked at each other and shrugged.

"What happened next?" asked Mother rather impatiently. "Did Dad come back right away? Did the nurses speak up and tell you that he wasn't dead?"

Grandma glanced up at us both with a smile then focused her

gaze toward me and replied rather coyly, "I guess Izzy Bee needs to keep reading for us to find out."

Mother huffed then raised her eyebrows in frustration at me. That was her cue for me to pick up where I had left off.

I chuckled in delight folding back the pages where my finger was positioned. I began to read again.

CHAPTER 19

December 12 & 13, 1970

ENTERING MARINA'S ROOM, I paused to stare at her lying there. I pulled the guest chair closer to the edge of her bed and took her hand in mine.

I sat there for at least a couple of hours, watching her breathe. Then her eyes fluttered open. She stared straight ahead, her bottom lip quivering. I squeezed her hand gently.

She turned her head toward me slowly. At first, she looked like she had seen a ghost, then her eyes opened wide and she burst into tears of joy. I rose from the chair and leaned over to embrace her.

"Will?" Marina exclaimed through her crying, "I thought you were dead."

"You can't get rid of me that easily," I whispered into her ear sarcastically with a slight chuckle.

She lifted herself and shuffled to make room on the bed. She patted the empty place, "Please Will."

I lay next to her and put my arm around her. She nuzzled into my shoulder. Soon, she was fast asleep.

The next morning, I was awakened by the nurse entering the room.

"That's a good sign," the nurse announced. "You are awake, and you are smiling. And you look rather comfy yourself, Mr. Massey."

I went to sit up and pull my arm gently from around Marina. She sat up and repositioned herself on the bed.

"Good morning, Mar," I whispered while looking into her beautiful green eyes.

She smiled. "Good morning, Will."

"How are you feeling? Does your head hurt? Does anything else hurt? Do you need anything?" I began to inquire frantically.

"I'll take it from here Mr. Massey," proclaimed Doctor Phillips. I hadn't realized that he had entered the room behind the nurse. "Marina, is it? May I call you Marina?"

Marina nodded in response to the doctor while peering my way with a joyful grin.

"Sorry Doc"

Doctor Phillips smiled at me in a reassuring manner, "No worries Mr. Massey. It's actually encouraging when our patients have such supportive loved ones around them."

I glanced over and noticed Marina staring at me. I motioned my head at her in the doctor's direction and smiled. She snapped out of her daze and turned her attention back to Doctor Phillips while taking a deep but relaxing breath.

As he gently pulled the bandage back from around her head, he inquired, "How are you feeling, in general?"

"To be honest, I feel rested."

He began to examine a couple of places on the left side of her head, nodded approvingly towards the nurse and mentioned something inaudible that she then wrote down.

"You're looking really good," he reassured. "The swelling seems to be receding very well. I think we made the right decision about the surgery."

Marina frowned, "Surgery?"

Doctor Phillips shook his head and sighed in displeasure with himself. "I apologize, let me start over."

He moved over and sat on the edge of Marina's bed. He took her hand into his hands, in the manner and style of anyone's favorite old grandfather.

"You and Mr. Massey were in a car wreck a few days ago. During the process of the wreck, you hit your head multiple times in the same spot."

Marina continued to listen intently.

"We estimate that during the accident, your head struck the window approximately four or five times before the glass shattered. Each impact caused your head to jolt violently, leading to your injury. The repeated trauma resulted in a deep laceration on your scalp and, more critically, a subdural hematoma. This is an accumulation of blood that formed between your brain and your skull. As the hematoma expanded, it started to exert increasing pressure on your brain, which was extremely concerning.

At that point, we faced a critical decision: either proceed with surgery to relieve the pressure or take a more conservative approach. After carefully evaluating your condition, we decided to avoid the risks of major surgery. Instead, we opted to stitch up the laceration and place you in a medically induced coma using sedatives. This allowed your brain to rest and gave the hematoma a chance to shrink on its own. Fortunately, this approach worked exactly as we had hoped, and your condition improved without the need for invasive surgery."

She nodded in appreciation.

"It actually worked faster than any of us had expected. You are a tough little lady."

Marina's mind seemed to be somewhere in between remembering the accident and understanding what Dr. Phillips had just explained to her.

"Marina? Do you understand what I am saying?" Dr. Phillips asked.

She popped her head up as though she were snapped out of a trance. "Yes, doctor, I understand."

He had a look of concern on his face, "Are you in any pain right now? If so, where and from a scale of 1 to 10, 10 being the highest, what level is your pain?"

"Just a little up here on the left side of my head. It's not bad though, maybe a 3 or 4."

Dr. Phillips smiled compassionately at Marina, then turned to make eye contact with me, "Mr. Massey, do you mind going down to the cafeteria and picking up some breakfast for yourself and Marina? Maybe something other than this lumpy thick oatmeal that I am sure has gotten cold by now. I'd like to have a private conversation with my patient."

"Of course, doc," I replied understandingly. I smiled at Marina and mouthed, "I'll be right back."

After a short visit to the cafeteria, I began my trek back with a tray full of morning snacks. I was intercepted by Dr. Phillips in the hallway. "Mr. Massey, I just had a revealing conversation with Marina," he began, his tone serious but empathetic. "She seems to be healing faster than we ever expected, however, I am concerned about her current stance on her cancer treatments. She seems quite reluctant to even discuss the matter, almost like she wishes to avoid it entirely."

I stood, absorbing his words, a sense of déjà vu washing over me. Marina's evasive response was eerily similar to how Susan had initially reacted when she was diagnosed; a classic case of denial.

Dr. Phillips continued, "She became noticeably irritable when the topic was brought up and seems intent on just leaving. I must implore you to speak with her and try to persuade her that beginning her treatments promptly could significantly improve her survival chances."

I thanked the good doctor and gave him my word that I would talk to her about it.

When I walked back into the room, she was staring aimlessly out the window from her bed. The sunlight was highlighting her dark hair that was hanging down below the bandages around her head.

I could tell that something was bothering her.

"What did the doctor say?"

She turned her head in my direction and gave me the best smile she could muster. "He said I could be discharged in the next day or so."

As I approached her bed, I could see that Marina's eyes were watering.

"What's wrong, Mar? Are you in pain?"

She began to cry uncontrollably. Between her hyperventilating cries, I could faintly make out, "We didn't make it Will. We didn't make it to San Diego and it's all my fault."

As I sat down on the edge of the bed, Marina buried her face in my shoulder and cried, "I'm so sorry Will."

"Mar, look at me," I whispered.

She shook her head without looking up, continuing to cry into my shoulder.

I leaned back slightly and placed my hand on her chin. I gently raised it up to make eye contact with her. "Mar, look at me, we're still going to San Diego."

She wiped her eyes and sniffled. "How are we going to do that Will, I wrecked my car."

I raised my eyebrows as though I had a secret to tell. "Well, the towing company gave me a little bit for your car, so I took that and went to a local dealer and got us a replacement."

Her expression went from complete hopelessness to that of disbelief, "You got us another car?"

"It's a sixty-six, not a sixty-five like yours, and it's a light silver blue rather than the turquoise color that you are used to, but it's a Mustang, and it will get us to San Diego."

Her face lit up, blood shot eyes and all. "Can we leave now?"

I smiled at her innocent reaction. "No ma'am, you must be cleared to travel first."

She puffed her bottom lip out and pouted playfully, "You're a party pooper, Will Massey."

I winked at her and gently pulled her to me for another hug while she continued to sniffle.

Leaning back I remembered. "I did call your Aunt Mildred and let her know what happened. I owe her an update, so maybe you could call her and do that? It would probably do her good to hear from you."

"I will do that today, right after I take a nap. I'm a little tired and my head is starting to ache a little."

I took a deep breath, and internally I thanked God that Marina was going to be okay.

"You know, I think I'm going to run a couple of errands to prepare for your discharge. Will you be okay by yourself?"

She cracked her eyes open and peered at me with her eyebrows raised. I knew from that look what her answer was, so I squeezed her hand and stood up to go.

"I'll give you some time to rest and I will be back in a couple of hours."

She smiled at me and asked, "You promise?"

I gave her a reassuring tilt of my head and answered, "I promise."

After leaving the hospital, I returned to the hotel room. I made a few phone calls and then decided to take a shower and shave, cleaning up after the day's events. The warmth of the hot shower was soothing, and standing there, I realized I had been neglecting my own aches and pains from the recent crash. *We were both very lucky*, I thought as I inspected the bruises that covered my body. The water cascaded over me while my thoughts drifted to Marina. I reminisced about her smile, her goofy smirks, and all the endearing expressions she had shown during our time together. But then, my thoughts turned to the future, stirring anxiety within me. I wondered, *what will happen when this trip ends?*

Trying to calm my rising worry, I tilted my head back, letting the water stream directly onto my face, which helped to wash away the intrusive thoughts. Once dressed, I made a couple more phone calls, and then went to handle some business at the bank.

Finishing up at the bank, I realized that it was mid-afternoon. I decided to pick up a couple of burgers, fries, and drinks to take back to her room, hoping to enjoy a simple meal together.

Marina was sitting up in her hospital bed talking on the phone when I walked into the room. I held up the bag of food. She mouthed '*Thank you!*' while smiling at me.

"Like I said, I am hoping they discharge me tomorrow. Listen, Will just walked back into the room with something that smells delicious. I will call you once we get to San Diego in the next several days." Marina continued listening to the voice on the other end of the line. "I will tell him. Yes, he has been a godsend." She winked at me casually with that comment. "I love you too Aunt Mildred. Talk to you soon, bye."

Marina hung up the receiver and glanced my way, "That was Aunt Mildred. I called to let her know that I was okay. She said to tell you 'Thank you' for taking care of me."

I didn't know how to respond so I just smiled at her compliment.

"So, what did you bring me? It smells really good."

"I brought us a couple of cheeseburgers, some fries and a Coca Cola for both of us. I thought you might enjoy having an early dinner with me."

Marina beamed as she took the cheeseburger from the side table. "More than anything in the world, Will Massey."

We sat there, eating our greasy burgers and fries.

"Oh my. This is so much better than hospital food, don't you think, Will?"

"Yep"

She glared over at me with a smirk as I smiled in response. My teasing reference to our initial one-line conversations wasn't lost on her.

"You did that on purpose, didn't you?"

"Yep," I replied again with a sheepish grin.

"Okay mister, what's the best burger you've ever had?"

"Hmmm, so we're back to the question game, huh? Let me see." I slowly put a French fry in my mouth and then responded, "I'd say it was a burger that I had at a little country store, in the Poconos several years ago."

I swallowed my food, took a drink, and drifted into a memory when Marina interrupted, "Was Susan there?"

Glancing apologetically back I answered, "Yes, she was. We had been dating for about a year and we decided to take a rare summer break and drive up to the mountains. We had gone for a hike up to see some waterfalls and then went for a swim in a remote lake. We stopped to get gas on the way back and had a burger at this little store. I'm not sure if it was really that great of a burger or if it tasted so good because we were just that hungry after a busy day."

We continued to eat in silence. It felt amazing to just share time with her again. I realized that I was craving conversation and interaction with her.

"How about you Mar, what's the best burger you've ever had?"

She held a fry in her hand as she raised her eyebrows. "That one's easy, Mildred's Diner."

"I think I sense some prejudice in that answer," I quipped playfully.

"Not at all," Marina responded. "Aunt Mildred decided long ago that she would only make burgers in her heavy iron skillet. Every customer that came in would rave at how she would make the perfect burger. It was soft and juicy on the inside, but the outside had almost a crunchy crust from the butter she would put in the pan. Then she would toast the bun just right."

I smiled at her thoughtful response.

"But this burger right here," she continued with a mouthful of food and while holding her half-eaten burger precariously in her hand, "it ranks a close second."

Again, awkward silence fell upon us while we finished up our meal.

"You know, I was thinking, if you get discharged tomorrow, maybe we could go see the Grand Canyon the next day."

Marina looked confused, "What day is today?"

I chuckled, realizing that she had lost track of days and time being in the hospital since the accident, "It's Sunday."

I reached into my back pocket and retrieved a brochure for 'Monument View Bus Tours' and handed it to Marina.

"I called this company earlier today and reserved us two spots. They do all the driving in a nice heated bus and we just sit back and enjoy the views of the Grand Canyon."

She looked a little skeptical, while peeking up from the brochure. But then she conceded, "Okay Will, I trust you. It would be nice for both us to not be driving."

I cleaned up the area after our little hospital room picnic and threw our garbage into the trash can. Time had passed quickly and the day with it.

"I was looking at the road atlas and mapping out the routes that would take us to San Diego."

Marina peered up out of the corner of her eyes and smirked.

Defensively, I began to explain that there really wasn't a direct route from Flagstaff, Arizona to San Diego, California. "I think the best route for us would be to travel to Palm Springs and stay there for a night before heading on to San Diego."

"Palm Springs? Isn't that where all of the movie stars go?"

Stumped by her question, I replied, "I'm not sure, maybe?"

Marina collapsed back into her pillow, as though she had fallen into a puffy cloud in the midst of a dream, "What if we see Lucy and Desi? I've read that they hang out in Palm Springs."

"I thought they were divorced," I responded.

Reacting like I had burst her bubble of happiness Marina remarked, "Whatever, Will."

She continued to gaze at the ceiling, smiling while imagining encounters with celebrities.

"You look like you are feeling better."

"I feel much better, Will. I hope they let me leave tomorrow."

"I hope they will too."

Marina stared at me warmly. "Will, you should head back to the hotel and get some rest."

"I'm not leaving you," I replied, shaking my head in defiance.

"I'm a big girl, Will," Marina countered playfully. "I'm feeling much better and I'd like to go to sleep so that tomorrow will come sooner."

Her response evoked childhood memories at Christmas time when we would all go to bed early just to make the time pass more quickly.

I nodded in agreement and stood from my chair. When I leaned in and kissed her on the forehead, she peered at me with a startled and confused look. It was then that I realized that every kiss I had given her to this point was while she was unconscious. I nervously made my way to the door in a mad dash.

"Goodnight, I'll see you in the morning."

She smiled and replied, "Goodnight, Will Massey."

CHAPTER 20

December 14, 1970

MY INTERNAL CLOCK roused me from sleep at exactly six o'clock in the morning. I lay on my back, gazing up in a daze, trying to discern shapes, faces, and designs in the popcorn-textured ceiling above me. The room was so silent that I could hear my own heartbeat echoing in my chest.

Something's off, I thought.

I turned to look at the bathroom door. There was no cheerful, slightly off-tune singing coming from the shower. No fragrant scents of soap, shampoo, or lotion drifting through steamy air; just the quiet, recycled mustiness of a dark hotel room encompassing me.

Is this what my mornings will be like after this trip is over? I wondered.

Lying there a while longer, a heavy lump formed in my throat, my heart started to pound, and a wave of fear and anxiety washed over me. My chest tightened, making it difficult to breathe deeply.

It was the same feeling that I had felt for five years straight, and I did not like it.

I leaned over the sink and began splashing warm water on my face, hoping that it would clear my thoughts. The water was helpful in rinsing the sleepiness out of my eyes, but it did nothing for my mind.

I stood there, staring into the mirror, thinking about the last two weeks of my life; the diner, the sleigh ride in Aspen, the wreck and then back to the thought of our trip ending soon.

This is not working, I thought angrily. I exited the room and made my way back to the hospital.

Walking through the lobby and past the main waiting area, I noticed a man dressed as Santa Claus. I paused and observed him. He greeted family members waiting for their loved ones, offering handshakes and comforting hugs to their children. It was remarkable to see how faces marked by worry, fear, and distress brightened into smiles. The presence of Santa seemed to instill a special kind of joy and warmth, transforming the atmosphere with a festive glow that only hope can allow.

I was instantly transported to the last Christmas that I had shared with my brothers and my parents. I could see the smiles on each of their faces while we opened our gifts to one another. It was like they were standing right next to me in the hospital. I realized that had we focused our thoughts on them heading off to war, that I wouldn't have that wonderful memory.

Try to enjoy today! I reminded myself.

When I entered Marina's room, I was stunned to see that she was sitting rather impatiently in the chair next to the bed, fully dressed from her head down to her shoes. Her hair was pulled back and gauze was still wrapped around her head. Her bags were set neatly beside the chair and she was holding her jacket and purse in her lap.

"What took you so long, Will?"

I felt terrible that she was waiting on me. "Have they discharged you already?"

"No. But they did come in this morning and removed the hoses and wires that were attached to me. The nurse said that I would be dismissed today."

"Did she say when?"

Marina turned her head in dissatisfaction, "No, but I'm not staying here any longer."

I wasn't quite sure what to do next. She had made her mind up and there wasn't anything that was going to stop her.

Not wanting to tempt fate with more awkward silence, I needed to do something. "I will go see if we can leave." I tried to sound determined and confident, but I could tell by her frown that she wasn't impressed.

I stuck my head out into the hallway, "Excuse me?" I attempted to get the nurses' attention. "Ma'am?" She continued to ignore me while she rifled through some charts and papers on the desk.

I slipped back into the room. "Mar, I think it might be a little while longer."

Marina glared at me and shook her head.

Knowing that she was not fond of silence or one-word conversations, I asked, "Would you like to get back onto the bed and just relax until they are ready to discharge you?"

Marina frowned, clinching her teeth together.

"Okay, that's a no," I stated out loud in a sarcastic tone.

She stopped glaring at me and turned her head to stare out of the window.

"Did you sleep well last night?" I asked.

"What do you think? I'm in a hospital bed with hoses and wires running from my body to that machine over there." Marina pointed at the large electronic device in the corner beside the bed that was now quiet.

I wondered if the nurses really turned that off or if she unplugged it herself.

"How did you sleep over at the hotel?" she asked in a derisive manner.

Before I could respond, the door opened up and in walked Dr. Phillips. "Good morning, Marina, how are you feeling today?"

She smiled at the grandfatherly doctor, "Much better Dr. Phillips. In fact, I am ready to be discharged."

Dr. Phillips looked at me and grinned before turning his attention back to Marina, "I can see that, but I will judge whether you are ready to be dismissed or not."

Marina scoffed, "I'm leaving today, one way or another."

Dr. Phillips leaned over in my direction and whispered, "You've got your hands full, son."

She glared at me with a look that said, *'Don't you dare respond to that statement!'*

I just smiled at her as Dr. Phillips moved closer and removed the gauze from her head and gently pulled back the bandage.

"Swelling appears to be almost non-existent; stitches look good."

The nurse who had followed him into the room took the old bandages and discarded them.

"If we didn't need the room so badly this morning, I would probably keep you for observation another day, but since you seem to be content on leaving us, I guess I can go ahead and let you go."

Marina peered at me like she had won a competition.

"I'm going to leave the bandage off so the air can get to it and help it heal. No water on those stitches for another forty-eight hours. In a week, I need you to come back in so that we can remove those stitches."

"I won't be here," she announced. "I will be in San Diego in a week."

I couldn't help but hear that she said 'I' rather than 'we' and I must admit that it bothered me. Maybe she didn't mean anything by it, but then again maybe she did.

"Okay," replied Dr. Phillips. "You find a clinic or hospital in San Diego and have them remove these sutures after seven days. Deal?"

"Deal," answered Marina.

"I will send the nurse back in with your discharge papers and some pain medication in case you need it, and then you are free to go. It was a pleasure meeting both of you and I wish you good luck and safe travels on your way to San Diego."

I shook the doctor's hand, thanked him and he left the room. Marina was standing up when I turned back around.

"Let's go see that hotel room that you got for us," she said in a snippy tone.

Luckily for us, the nurse came back in with the discharge papers. "Ms. Payne, if I could get you to sign right here, then I believe Mr. Massey has taken care of everything else. You can be on your way."

Marina gave me a curious stare before being interrupted by the nurse. "I have a wheelchair right outside the door for you."

"No, that's okay, we'll manage," I interjected before Marina could respond.

"I must insist," replied the nurse. "It's hospital policy."

After pushing through her pride, Marina sat in the wheelchair for the short ride out of the hospital. While loading Marina's remaining belongings into the trunk, I noticed her walking around the car slowly and checking it out from every angle.

"Nice car, Will."

I simply nodded and opened her door.

It was a quick trip from the hospital to the hotel. She spent the majority of the time looking over every inch of the car.

"You did well," Marina complimented again with a smile.

I parked and then ran around to her door and opened it for her. She smiled meekly in response.

When we walked into the hotel room, I noticed her chuckle after seeing the two beds.

She sat quietly on the edge of the bed that I had not disturbed. I thought she might say something, but instead, she slowly stood up and made her way into the bathroom and shut the door. A few minutes later, I heard the water from the shower come on.

I darted over to the bathroom door and knocked, "Hey Mar?"

"Yeah?"

"You know you aren't supposed to get your stitches wet, right?"

The door cracked open and Marina poked her head around from the other side. "That's what shower caps were made for, Will." She pointed to the hotel provided shower cap that was now covering her head. "But thanks for thinking about me." She gave me another playful smile and shut the door.

I lay down on my bed and stared at the ceiling. The smell of clean soapy steam began to make its way into the room. I closed my eyes and listened to the most beautiful rendition of *Silent Night* that my ears have ever heard. My eyes began to water from emotions. To say that I was very thankful that Marina was going to be alright was indeed an understatement.

It wasn't long before she exited the bathroom, fully dressed and looking refreshed from the shower.

"That was one of the best showers I have ever had."

"How are you feeling?" I asked.

"I'm feeling fine, Will. In fact, I was thinking that maybe we could go for a drive this afternoon. I want to get comfortable riding in the car, before we leave Flagstaff for a longer duration."

"Are you sure that's a good idea?"

Marina just glared at me.

"We could do that. We might not be able to do all three, but I think the Petrified Forrest, the Painted Desert and the meteor crater are all within two hours of here. But are you sure that you are up for it?"

"Let's go," she replied.

On the way out of Flagstaff, we stopped at a small deli and grabbed a couple of sandwiches, a bag of chips and a bottle of soda for both of us. It was a beautiful day, not a cloud in the sky. We were quickly reminded that it was still winter as a December chill was in the air.

Marina was quiet during the drive. Every few minutes she would read off some interesting facts while browsing through the tourist brochures that I had kept for us.

After almost two hours of driving, we arrived at the Painted Desert Visitor Center. The small building was full of petrified rocks, pictures and geological displays explaining the colors of the terrain. Exiting the building, we walked along a short trail, admiring the layers of colors on the rocky horizon. Marina bent down slowly and retrieved a small stone that looked like the stub of a branch. Tracing its woody yet stony texture, she glanced at me with a look of fascination. "It's hard to fathom how old this rock is." She handed it to me, and then pontificated, "It's humbling to think how short our lives are in comparison."

Her choice of words struck a nerve deep inside of me. I slipped the rock into my pocket and we retrieved our lunch from the car. Sitting down at a nearby picnic table, the warmth of the sun married with the chilly December air felt soothing. Marina continued to act strange and kept to herself. I wasn't sure if she was experiencing pain from the wreck or if she was upset with me, but the silence was deafening.

Feeling the need to break the silence, I stated, "So, I guess it's my turn?"

She peered at me in between taking a bite of her sandwich and sipping from her soda. "You think it's your turn? Wasn't I answering your question when we had the wreck?"

"Oh yeah," I conceded, although I seem to remember being asked about the best burger I had ever had just the day before. "What would you like to ask me?"

She took another bite and chewed slowly. Her eyes shifted away from me and down to her sandwich and chips.

"What are you going to do after we get to San Diego and the trip is over?"

Her question caught me a little off guard, so I turned and stared toward the beautiful horizon and considered my answer.

"I guess I must get on with my life, since I promised a friend of mine that I would."

I could tell that comment inspired Marina to raise her head up and look at me. I continued to stare out at the sun dancing on rock formations in the distance.

"Maybe I can fall in love again. Someone who will challenge me; Someone who will make me want to live every day like it's my last; Someone who will love me and grow old with me and maybe have a family. I think I'd like to be a father. You know, I met a young man at the hospital who was beaming at his newborn baby girl in the nursery and I began to yearn for that kind of happiness.

After this trip, I think I also want to travel more. All in all, I guess I will stop thinking and start doing."

I turned and noticed that Marina's head was down and she was wiping her eyes.

"Mar, are you okay, are you in pain?"

She kept her head down and shook her head, "No, I'm okay Will; I think some dirt just blew up into my eye, that's all."

"Are you sure?"

"I'm fine, Will, but I am starting to get a little tired. Can we head back now?"

"Of course we can." I was truly concerned that the two-hour drive was too much, too soon for her and now we would be driving two more hours to get back to the hotel.

The return trip to Flagstaff was eerily quiet despite Christmas music on the radio.

As the sun dipped below the horizon in front of us, the sky transitioned from a deepening blue to a stunning tapestry of purple, pinks, and orange. It was a breathtaking spectacle, yet I noticed Marina was absorbed in her own thoughts, gazing out the passenger window, not even noticing the sunset.

When we arrived back at the hotel, I hustled around and opened the door for her. She barely cracked a smile to me.

I fumbled with the room key and opened the door. Marina whispered, "I'm really tired William, I think I will go ahead and lie down for a while."

"That's fine, Mar. Can I get you anything?"

Shaking her head, she pulled the covers back and crawled into her bed. It wasn't long before she was sound asleep. I watched her sleeping for at least an hour. My nerves were shot. I lay there trying to sleep but all I could do was worry about her. Eventually my exhaustion won over, and I drifted off to sleep.

CHAPTER 21

December 15, 1970

MY EYES OPENED to the sight of daylight sneaking past the crack in the curtains and onto my bed. I peered over at the alarm clock and realized that it was already 8:30am. I thought, *when was the last time I slept this late?* It was one of those nights where you close your eyes, then open them. There were no dreams that I could remember, in fact my entire night's sleep felt like it passed during the flick of a finger.

I then looked over to see that she was still asleep.

Sitting up on the edge of my bed, I yawned and then took a deep breath before deciding that I needed the warmth of a shower. I proceeded into the bathroom and brushed my teeth before turning the shower on and stepping inside. I stood there for a few minutes letting the water run down my face. My moment of peace was interrupted by a soft knock on the door.

"Will? I need to use the restroom, may I come in?"

"Of course, Mar."

"Will?"

"Yes Mar?"

"Promise me you won't peek!"

Her statement seemed strange to me. Why would I peek? Who wants to see someone relieving themselves? If anything, I should have asked her not to peek, I mean, I was the one completely naked.

"I won't peek if you won't peek," I replied mockingly.

A few seconds later, I heard the toilet flush.

I finished my shower and then peered around the shower curtain to ensure that Marina was no longer in the bathroom. Exiting the bathroom, she was sitting cross-legged on top of her bed that she had already made. "Thank you for not peeking," Marina expressed almost apologetically.

I nodded, graciously accepting her thanks. "I'm just curious, if you had been in the shower and I had knocked, needing to use the bathroom, would you have let me?"

Her solemn expression changed to a grin. "Heck no, I would have told you to go use the lobby restroom."

She began giggling at her answer. Her laughing warmed me throughout. I had begun to think that I had done something or said something wrong and even a small glimpse of her sunny personality was a needed jolt to my system.

As her amusement subsided, she apologized. "Will, I am sorry that I was such a fuddy-duddy yesterday, can you forgive me?"

"Nothing to forgive, you were really tired. I think we both were, to be honest with you."

Marina grinned while another episode of uncomfortable silence fell upon us.

"What's the plan for today? I know you have one," she jokingly prodded.

"Well, today is the tour of the Grand Canyon I mentioned a few days ago at the hospital. That is, if you feel up to it."

"Of course I do. I had forgotten all about it."

"We need to meet the tour group in about an hour. It includes lunch, so I guess they will provide that once we are at the canyon."

"Then I better get ready," Marina declared.

A light snow flurry had begun to wisp around us. After a short time, we parked the car then checked in at the main office for Monument View Bus Tours.

We boarded an old Greyhound tour bus and noticed that we were the only people on board. I turned and asked the driver "Is one side better than the other for the views?"

He shook his head, "Not really, but you might want to be on the left side if you don't want the sun in your eyes coming and going."

Marina led the way and found us a pair of seats on the left side of the bus about half way back.

"This is nice," I announced. "Maybe there won't be many on the tour?"

Over the next fifteen minutes, the bus slowly filled with people. Two here, three there; they just kept coming until the entire bus was full and there wasn't an empty seat to be found.

"Well, I guess I spoke to soon," I admitted. Marina just looked at me and raised her eyebrows in agreement.

Finally she decided to break her silence. "Will, do you notice anything peculiar?"

I looked at Marina up and down, and then proceeded to check myself. No stains, no buttons missing, no zipper left unzipped.

I shook my head in confusion.

She gave me a frustrated look and then whispered, "We're the youngest people on this bus."

I began to look around at the people on the bus, and realized she was correct; we were the youngest people on the bus.

She elbowed me in my ribs, "Stop staring Will, that's not nice."

"Welcome to Monument View Tours," a deep, older voice boomed through the speakers. "I am your tour guide, Jerry and it's my job to make sure you have fun and enjoy this tour of the south rim."

Jerry was an older man with a portly figure. He had a round face and a thick white walrus mustache that seemed to capture his personality completely. The green jacket that he was wearing was covered in patches, which gave him the appearance of a park ranger, although upon further inspection, they were a variety patches that he had collected from being a military veteran and from working as a tour guide.

"Now I know you folks probably want to rest before we get where we are going, but let me go over a few things first."

Marina leaned toward me and put her head against my shoulder, then quickly pulled back up and asked, "Is it okay if I put my head against your shoulder?"

I couldn't believe that she felt the need to ask. "That's perfectly fine, Mar."

Jerry continued, "Our travel time up to the park will be a little over an hour. Once we get there, we will make a quick stop and get our first look of the canyon for about fifteen minutes, stretch our legs, take a few photos and just enjoy the brisk December air."

I glanced down at Marina and noticed that her eyes were shut. I wasn't sure if she was just resting or if she had fallen asleep.

"Our final destination on the tour will be Grand Canyon Village, where you will be served a delicious lunch and you will have a couple of hours to walk around and take in the sights. After that, we will board the bus and get you folks back to where we started in Flagstaff."

I stared out the window for a while, watching the small junipers race by. Every few seconds, it seemed the same stretch of road and scenery would repeat. Although redundant, it was soothing in its own way.

"Do we have anyone with us today from another country?" Jerry inquired through the speakers.

Someone behind us must have raised their hands because he called on them and they replied with, "Montreal, Canada."

"Welcome, eh!" joked Jerry, garnering a few chuckles from the passengers.

"Anyone else?" Jerry asked. His eyes perusing the tourists on the bus.

At that moment, his eyes made contact with mine, "How about these two young lovebirds here, where are you from?"

I raised my eyebrows, non-verbally questioning if he was talking to me. "Yes, you two; what are your names and where are you from?" Jerry responded.

"I'm William and this is Marina. We're from Ohio."

"William and Marina from Ohio… are you on your honeymoon or just vacationing?"

I peered down to see her peeking up at me with one eye open while biting her upper lip to keep from smiling. She knew how uncomfortable this was for me. "Traveling through," I responded.

"Welcome to Arizona, William and Marina, glad you could make it."

While Jerry continued his routine, I turned my attention back to Marina and jokingly whispered, "Thanks for abandoning me on that one. I should've said 'honeymoon'."

She just nudged me playfully with her shoulder and replied, "You wish."

The bus was cozy and warm and the steady vibration from the road was enough to lull us both to sleep. When we reached the South Rim Scenic Road we were startled from our nap by the sound of Jerry's voice, yet again. "Okay adventurous travelers, we have reached the south rim of the Grand Canyon. We will be pulling into the parking area for Mather Point. This overlook was named after the first director of the National Park Service, Stephen Tyng Mather. It's a clear but cold day today, so you can see over sixty miles to the west and about thirty towards the east. You may be able to make out small stretches of the Colorado River down below and always keep an eye out for wildlife."

As we all slowly exited the tour bus, Jerry continued, "Please watch your step and don't get too close to the edge. If everyone can meet back here in twenty minutes, we will head on to our next stop."

We buttoned up our coats and started the short walk to the overlook. I took Marina's hand in mine. "It might be a good idea if we hold each other's hand, you know just in case one of us stumbles or loses our balance."

She rolled her eyes at me with a playful smirk. I could tell that she was perfectly fine, if not pleased with me holding her hand.

The canyon was vast, the river down below was tiny, and the red rock formations reflected a beautiful mosaic of colors and layers. I whispered under my breath, "I can't believe I almost missed this."

Marina gave me a look of surprise and understanding, then smiled and squeezed my hand.

"It's bigger than I could have ever imagined," proclaimed Marina. She gazed from east to west with the exuberance of a child.

"Stand over there next to the edge," I directed while reaching into my coat pocket and pulling out the camera.

She moved over near the edge of the railing, "Is this good?"

I held the camera up and instructed, "Say cheese!"

At that point she thrust both hands up and out and said, "Cheese!"

Marina then came toward me with a huge smile on her face, "Let me take one of you Will." She took the camera out of my hands and pointed to where she wanted me to stand, "Over to the left a little more. Perfect. Now take your scarf off or at least pull it down so I can see your face."

"Is this good?"

"Just be still," she commanded with a smile. "Hold on, one more second."

"Can you just take the picture already, it's getting colder out here and the wind is making it worse."

She gave me a look with attitude as she lowered the camera, "No complaining Will."

"Oh, come on Mar."

She just laughed, "On three, okay? One, two, three..."

Marina rolled her eyes at me and kept laughing.

"What's so funny?"

"You," she stated. "You have your arms crossed and you are barely smiling, loosen up Will Massey."

I took the camera back from her. "Maybe one of these people wouldn't mind taking a picture of both of us," I suggested. Marina's smile and her facial expression let me know that she approved. "Excuse me sir, would you mind taking a picture of us?" When he turned around, I noticed that it was Jerry from the bus.

"That's what I am here for," replied Jerry.

I put my arm around her as she leaned into me, Jerry snapped the picture.

"How about I take one more? Just in case that one doesn't turn out," Jerry proposed.

"Are you ready?" he asked. In one fluid motion, I reached

down and scooped Marina off the ground and cradled her in my arms as Jerry took the picture.

"Why Will Massey, you do have a spontaneous bone in your body."

I just smiled and rolled my eyes at her, and then set her gently back down on the ground.

"Time to get back on the bus," Jerry exclaimed in a very loud voice for all to hear.

The bus was nice and warm and felt comforting after being out in the cold air.

"Next stop, Grand Canyon Village and lunch," announced Jerry enthusiastically.

We were only on the bus for fifteen minutes or so before we pulled into another parking lot; this time in front of the Fred Harvey Hotel in the village.

"Okay folks, once you get off the bus, you're going to walk into the building then take a left and lunch will be straight ahead. Once you've finished eating, feel free to walk around and check out the village. We will all meet back here at the bus a little after one thirty. That should give everyone plenty of time to eat, check out the overlook and shop for some souvenirs. We will depart for Flagstaff no later than two o'clock."

We hurried off the bus and into the hotel lobby and that's when I noticed a strange look on Marina's face.

"What's wrong?"

"That smell… I've smelled it before."

"What smell are you referring to?"

"A few years ago, I accompanied Mildred to visit one of her close friends. She was an elderly lady, advanced in age and without any family to care for her. She lived in a quiet little nursing home. I remember the visit vividly. The three of us sat together in the modest dining area as she ate her lunch. There was a distinctive smell that permeated the air, a mix of antiseptic, overcooked food, and the faint mustiness of age. It smelled just like this."

I chuckled at Marina's description and frown.

We entered a small room off of the lobby. There was a line forming at a buffet that had been laid out for our tour group.

I noticed the worry on her face so I tried to reassure her, "It can't be all that bad, right?"

The look on her face seemed to say, *you silly little man.*

We both grabbed a tray and began to make our plates.

"Will, is this cabbage?"

I nodded, holding back my snickering.

I placed a spoonful of mashed potatoes, some cabbage, and some pinto beans on my plate. Amusingly, she mimicked each selection that I made. Marina continued to contort her face in ways that she probably couldn't replicate if asked to. The meat appeared to be something sliced and completely submerged in a vat of brown gravy. I assumed that it was roasted turkey and placed two pieces on my plate and then added a yeast roll. We proceeded to one of the large tables they had arranged for us and sat down.

"Would you like a glass of water?"

She nodded while staring at her plate with disdain.

I stepped over to the drink table and retrieved a glass of water for both of us. Before returning to my seat, I noticed the dessert table that we had missed.

I placed our waters down, and then I set a small parfait next to Marina. It was green gelatin on the bottom, colorful small marshmallows on top of that, and then what I believed was a pistachio pudding, topped off with whipped cream and a cherry.

She scowled at me and I had to look away for fear that I would erupt in laughter. I tasted each serving on my plate and I decided that I would focus on the potatoes, yeast roll and gravy.

Marina nudged me with her elbow and whispered, "Did you try the meat? What is it?"

"Chicken livers," I teased.

She frowned at me and clinched her jaw.

"I'm just teasing. I'm fairly confident that it's roasted turkey."

She tasted the turkey and then took one of her yeast rolls and flattened it with her hands. Placing a piece of the turkey on the roll along with a small dollop of mashed potatoes, she pulled the edges up and created a fold over sandwich. Content with the sandwich, she completely ignored the rest of the food on her plate.

I pushed away from the table to get us both some refills on our water. When I returned, I noticed that Marina had decided the dessert wasn't bad at all and had eaten her way down to the marshmallows and gelatin. I could only smile in response.

While several others decided to hit the buffet for seconds, we were both eager to see more of the Grand Canyon. Having plenty of time on our hands, we headed up the street and across the railroad tracks to the rim trail. There was a beautiful rock wall that protected curious travelers from getting a little too close to the edge. The views were spectacular.

There were several areas where the rock wall was further back from the edge of the canyon. As we strolled along, I noticed a mischievous look on her face. She unlocked her arm from mine and proceeded to climb over the rock wall.

"What are you doing?" I questioned in a panic.

"I've got an idea, Will."

Although I've heard it throughout my life, I always cringe each time I hear, "I've got an idea Will" coming from Marina.

"I'm going to crouch down and stretch one arm up and grab

the top of the wall. Take your camera out and try to take a picture that doesn't show the ground I am sitting on, but does show the vastness of the canyon behind me."

I wasn't so sure about this idea, but I retrieved the camera from my coat pocket and lined up the shot the way that she had requested. It was crazy, but she was right, it really did look like she was holding on for dear life. I took the picture and then helped her back over the wall.

She noticed me smiling and shaking my head in disbelief when we continued our stroll.

"What's wrong Will Massey, did I scare you?"

"Scare me? No. Amaze me again, yes. Scare me, no."

She smiled and bit her bottom lip at my response. Her eyes sparkled as she looked up at me. Again, I wondered what was going through her mind.

We followed the trail around the rim to a covered overlook named The Lookout Studio. It was a rustic structure built on the rim of the canyon that had amazing views and a plethora of souvenirs, but more importantly, it had heat. After browsing for a few minutes and allowing both of us to warm up some, I bought a few postcards and then we continued our walk around the rim.

Glancing down at the map, I stopped in my tracks. "It says here that we should be at Matrimony Rock or Heart Rock."

I handed Marina the map, while I surveyed the canyon out in front of us.

"Do you see it?" she asked.

I continued looking, back and forth across the canyon. "If it's out there, I'm not seeing it. Does it say what I should be looking for or in what general area?"

"It says that it's a heart shaped rock," she replied with a sarcastic grin on her face.

"What about that outcropping way over there? Do you see it Mar? Does that look like a heart? I'm thinking that's it." I pointed across the canyon to a silhouette of a rock protrusion.

"I see it, and that's not it," Marina answered in her smart-aleck voice.

"Where is it?"

She grabbed my arm and pulled me back away from the rock wall. "Will, take a look at the wall."

When I refocused on the wall rather than the canyon, I noticed it. It was a natural rock, almost the size of a car tire that was in the shape of a heart. It had been set within the wall on the walking path for all to see and admire.

"Well look at that, right in front of me."

"Yep," remarked Marina, "You tend to miss things that are right in front of you Will Massey." She sashayed ahead of me while I paused, letting her words sink in.

"Wait…What do you mean; I 'tend to miss things that are right in front of me'?"

Marina rolled her eyes at me and smiled while spinning around in a light-footed manner. "I'll let you figure that one out on your own." She giggled as she twirled a stray lock of her with her index finger.

I wanted to be insulted by her statement, but instead I relished every flirtatious comment that she could muster. I glanced at my watch. "We still have about an hour left before we need to be on the bus. Do you feel like checking out this El Tovar Hotel restaurant with me?"

"I thought you'd never ask."

Lucky for us the restaurant wasn't very busy. The maître d' sat us at a table near the fireplace. The table was covered with a white linen tablecloth and place settings were set with precision. A small candle sat in the center of the table surrounded by a wreath of young evergreen twigs.

The waiter arrived after a few minutes, "Welcome to El Tovar, can I start you off with something to drink?"

"I already know what I'd like to get, how about you Mar?"

Marina nodded and replied to the waiter, "I will have a glass of water and a bowl of your French onion soup."

I smiled at her, turned to the waiter and responded, "I'll have the same."

He gathered up our menus and headed back to the kitchen. Marina began gazing into the flames of the fireplace with a gentle beam on her face. It was breathtaking to see the shadows from the flames dancing on her dark hair and her cheeks. I couldn't stop staring at her, wondering what was going through her mind.

"So today is my day to ask a question?" I asked.

She slowly turned her attention back toward me with a playful yet concerned smirk, "Go ahead."

"What will you do after we reach San Diego?"

The question caught her off guard but she quickly recovered and responded, "I would like to go for a walk on the beach and watch the sunset."

I nodded and smirked unsatisfied with her answer, "What about after that, what are you going to do once we aren't traveling anymore?"

Her smile melted away, and she turned her gaze back to the fireplace. "You think too much, Will Massey."

Before I could press her further our waiter appeared with our soup and some bread. "Here you go," he interjected. "Let me know if you need anything else."

We both nodded at him with appreciation. The soup felt good and warmed me from the inside out. She must have felt the same, closing her eyes while savoring the taste and swallowing her first spoonful. I decided to be persistent.

"I don't think I'm thinking too much, just curious I guess."

Marina twisted her spoon in the soup then shrugged her shoulders, "I don't really know. Maybe I will find a waitressing job and a place to stay. I really haven't thought that far ahead."

"Remember that you will need to find a doctor to take those stitches out."

She smiled at my comment while enjoying another bite. "I will need to do that," she confirmed while grinning and nodding her head.

We finished eating our soup in relative silence.

The waiter arrived to check on us again. "How are you two doing, can I get you anything else?"

"Do we have time for a hot chocolate, Will?"

I peeked at my watch and nodded, "We have about forty-five minutes before we need to be back on the bus."

Turning back to the waiter, she asked, "May we have two hot chocolates please?"

"Yes ma'am," answered the waiter as he took our empty bowls and turned back toward the kitchen.

Marina straightened her napkin in her lap and then looked directly in my eyes. "Will, I would like to focus on enjoying every day that I have remaining on this journey. No worrying or planning about what happens after the trip, okay?"

I could tell from her body language that she was worried, but I wasn't sure about what. Was it the cancer, was it the lack of planning around being in San Diego, or was it that this fun road trip was about to end?

I nodded to show my understanding and willingness not to press any more.

The waiter appeared with a mug of hot chocolate for both of us. They were like bowls with handles and I believe there was more whipped cream on top than there was hot chocolate underneath. I began to use my spoon to mix some of the whipped cream into the hot liquid.

"Yum," Marina sighed, taking her first sip. I grinned at the sight of a large amount of cream that had settled on her upper lip. Without any hesitation she extended her tongue and pulled that cream down in one motion.

"Is it good?" I asked.

"Oh yes," she exclaimed. "Haven't you tried it?"

"I was waiting for it to cool off a bit."

"Waiting for it to cool off a bit?" Marina questioned flippantly. "It's hot chocolate Will. It's supposed to be hot."

I just rolled my eyes and smiled at her remark. She watched me with bated breath while I took my first sip.

"What do you think?" fluttering her eyebrows inquiringly.

"That's pretty good, especially knowing that we are going to be going back out into the cold in a few minutes."

She wrinkled her nose at my answer and pouted her lips. We spent the next few minutes smiling and giggling like school kids back and forth, competing to see who could accumulate the most whipped cream on our upper lips. Marina won.

I snuck a peek down at my watch and relayed, "We should probably finish up and head back to the bus."

"I know," Marina huffed, scrunching her face once again.

I paid our bill and we bundled back up before heading outside. The wind had picked up some and the temperature had definitely fallen.

"Let's hurry Will, it's getting colder out here."

We walked down the street with haste and over to the parking lot where the bus was parked. Climbing aboard, we took our seats. It was a few more minutes before everyone returned and even more for everyone to get settled. With the temperatures falling outside, it was easy to sense that the heat on the bus had risen, probably to compensate for the cold.

"It's hot in here," Marina whispered.

"Welcome back everyone," Jerry announced. "I hope you enjoyed your time in the village. Did everyone get enough to eat?"

We could hear a majority of people on the bus replying with a resounding 'yes' and other groaning affirmatives.

Marina leaned over to me and whispered, "Blah! That food was nasty, but our soup and hot chocolate was fabulous. Thanks, Will."

I flashed a smile and winked at her. The bus started to roll and she snuggled into my shoulder comfortably, closing her eyes. Outside, a light mix of rain and sleet began to fall as we made our way down the road. Gazing out over the canyon, shrouded in low clouds, I marveled at the spontaneity of it all—just two weeks ago, I could never have imagined I'd be here. Soon, my view was obscured. The bus windows had fogged up from the cold precipitation outside and the warmth inside.

As we moved away from the canyon and headed back toward Flagstaff, I let my head rest on Marina's, taking care not to cause her any discomfort.

We had been on the bus for a while when my peaceful state was interrupted. Marina pulled her head back and gave me an inquisitive look.

"Will, is that you?"

Her question made no sense to me. "Is what me?" I whispered back.

Before she could answer, I smelled something that really

cannot be described to its fullest effect. Someone on the bus was having internal issues with the food from the buffet.

Marina pulled her coat up from her lap, buried her face into it and began to mix muffled laughter with bouts of saying "NO".

I pulled my left arm up and tried to cover my nose with the crease of my elbow.

"Open the window, Will."

I motioned to the frost covered window and the rain pouring down outside. "I can't do that, it's too cold outside and the rain would pour in on everyone."

Marina laughed out loud while burying her face back into her coat, "This is awful."

Luckily for us, the ride didn't seem to last that long on the return.

We fled from the bus and jumped into the car. Before I started it, we looked at each other and broke into a frenzy of laughter as we contemplated what we had just experienced.

I started the car and looked at Marina, "What else would you like to do today?"

"Can we just go rest in the room tonight, before we leave tomorrow?"

I smiled and nodded, "That sounds like a great idea."

Arriving back at the hotel room, we both peeled off our coats, hats and shoes. My back was toward Marina, so I didn't notice that she had made her way toward me. I turned around and to my surprise, she was standing within inches of me.

She looked into my eyes and flashed a smile, then began to speak, "Thank you for another beautiful day that I will never forget."

I started to say something, but Marina lifted her hand up toward my lips, "Don't," she whispered, "I'm not finished."

"Thank you for staying with me through the hospital stay; thank you for being you."

A nervous flutter raced through my body from my heart to my stomach. My mind flashed; *does she want me to kiss her? Should I kiss her? What if I kiss her and she didn't want me to kiss her and then everything will be awkward?*

Before I could react, Marina wrapped her arms around me, holding me close in a long, emotional embrace.

She released her hold and announced, "If it's okay, I think I am going to go take a shower. Something about the cold and the bus trip just makes that shower sound very inviting. I think I'm beyond not getting my stitches wet."

I nodded in approval then suggested, "Maybe we can order some room service for dinner and then just turn the radio on and play some backgammon tonight?"

She responded with a huge smile and then hugged me one more time before turning for the bathroom. "Why don't you go ahead and order room service, Will. You know what I like by now."

The bathroom door shut and I sat there letting the moment sink in.

I ordered room service for us and we played backgammon and sang along to the radio on Marina's bed until late in the evening. Eventually, she became exhausted from the day and shifted over next to me and fell asleep while we listened to the radio.

I closed my eyes soon after, feeling as happy as I had ever felt in my life.

CHAPTER 22

December 16, 1970

AFTER A LONG night's sleep, I woke with Marina by my side. I thought, *if nothing else, I've made a close friend on this journey.* I was enjoying the moment, but at the same time my mind was already stressing over the travel time and wanting to get to Palm Springs before nightfall. I rose from the bed, making every effort not to wake her just yet.

I shaved, washed my face and brushed my teeth before poking my head out of the bathroom to check on Marina. She was sitting up against the headboard, lost in that state between deep sleep and being awake.

I gathered my things from the bathroom and stepped back into the room. "Good morning sunshine, ready for a long day on the road?"

"As ready as I am going to be," she replied with a sleepy grin.

After a short amount of time, we were headed through the door and out to the car.

"I think we should stop, get fueled up and maybe purchase

some snacks to take in the car with us. There doesn't appear to be many large towns on our route, so the more prepared we are, the better."

Marina found my compulsive planning to be humorous, although she did try to mask her chuckling.

We stopped and topped the car off with gas, bought ourselves some snacks and then pulled back on to the interstate. I tuned the radio to a station out of Flagstaff and Marina situated her pillow against the window so she could nap.

"Is it okay if I shut my eyes for a while," Marina asked.

"Not a problem at all. Your head isn't hurting, is it?"

"Just a little, but nothing a little rest won't cure."

The terrain around Flagstaff was hilly and the road seemed to be encased in tall pine trees. A blanket of old snow was still hanging around under the trees, and where there was no snow, there was dirt, rocks and dormant grass and weeds. I realized after about an hour of driving that the radio station was out of range. I remembered seeing an eight-track tape in the glove compartment that must have been left by the previous owner, but Marina was sound asleep and I didn't want to wake her.

The silence, along with the monotonous whoosh of pine trees flashing by in my peripheral vision, began to weigh on me. Realizing that I needed to do something, I pulled over and retrieved the eight-track tape.

Looking closer at the tape I read, *Sgt. Pepper's Lonely Hearts Club Band.* I had heard about the Beatles, but really never listened to them much. I put the tape into the player and pulled back onto the road, Marina none the wiser.

The countryside was transforming the further west we drove. Gone were the tall pines and the denser vegetation, I was now staring at an endless horizon of dry short grass, dirt, sparsely disbursed evergreen shrubs interrupted occasionally by a few hills off in the distance. With Marina sleeping, the mundane backdrop of the landscape and the curious lyrics of the music, my mind began to wonder in a thousand different directions.

I began to question how I could feel so isolated and lonely yet fall for this woman in such a short amount of time.

I wasn't doubting the love I shared with Susan, but I was beginning to wonder, *why didn't I feel this way with her?*

What I felt now was different; it was both new and familiar at the same time. *Is this truly love, or is it merely convenient because it's new?* A pang of guilt towards Susan crept in, but I knew deep down that she would have been happy knowing I had found a way to live. Each time I would glance over at Marina sleeping, I would smile. She was now a part of my life, regardless of where we went from here.

I had noticed that gas stations were few and far between on the road, so when I saw a sign indicating that a truck stop was up ahead, I immediately pulled off to fill the tank for the remaining drive.

As I came to a stop, Marina woke from her nap and sleepily looked around at where we were. "Where are we?"

"Kingman," I replied.

"It looks pretty desolate out here."

I smiled and nodded, knowing how much of an understatement that was given the last hour of driving.

"How long have I been out?"

"Almost two hours."

Marina seemed shocked that she had slept for so long.

"It's beautiful out here, in its own unique way," I explained. "But after a while, it's a little redundant. I'm not sure you've missed much."

Pulling back onto the highway, she continued to probe, "So we are still in Arizona?"

"Yes, but not for much longer, I think we should be in California in less than an hour."

Marina nodded, seemingly pleased with that answer. She stared out the window, taking in all of the nuances of this land that she had never experienced before. Since the wreck, it had become more apparent to me that her mind was wandering more and more. My protective nature wanted to fix it, but my self-conscious cautious side worried about crossing any unspoken boundaries. I began to notice the uncomfortable silence again, so I reached for the stereo volume.

"Oh, by the way, this car has an eight-track player, and I found a tape in the glove compartment."

Marina seemed captivated. She examined the player that was installed in the cars dash, pushing the buttons and determining what each would do. Feeling relieved that I had found something positive to distract her; I turned the music up.

"Is this the Beatles?" she asked with a smile.

"It is."

A few minutes passed and the song "When I'm Sixty-Four" came through the speakers. I could tell that her mind was a thousand miles away again as she listened to the words.

She reached and turned the volume of the stereo down completely and shifted her body, facing me from the passenger seat.

"It's my day to ask a question, right?"

She hadn't really answered my question on the previous day, but not wanting to be difficult, I yielded, "I think so."

Marina hesitated uncomfortably and I could tell she was struggling with her question or how to ask it.

"Something has been bothering me," she began. "Wait, that didn't come out right... I mean, I'm curious about this..."

I raised my eyebrows in baited anticipation.

"Were you really going to kill yourself?"

My face must have communicated the awkwardness and shock of the question because she quickly reframed it, "You know, were you really willing to die? Were you not scared of death?"

I paused, staring straight ahead at the road while collecting my thoughts.

Again, she tried to elaborate, "What was your mindset that drove you to that point?"

I reflected on my feelings for the past five years and earnestly tried to unpack them in relation to her line of questioning.

Realizing the awkwardness of the inquiry, she began to apologize. "I'm sorry Will. I shouldn't have asked that. You don't have to answer."

"No, no, it's okay. It's a valid question, albeit very deep and complex."

I continued to stare forward, fighting through the emotions in my head. "I think I had built my existence; who I was; my self-identity, so tightly with Susan, that when she died, it was like a flood washing away a house that didn't have a strong foundation."

Based on her facial expression, I could tell that my first sentence seemed to confuse more than enlighten.

"When Susan Jane died, I lost my best friend. In fact, I've always had acquaintances in my life, but very few true friends. So, I immediately felt a loneliness that was painful."

Marina seemed intrigued by my answer. I noticed the intensity in her eyes. She waited for more, almost needing my answer for herself.

"Minute after minute, hour after hour, day after day, week

after week, month after month, the cycle of seclusion just built on itself. The emotional pain continued to grow."

Marina nodded and tilted her head as she tried hard to take it all in.

"Susan Jane was my hope. With her gone, I guess my hope for the future seemed to vanish. There was nothing to live for. My will to live slowly eroded away. Add to that, the feelings of guilt that I couldn't do anything to save her, and it made living more difficult than dying."

As Marina continued to listen, she turned her face toward the road ahead. Her body language seemed to indicate that she was sympathetic to my answer.

"I've always been a morning person, but thinking back, after she died, I really didn't look forward to each day. Many days, I would just lie in bed and sleep until the afternoon. Life wasn't enjoyable anymore."

Marina chuckled and turned her face back toward me. "You, sleeping in until the afternoon?" she joked nervously, attempting to deflect her emotions

"I know, right?"

She smiled apologetically.

"It wasn't uncommon on any given day for me to look back and not remember what had happened during the day." I shook my head as recalled one specific event. "I remember, about a year or so after Susan died, where I got up and went to work. At some point I left the office and ended up at a park where Susan and I had visited one time to have a picnic. I couldn't remember the drive that got me there and I couldn't remember when I left work or how long I had been at the park. The sun started to set and I felt cold, alone and confused. It was like I had been spending time with her, and then she wasn't there."

After seeing the melancholy look on Marina's face, I really didn't want to continue with the topic. We had crossed into California and neither of us had even noticed.

"Please continue," she pleaded with all sincerity.

I took a deep breath. "I guess the only day I looked forward to and thus I would wake up early to get going, was each year when I would drive down to visit her grave."

"Why is that?"

"It sounds weird, but my brain knew that her body, deteriorated as it might be, was just six feet away. I imagined her resting in that box; right there, that close to me; still able to hear me somehow. It was comforting, in a strange way. I would sit out there all day. At times I would just sit quietly, listening to the birds and the wind, and other times I would talk until the sun went down."

Marina's face was etched with a deep, solemn expression. Fear gnawed at me, worried that my words might only deepen her anxiety about the struggle she was soon to face. Yet, despite my urge to fall silent, an even stronger desire surged within me; a longing to share these stories with someone. I couldn't help but snigger as a memory washed over me.

"I think it was two years ago, on a bitterly cold and wet day. I had made my annual pilgrimage to her gravesite. The rain was relentless, pouring down in sheets. It was so frigid; I was sure it would start snowing at any moment. Utterly miserable, but I kept telling myself that I had no right to complain. I was alive, while Susan Jane didn't even have a choice. I sat there all day, grumbling about the rain and the cold. My clothes were soaked through, my shoes squelched with every step, and by the time I left the cemetery, my fingers were wrinkled and water-logged."

She shook her head in disbelief, looking at me compassionately.

I noticed her swallow deeply, trying hard to keep her eyes from watering.

Realizing that maybe I hadn't answered her question I explained, "Back to your original question; I guess I had decided that I had died as well when Susan passed away. I wasn't really afraid to die, because I was already dead."

The profoundness of that statement hit me when I said it. I hadn't really given too much thought to it. In fact, it was only a little more than two weeks since I had felt that way.

"What about now, Will?"

"What do you mean?"

"Do you still feel dead?"

I smiled while glancing at Marina. "No. I've visited my childhood home, feared for my life from an angry rattlesnake, experienced a powwow, viewed the heavens above from eleven thousand feet and visited the Grand Canyon. Heck, I've even eaten a bull's balls."

She laughed out loud and her face filled with grateful delight at my response. I had a hard time keeping my eyes on the road, every ounce of me wanted to soak up that joy from her.

"I met a beautiful young woman who has shown me how to let go. I shared a most amazing dance with her, went on a sleigh ride through the heavens and survived a death-defying crash with her. Oh, I'd have to say, I'm very much alive." She appeared stunned and embarrassed by my remarks.

Not wanting to make eye contact with me and appearing to fight back tears, she was looking around frantically to find anything to focus her eyes on other than me.

I grinned, reached for the stereo, and turned up the volume. We listened to the Beatles sing for the next hour, periodically smiling at each other and trying to sing what words we could make out. It was a nice feeling.

Approaching Yucca Valley, we noticed a sign that read, *Palm Springs 40 miles*. We ejected the eight-track tape and found a radio station out of Palm Springs.

"Where should we stay, and for how long?" I asked.

Marina had a look of contemplation on her face. "It would be nice to stay at a place where celebrities and movie stars have stayed or maybe stay."

I waited then gave Marina a look of *'And?'*

"I don't know Will, maybe we just stay for one night? I'd really like to get to the coast and see the sunset over the ocean soon."

"Let's start with one night, and go from there. We'll stop for gas when we come into town and just ask someone for a recommendation on where we should stay."

She seemed pleased with my plan.

Turning onto Indian Canyon Drive, we began our approach into downtown Palm Springs. I pulled into a small gas station to fill up the tank and ask for directions. Marina rolled her window down and leaned out taking in a deep breath.

"The air smells different here. And it's so warm."

After two weeks of colder temperatures, it was nice to feel a warm breeze. I decided to roll my window down in response and take a breath. "I just smell gas," I quipped.

Marina rolled her eyes and sniggered at me.

The attendant came up to my window after topping off our tank and washing our windshield.

"Thank you, sir, where would you recommend that we stay if we want a chance at seeing a famous person?"

The attendant chuckled as though he could predict that I would ask him that question. "You should try out the Riviera

Hotel. Keep heading down this road and turn left at East Vista Chino. It will be on your left after you turn. I can't promise that you'll see any celebrities, but you could always ask if someone is putting on a show tonight."

"Much appreciated," I replied. "Can you recommend a good place to eat?"

"Oh, that's easy," he replied. "Las Casuelas is just further on this road in the downtown area. I'd also recommend Sherman's. It's more of a deli, but unbelievably popular and delicious."

"Sounds like we should check out the Riviera," I declared, pulling back onto the main road.

Marina was dying to spot someone famous. This fact was very apparent as she stared down every pedestrian and passenger in every car. "Wouldn't it be so cool to see a celebrity?"

I nodded and smiled at her exuberance.

After a few more minutes, we pulled into the Riviera. Entering the main lobby, the scale of the hotel hit both of us. The grandeur and style captured the glamour and glitz of a time gone by.

Approaching the reception desk, Marina's eyes danced and glistened with excitement.

"Welcome to the Riviera, my name is Sophia, how may I assist you today?"

"Hi Sophia, we are traveling through and we need a room for the night. We may choose to stay longer, but we're undecided at this point," I relayed.

"We do have availability, what type of room would you like?"

"A room with two queen beds would be our preference."

Marina smiled innocently at my reply, then decided to chime in, "Are there any celebrities here right now?"

Sophia grinned at the inquiry then replied, "I'm sure that there are some celebrities in Palm Springs right now, but I cannot divulge any who might be staying in our hotel at this time in respect of their privacy."

Marina looked noticeably disappointed but appreciative of the response. "I understand."

Sophia smiled sympathetically and confessed quietly, "I'll hook you guys up with one of our suites for the same price of our basic room." She then addressed Marina directly, "Many guests in the past, like Lucille Ball, Desi Arnaz, Marilyn Monroe, Dean Martin, and others have stayed in our suites."

Marina straightened up her posture and glanced around, smiling while biting her bottom lip. Her giddiness was enough of an indicator that we had selected the right hotel.

Sophia handed us our key along with a map of the property. She traced a path on where we should park and how to navigate to our building and our room.

I suddenly remembered the gas station attendant mentioning shows at the Riviera. "Are there any shows scheduled for tonight here at the hotel?"

"There is always some live music going on late in the Riviera Room. You can choose to just sit in the bar or lounge or you can go for the restaurant seating and enjoy dinner. I don't see a big show tonight, but it's still worth a visit. The poolside bar can also be a happening scene."

We thanked Sophia and headed back out to the car.

"Should we check out the room and unload our stuff, then maybe try the restaurant that the gas station attendant recommended?"

"That sounds fine to me, Will."

When we entered the suite, we were both in shock. It had a living room, bedroom and a small kitchen. The balcony looked out over the pool that seemed to be the hub of the entire property.

"Will, this is like an apartment," Marina exclaimed in disbelief.

"I wonder if they are trying to get us to stay longer," I speculated. Marina shrugged.

We both freshened up and then headed back out into the night. Las Casuelas was an amazing experience. Neither of us had eaten much Mexican food in our lifetime, but both of us were immediate fans of the food. The ingredients were so fresh and the complexity of flavors from the seasonings and spices were so new and liberating for both of us. After our nice dinner we returned to our suite. Both of us not wanting to go to bed, but being fully exhausted from all of the time in the car, we decided to walk down to the bar at the pool and then bring our drinks back to the room.

"This is so nice," declared Marina, settling into a small chair on the balcony. A Latino inspired band was playing some upbeat music in the pool area and the sound was a perfect volume to enjoy from the comfort of our room.

"Very nice," I concurred, while continuing to sip from my old fashioned.

We sat on our balcony, staring up at the stars, watching the activity around the pool and enjoying the music. For a minute, all of our cares were gone. But then I ruined it.

"I can't believe that tomorrow will be the last day of our journey."

Marina remained quiet and all of the energy and joy that was just on her face faded away. I knew immediately that I had spoiled the moment.

"At least the trip tomorrow should only take around three hours or so," I opined, hoping that was a positive observation.

She sat there quiet and finished her drink, then turned toward me slowly, "I'm a little tired, Will. I think I'm going to get some sleep."

"Okay," I replied. "I'll be right in."

Walking in a few minutes later, I noticed Marina had already turned the lights off and had buried herself under the covers of her bed.

Most of the night was spent tossing and turning, unable to sleep. Despite my best efforts to relax and calm my mind, the restlessness persisted. Tomorrow, we would arrive in San Diego, marking the end of our journey. The thought of potentially never seeing her again weighed heavily on my heart. The uncertainty of our future, coupled with not knowing what decisions she would make, filled me with anxiety and stress.

As the night crept towards the early hours, my body finally succumbed to exhaustion. At around 1:20 am, I drifted off into a deep, albeit uneasy, sleep.

CHAPTER 23

December 17, 1970

WE MADE IT to San Diego. Walking from the hotel to the beach, the sun was beginning to set and the breeze off the ocean was picking up. The air was crisp and cool but the sand was warm beneath my feet. Marina was further ahead of me. I felt a sharp pain as a stepped on a broken shell. Lifting my foot up, I brushed the jagged pieces away and set it back down. Peeking ahead to locate Marina, I couldn't find her. I began to walk faster until I was almost at a full run.

"Marina!" I yelled. "Marina, where did you go?"

Now in a full panic, I looked up the beach, then down; scanning the shoreline and the water to no avail. She had vanished, and while my heart was racing, my stomach was all in knots. A storm had come upon the beach quickly and dark clouds churned above.

I screamed at the top of my lungs, "MARINA!"

At that very instant a loud crack of thunder and burning flash of lightning hit right in front of me.

Waking up, I sat straight up in my bed disoriented. My heart was pounding in my chest and my breathing was erratic. Glancing over, I noticed Marina was still asleep, lying peacefully in her bed with one leg out from under the covers.

It was just a dream.

Rolling over and looking at the alarm clock, it read *8:22 AM*. The morning sun was peeking through the glass window behind the curtains, casting a beautiful rainbow upon the wall. Luckily, the peacefulness of the colors and quietness of the room calmed my elevated heart rate.

I slid out of bed and escaped to the bathroom and began rinsing my face over and over. Leaning on the countertop I stared into the mirror and thought about the vividness of my dream. Just then, a knock on the door of the suite broke through my strange reflection. I hurried to open the door.

"Good morning, sir, room service?" stated a young man in a hotel uniform, holding a loaded tray and standing patiently at the door.

"Oh yes," I acknowledged, remembering that I had ordered a full breakfast for us before heading to bed the night before.

Bringing the tray back into the room I placed it down on the table. Marina awakened from her sleep and cried out, "Who was at the door?"

"I ordered breakfast for us last night; it was just room service delivering it."

The surprising glow on her face let me know that it was a good idea. "Let me get dressed and we can have breakfast on the balcony," Marina exclaimed.

I poured us both a cup of coffee and she joined me on the balcony.

"This is wonderful, Will, thank you."

"The last day of our trip, I thought we could use a nice breakfast together."

She picked up her small glass of juice, held it up, and proclaimed, "A toast!" She smiled and continued, "Here's to a trip that I thought would never happen, and to a friend who I couldn't have done it without."

We both touched glasses and took a drink.

"It looks like it should only take us about three hours to get to San Diego, anywhere in particular you want to go?"

Marina contemplated the question while slathering an excessive amount of blackberry jelly on a piece of toast. She noticed me watching her. "What? Blackberry jelly happens to be my favorite," she retorted.

I kept my mouth shut and smiled at her. If only she knew how these little observations were affecting me.

She held that half-eaten piece of jellied toast in her hand while sharing her thoughts. "There's a hotel that I read about a few years ago. It's a place where Presidents and foreign leaders have stayed, and many Hollywood celebrities. I think that 'Some Like it Hot' was even filmed there. The *Hotel Del Coronado* is the name of it and it's supposed to be beautiful."

"Then that's where we shall go," I stated with conviction. "What time should we leave?"

She took a sip of coffee to wash down the jelly and toast that she had just consumed. She contemplated my question then responded, "It would be nice to watch the sunset on the beach tonight."

I nodded in agreement, and we finished our relaxing breakfast on the balcony. Soon enough, we were back on the road.

After an hour of solemn quietness in the car, I could tell that something was bothering her. I decided to break the silence. "I guess it's my turn."

"Your turn?" she questioned.

"You know, my turn to ask a question," I explained, oblivious to her sarcasm.

"Go ahead," she conceded with a smile.

I took a deep breath and then probed, "Why are you really taking this trip?"

She appeared stunned at my question and slightly irritated. "What do you mean? I've told you that I wanted to see the coast, and I wanted to just experience things I haven't experienced before."

Pushing harder, I asked, "Mar, is there something that you are not telling me?"

Marina became really flustered at this point and continued her denial, "No, William, nothing. You're really starting to irritate me with this line of questioning."

I took a deep breath. "Why didn't you tell me about the cancer?" There it was. I said it. That question had been eating me alive, and I knew I was risking it all by even asking.

Her mouth gaped open, and the color drained out of her face before responding with exasperation, "How do you know about that?"

I exhaled noticeably then explained, "After the wreck, the doctor at the hospital called and received your medical records. He asked me why you haven't had any treatments or been back to take care of it. He also said that you seemed to be avoiding the topic of treatment altogether."

"No," Marina fired back. "When you left the hospital room, that doctor upset me. He just started attacking me, like I was guilty of getting cancer or something. I told him that I can't afford the treatments and he just kept going on and on like that wasn't a valid reason. I told him that I have no family aside from Aunt Mildred. I have no options."

Her eyes began to well up.

"When did you receive the diagnosis?"

"Back in the spring, in April. I went in for a checkup and mentioned a strange lump under the skin up in this area." She motioned up near the side of her left breast. "The doctor immediately wanted to remove it and test it."

"A biopsy," I mumbled in complete understanding.

"Yeah, that's it. They called me the next week and told me it was cancer and that I needed to come back in so they could do more surgeries and start some new trial treatments. Aunt Mildred and I couldn't even pay that bill, there's no telling how much a follow-up would have cost us."

"So, this is just your quest to see and experience what you can before you die? Isn't that just giving up?"

"I told you Will, we couldn't afford it. I was just going to become a burden for Aunt Mildred."

"Why didn't you tell me? Maybe I could help."

"No, don't you dare do that."

"Do what?"

"This is why I didn't tell you. You're such a nice guy and I knew you'd want to help somehow. I'm not Susan Jane. You can't fix this."

With that last statement, I clammed up. I stared straight ahead, focusing on the road while I battled with the emotions running through my head and my heart.

Marina rested her head back against the seat and gazed angrily out the passenger window.

We reached San Diego later in the afternoon and I followed the signs to Coronado Bridge.

Crossing the bridge, I noticed a slight smile appear on her face as the Pacific Ocean came into view. It dawned on me how important this was for her. At the sharp curve in the bridge, I saw the sprawling white facade of the Hotel Del Coronado with its clay-colored roof. Pulling the car up to the hotel, I turned it off, looked over at Marina and offered up a compromise. "One more evening, and then we can determine what we're both going to do tomorrow?"

She nodded timidly then quietly responded, "Thanks Will."

After checking in at the front desk and unloading the car, we settled into our room. It struck a perfect balance between elegance and practicality, blending historic charm with modern amenities. Despite the room's impressive features, a palpable cloud of gloom hung over it. I noticed that Marina had slipped back into a somber state; her body language and facial expressions had become subdued and withdrawn once again.

I must confess, I was struggling with a similar melancholy, realizing that our road trip had come to an end and I was merely a passenger now on a train that had arrived at its destination. Determined to lift our spirits, I put on my best smile and asked, "So... what would you like to do first?"

As she turned toward me, her head bowed, she responded in a soft, hesitant voice, "I would like to go down to the beach and watch the sunset. Would you like to join me?"

"I wouldn't miss it for the world," I answered, my smile genuine and unrestrained.

We wandered through the hallway until we came across a sign that read *Beach*, with an arrow pointing toward an exterior door. Reaching for the door, a sudden flash of lightning and a loud clap of thunder startled us. The skies had opened up, and rain poured down in sheets.

"So much for that idea," I remarked, a bit disappointed.

Marina clenched her teeth and scowled. "I can't seem to catch a break," she mumbled under her breath as her eyes began to well up.

"How about we try the hotel's restaurant? See if it's any good? We still need to eat, and as for the sunset on the beach, there's always tomorrow," I offered.

She just nodded, turning around slowly, her expression muted.

The hallways were adorned with dark wood wainscoting, intricately patterned carpets, and ornate light fixtures. Large windows offered views of the lush gardens and ocean, strategically placed to enhance the ambiance. Walking through the corridor, we paused occasionally to admire historic photographs along the walls that offered a glimpse into the hotels storied past; there were photos of celebrities and diplomats, presidents and members of Congress, and even a picture of Lassie, the movie star dog.

Entering the lobby, I was struck by the soaring ceilings, rich wood paneling, and intricate crown molding that contributed to a grand, welcoming atmosphere that beautifully melded historic and contemporary elements. A large Christmas tree adorned with colorful lights stood like a centerpiece in the wood-stained lobby. Vintage light fixtures cast a warm, inviting glow, while garlands wrapped around the balcony railings shimmered with thousands of multicolored lights. The mix of antique furnishings, plush seating, and impressive artwork reflected the hotel's rich history. Comfy sofas and armchairs were arranged into cozy seating areas for guests to relax.

The hotel interior was a perfect harmony of historic charm and modern luxury, enhancing the uniqueness of our experience. Continuing on, Marina slowed down to peek into the gift shop, her gaze lingering on several items commemorating Marilyn Monroe's visit to the hotel.

"Should we try some Polynesian food?" I asked, hoping to pique her interest.

She shrugged, her expression showing only faint curiosity. I could tell her thoughts were elsewhere, probably still lingering on our earlier conversation about the cancer.

We spent about an hour in the Luau Room, surrounded by its vibrant, tropical decor. Marina took only a few sips of her fruity tropical drink and picked at her meal without much enthusiasm. Wanting to do something, I questioned the best approach—whether to give her some space or try to engage her in conversation to draw her out of her shell.

Making our way back toward the lobby, I watched her intently, noting how she walked right past a vintage photo of Lucy and Desi without a glance. It was clear her mind was preoccupied. When we rounded the Christmas tree in the bustling lobby, she suddenly collapsed. Reacting swiftly, I caught her just before she hit the ground.

"Oh my God! Are you okay? Are you alright?" I blurted out, my voice tinged with panic.

"I just slipped on the wet floor. Stop it Will. Quit treating me like I'm dying!" she snapped.

The eyes of everyone in the lobby turned toward us, and I could see the embarrassment flush on Marina's face. I tried to offer some comfort as we retreated to our room, but the atmosphere was tense.

"Marina, talk to me please. What's going on?" I pleaded, hoping for some insight into her feelings.

"You're treating me like I'm dying and like I'm helpless. That's what's going on," she responded, her frustration evident in her tone.

She hurried into the bathroom and slammed the door behind her. From the other side, I could hear the muffled sounds of her crying.

"I'm sorry. I'm just worried about you."

"I don't need you to worry about me," came her sharp reply through the door.

"There's something I need to tell you. Susan and I... we started an industrial supply company right out of our garage. It was our work, but it was our family too, in a way. We expanded to a warehouse, and eventually, we had several locations throughout Pennsylvania."

"Why are you telling me this, Will?" her voice straining through the question.

I took a deep breath. "Ever since Susan passed away, I've been pressured by an investor to sell. While you were in the hospital, I made some calls... and I said yes. I sold my company for a considerable gain. Whatever it takes, whatever it costs, we'll beat this cancer, together."

The bathroom door flew open. Marina looked both distraught and incredulous. "Why would you do that?" she asked angrily.

"Because I want to help pay for the treatments you need," I explained, my voice firm yet gentle.

"I didn't ask you to do that!" she exclaimed, her voice rising with frustration.

Confusion, worry, and anger swirled within me, leaving me speechless. My emotions were a wreck.

She continued, "Aunt Mildred was going to sell her diner to raise money for the treatments, and I told her no! WHAT IS WRONG WITH YOU PEOPLE?"

My emotions peaked, my heart pounding inside my chest. "We love you! I guess that's what's wrong with us!" I said it, well sort of. I didn't mean to say it, but I certainly meant it. The air thickened with an anxious pause between us.

Finally, she spoke: "Well, I don't love you!"

Her words stuck like a dagger. In that moment, my worst fears were confirmed, my feelings for Marina were not reciprocated. The silence that followed was deafening. I felt my heart shatter. A lump formed in my throat while a wave of nausea washed over me. With a heavy heart, I whispered, "Maybe I should go get my own room."

"That's probably not a bad idea." Her voice breaking as she wiped away the tears that were streaming down her face.

With a heavy sigh, I stooped to pick up my duffel bag. "Goodbye, Marina," I said, my voice barely a whisper as I turned to leave the room.

That was one of the worst nights of my life.

CHAPTER 24

December 18, 1970

AFTER A RESTLESS night of tossing and turning, I ended up standing at my hotel window the next morning, gazing out at the Pacific Ocean. The sky was a tapestry of grays, the morning rain drizzling down in a steady, melancholic rhythm. The weather forecast promised some relief with a break in the clouds expected later in the day, but my mood mirrored the dreariness outside; I wasn't holding out much hope.

By the time the clock struck 1pm, I felt a need to do something productive, I would visit the concierge desk and ask for assistance in planning my return trip to Cleveland. Walking through the corridor, my thoughts inevitably wandered back to Marina. I replayed our last conversation, puzzled over how our connection, which had seemed so promising, had soured so swiftly. The desire to make amends with her weighed heavily on my heart, yet I was baffled by the rapid downturn our relationship had taken. How could something so good unravel so fast? The question haunted me as I made my way to the lobby, lost in my thoughts.

"Good afternoon, sir. How may I assist you today?" the young man behind the concierge desk greeted me with a polite nod.

"I need to arrange a flight from San Diego to Cleveland, Ohio. Is that something you can help me with?" I inquired, hoping for a straightforward process.

The young man hesitated, his expression turning uncertain. "Well… I… you see…" He stumbled over his words, clearly struggling to formulate a response. "Yes… but no."

Given everything that had happened the night before, this confusion almost made me expect Rod Serling to appear and announce that I had entered another dimension.

"What I meant to say is, we can definitely assist with that, but unfortunately, I personally can't help you," he clarified somewhat sheepishly. "Mr. Eden, who usually handles travel bookings, had to leave early today. I'm really sorry. If it's urgent, I could give you the phone numbers for the airlines?"

"No, that's okay. I'll just come back tomorrow and speak with Mr. Eden. There's no rush."

"Sorry about that," he apologized again, his tone sincere.

"No worries," I reassured him. Then, seizing the opportunity to salvage the day, I asked, "Could you perhaps direct me to the Casino Lounge?"

"Now that, I can do," he replied, his smile returning while providing me directions to the lounge.

I settled onto one of the red leather stools at the bar, the plush material sinking under my weight. It was early afternoon, and the lounge was nearly empty, save for a couple of patrons scattered around the dimly lit room. I sat alone at the bar, the only customer in immediate proximity to the bartender.

"What can I get you?" the bartender asked; his tone friendly as he polished a glass.

"I'd like an old fashioned," I started, then hesitated, memories flashing through my mind. "No, wait. Make that a Manhattan; with extra cherries," I ordered, recalling how Marina liked hers.

"Coming right up," he replied with a nod.

I managed a half-hearted smile, my thoughts drifting to Memphis and the delight on Marina's face when she tasted her first sip of that very cocktail. Or the accidental way she called it a 'Manheim' back in Denver, her mispronunciation a charming highlight.

"Here you go," the bartender said, setting the drink in front of me. He paused, studying my face before asking, "You want to talk about it?"

His question caught me off guard. "Talk about what?"

He continued putting away some freshly washed and dried glassware, his movements methodical. "You look like you've lost your best friend, that's all."

"That obvious, huh?" I sighed, not realizing my emotions were so transparent.

He nodded, slinging his bar towel over his shoulder with a practiced gesture.

"Her name is Marina," I began, my voice shaking. "Fate brought us together a couple of weeks ago in Ohio." I took a long sip of my Manhattan, and then peered down into the glass, lost in thought. "She likes Manhattans, with extra cherries." A smile flickered across my face as I remembered more. "She has this adorable reaction when she doesn't like the taste or smell of something, she scrunches up her face in the most irresistible way."

I reached into my glass, pulling out a cherry by the stem. I twirled it thoughtfully before popping it into my mouth. "She's got this incredible spirit, unafraid to live life fully. And planning? Forget about it, she shines her brightest when she's spontaneous."

My smile widened while I drained the rest of my glass. The bartender caught my eye, and I nodded for another. While he started mixing the drink, I fished around for the remaining cherries, reflecting aloud, "We traveled across the country together these last few weeks."

"Is that so?" he inquired, intrigued.

"We've shared unique experiences and created memories more vivid than any I could've dreamed up. We've exchanged secrets and confessions that no one else knows. She doesn't realize it, but she has become an essential part of me, forever a piece of my heart."

I savored another cherry before he handed me the fresh Manhattan. "So, what happened?" he asked, leaning toward me.

I sighed, the weight of recent events pressing down. "I found out she's sick, and instead of making her feel supported, I ended up making her feel fragile and helpless. Now, I'm terrified I might never see her again, and I'm not sure how I'll cope with that."

"Hmmm," he murmured, wiping his hands on his bar towel. Then, with a lighter tone, he asked, "So tell me, what does this angel look like?"

I chuckled softly. "Angel is the perfect word for her." I paused, picturing her vividly in my mind. "Her hair is dark and flows in waves down to the middle of her back, stirring ever so slightly with each breath she takes. She has this playful curl that sometimes falls across her face, prompting her to either blow it away with a pout or brush it aside with a gentle hand." My gaze drifted, barely touching the drink in front of me. I quickly got lost in the details. "Her eyes are green, though the left leans a little towards hazel. They sparkle like emeralds when she's happy, brightening even the darkest places."

"Sounds like a beautiful woman," he said with a warm smile, then proceeded to stroll to the other end of the bar.

He just walked away. Who does that? I thought.

Just then, a familiar voice from behind me drew my attention. "I don't know that she's that beautiful."

Turning around, my eyes met Marina's. She was standing there in the lounge. "How long have you been there?" I asked, my heart skipping a beat.

"Fate, huh?" she said with a hint of playfulness.

Before I could spill out a torrent of apologies, she cut in, "You promised you'd get me to the beach to see the sunset. We're not finished, Will Massey."

The bartender winked at me and smiled as I stood up to join Marina.

We stepped out onto the walkway. The dimming light and the cool ocean breeze hinted that sunset was nearing. Marina paused to slip off her shoes, and I did the same. Together, we walked across the soft sand, drawn toward the rhythmic dance of the ocean waves. The wind was brisk, yet the sand remained pleasantly warm beneath our bare feet.

Suddenly, I stopped, wincing from a sharp pain underfoot. Bending down, I carefully picked out a few small seashells nestled in the sand. They were perfectly intact, their intricate patterns catching the fading light. I admired their delicate beauty before slipping them into my pocket. When I looked up, a brief wave of panic washed over me, fearing I had lost sight of her like in my dream. But she was right there beside me, her gaze fixed on the descending sun.

We continued our walk in quiet harmony, attuned to the soothing symphony of crashing waves. The sound seemed to cast a spell over us, its mesmerizing cadence wrapping us in a blanket of calm. I watched as she closed her eyes and took deep breaths, each one seeming to fill her with peace and a sense of triumph. Indeed, it was a victory for her. A moment of pure bliss and a goal she had waited a long time to achieve.

"Marina, I have a confession to make," I said, my voice shaky with nerves.

We paused at the shoreline, the water swirling around our feet, mingling with the crushed shells and coarse sand. We faced each other, the setting sun casting long shadows on the beach.

Her expression grew to one of concern. "What is it, Will?"

"When I walked into Mildred's Diner, and I heard that bell over the door jingle, followed by the sound of your footsteps drawing near, I didn't expect... you."

Marina's attention intensified, her eyebrows furrowed in a mix of confusion and fascination. She shook her head softly, her eyes wide with a look of awe and curiosity, hanging on to each word as if trying to piece together a puzzle.

Summoning all the courage within me, I took a deep breath, becoming completely vulnerable. "I shouldn't be here today, but I am. I'm here because of you. Maybe it's fate, maybe it's divine intervention, but something extraordinary brought me to you and you to me," I confessed, the words pouring out with a mixture of fear and fervor.

"From the second you leaned your knee on the chair across from me and brushed back your hair to reveal those stunning green eyes, to the first time I watched you laugh over a meal. Every time you sing in the shower, I lie there, captivated like I am listening to my favorite songbird." My voice trembled with each memory that I recounted, each one etching deeper into my heart.

"I've seen your joy, and I've seen your tears. I'll never forget seeing you hanging upside down in the wreckage, blood trickling from your ear and nose, the terror of possibly losing you haunting me. Last night was awful—I couldn't sleep, and my stomach was in knots."

I paused, closing my eyes to gather strength. When I opened them, they were filled with resolve. "I don't ever want to feel that way again. Marina, I've thought about this a lot. I have fallen deeply in love with you. I can't… I don't want… to spend another day of my life without you."

She turned her back to me, facing the sun while her hair danced gracefully in the ocean breeze. I stood there, waiting for her response, each second stretching into what felt like an eternity.

Suddenly, Marina's voice broke the silence. "I lied," she proclaimed loudly, her back still to me.

My heart raced.

"When you asked me right before the wreck if I had ever known a man who I was in love with… I lied. There was no George… I was talking about you."

Her words were pleasant to my ears, yet I detected a hint of hesitation in her tone—a signal that there was more to come.

"You've been strong, yet gentle. You've treated me with nothing but respect and kindness, always putting me first. Your voice is kind, your soul is gentle. Your presence brings me warmth, and your absence would leave me with a chill," she expressed with a trembling voice.

Turning to face me, tears streaming down her cheeks, Marina confessed, "I didn't mean it when I said I don't love you last night. In fact, I have fallen in love with you and I don't know what to do."

"What do you mean, 'You don't know what to do?'" I asked, my voice filled with urgency and confusion.

"I've wanted to kiss you and tell you since before the wreck that I am falling for you, but…" she hesitated, her voice faltering.

"But what?" I pressed, my anxiety peaking.

"But I don't want to be the reason you walk into some diner and order ice water to go in a few years. I don't want to make you feel alive only to rip your heart out when I'm not here." Her voice cracked with emotion. "I love you, Will Massey, but I can't bear the thought of being with you, knowing I'd be the second great love of your life to die of cancer."

She paused, a look of profound shock and realization crossing her face, "But I don't think I could live one day without you. I'm so scared. I don't want to die, and I don't want to be a burden. I don't know what to do."

With that, I stepped forward and pulled Marina into my arms, our lips meeting for the first time as the sun dipped into the ocean behind us. All the pent-up emotions poured out in our embrace. We kissed passionately, clinging to each other, neither of us willing to let go, lost in a moment of raw vulnerability and profound love. It was as though a weight had been lifted off both of us. As our lips parted, our foreheads gently pressed against each other.

Staring into her eyes I whispered, "I'll never leave your side, Mar."

"And I'll never leave your side, Will Massey," she replied.

As we began to stroll along the beach, a sense of relief seemed to wash over both of us. The ocean waves carried away all our burdens. The sky began to darken into twilight, and impulsively, I stopped and reached for the locket dangling around my neck.

"What's wrong?" Her voice tinged with concern. She tightened her grip on my hand.

"My heart belongs to you now," I declared, emotion swelling within me. I pulled back my arm, ready to hurl the locket into the welcoming depths of the ocean.

"No!" Marina exclaimed, her reaction swift, catching my arm

mid-swing. "Will, your heart is big enough for both of us, and I am okay with that."

She placed her hands gently around the base of my neck and drew me close, sealing her words with a loving kiss that spoke volumes of acceptance and shared futures.

In that moment, I realized that our journey together wasn't ending—it was just beginning.

———————

I read a poem once by a poet named Frost. I don't remember every line word for word, but the way I interpreted it is that there is a man who comes to a place in his life where he must choose which road he would take. Rather than choosing the one that seemed to be the easiest or offer fewer unknowns, he chose the other road, and that made all the difference in the world, and he never once regretted it. I was inspired to write my own.

———————

The Other Road, by William Massey

I thought I knew what road to take;

I'd finally set my mind.

But then a simple twist of fate,

and footsteps from behind,

Steered me down a different path,

a path I could not plan.

Stop thinking and start doing,

was so hard to understand.

I held my breath and took a step,

a leap of faith with you.

I saw the world a different way,

and experienced life anew.

We shared a ride along the way,

two people, but as one,

Neither of us realized,

our journey had just begun.

Now gazing through the rearview mirror,

at everywhere we've been.

I yearn and ache so deep inside,

to do it all over again.

I reflect on life and think of you,

the love I've been bestowed.

And I thank the Lord each and every day,

I took the other road.

CHAPTER 25

Present Day

I SET THE STACK of papers back down onto my lap. Mother and I looked at each other in amazement, before turning our gaze upon Grandma. She sat there in her chair smiling. We could tell her mind was a thousand miles away.

"What do you think? Did Pawpaw get it right?"

Grandma hesitated for a minute and then answered, "Yes Izzy, he captured it perfectly."

Mother stood up from the couch and made her way to the curio and retrieved the picture of Susan Jane. "So, this was Susan Jane?" Mother asked with a smile.

Grandma nodded.

"Dad wanted to name me after her?" Mother inquired curiously.

Grandma shook her head, "No sweetheart… I did."

Mother appeared confused and in need of more explanation.

Grandma obliged. "I have always been very thankful of Susan Jane. She didn't choose to get cancer, or die so young, but she loved my William until her death. Then her death became the catalyst that brought us together. Without Susan Jane, there would have never been a William and Marina."

I could tell that Mother was struggling to comprehend Grandma's deep and wise deduction.

"You were the child that Susan Jane always wanted, that I always wanted, and William always needed. The more that I learned about her, the more that I knew I had to honor her. Trust me, you should be honored."

Mother smiled and nodded in agreement.

"All of this stuff, it's from your trip?" I asked.

Grandma nodded.

I picked each item up from inside the lockbox. "Pawpaw's pocketknife from his brother? The frog from the pow wow? The bracelet from your hospital stay after the wreck? The locket with Susan Jane's picture? A seashell from Coronado? What about this rock?"

"That's a petrified rock from the Petrified Forrest, it was illegal to take that, but we didn't know it," she whispered. "Maybe you can return it one day for me?"

I smiled and nodded at her suggestion.

"I can't believe that you fell in love during a road trip," said Mother.

"You'd be amazed at what a 'road trip' can do for a relationship," quipped Grandma.

I smiled at her response. Her edginess combined with her tenderness was a mix of qualities that I often recognized in myself, to a fault.

"What should we do now?" I inquired.

"That was a long trip down memory lane for me. I think I will go lie down for a while."

Grandma stood up from her chair and slowly stepped over

to Mother on the couch who was still staring at the photo of Susan Jane.

"I love you, Blue Jay. Thank you for being here for me." Grandma leaned down and gave Mother a soft kiss on the cheek.

I stood up and met her halfway as she turned toward me, "Go take a nap Grandma. Mother and I will determine what we do later."

"You remind me of me," she whispered, "so full of energy and life. You should keep an eye out for those who will compliment you and balance that reckless spirit a little."

I snickered at her advice, knowing that it was more valid than I wanted to accept.

"I love you Izzy Bee. I'm so glad you came, and I know that Pawpaw is also glad you came."

"I love you too," I whispered while giving her a long hug.

Grandma turned and headed toward her room still grasping the picture of Pawpaw. "You two keep it down out here, and don't get into any trouble."

"Do you need me to help you to your bed Mom?" Mother asked.

Grandma turned to stare at her and responded, "I am a grown woman, Susan Jane. I can take care of myself!" And with that she glanced over at me and smiled with a faint wink of her eye.

That was the last thing that we heard Grandma say. She climbed into her bed and never opened her eyes again. I like to think that she just couldn't bear to go one more day without him. Or maybe he was waiting around for her.

We held a memorial service for them several days later. There they were, side by side in beautiful matching urns with an enlarged photo of the two of them on Coronado beach.

Once all of the family friends had paid their last respects,

Mother and I spent time getting everything in order and filtering through all of their stuff.

I discovered the day after Grandma passed away that Pawpaw had left me their cherished '66 Mustang. The memories of those joyous rides with him along the breathtaking coast flooded back to me. As a little girl, I never understood the significance of that car. Pawpaw had lovingly preserved it, storing it away like a hidden treasure, only taking it out for rare, nostalgic drives and occasional maintenance. It was more than a car; it was a piece of their shared history, our shared history; a testament to his love and to the important role that it played in his life.

Two weeks later, Mother and I loaded that car with a few items from the house along with our suitcases. Shutting the driver's side door and starting the engine, I could imagine them in this car, driving down the road.

"Are you ready for this?" I asked.

Mother smiled from the passenger seat and nodded. She then glanced at Grandma and Pawpaw in the back seat, comfortably strapped in. "Keep your hands to yourself, Will Massey," she quipped with a huge smile on her face and tears in her eyes.

I laughed at Mother's comment, and then I yelled out the window, "Hudson, Ohio, here we come!"

ABOUT THE AUTHOR

S.L. ARRINGTON has been storytelling his entire life. Whether through poetry, music, art or writing, he loves creating stories that explore the intricacies of the human spirit; especially the inner conflicts we wrestle with as we navigate through relationships and interactions in our lives. His stories are founded on experiences, expectations and revelations that he has encountered in his lifetime. He lives near Nashville, Tennessee and is surrounded and supported by his beautiful wife, Ginger, a son and three daughters, along with twelve grandchildren.

www.ingramcontent.com/pod-product-compliance
Lightning Source LLC
Chambersburg PA
CBHW022120310726
48972CB00007B/2125